TOP DOG

KERRY KAYA

Boldwood

First published in 2019. This edition first published in Great Britain in 2022 by Boldwood Books Ltd.

Copyright © Kerry Kaya, 2019

Cover Design by Colin Thomas

Cover Photography: shutterstock

A CIP catalogue record for this book is available from the British Library.

Paperback ISBN 978-1-80162-986-7

Large Print ISBN 978-1-80162-987-4

Hardback ISBN 978-1-80162-984-3

Ebook ISBN 978-1-80162-988-1

Kindle ISBN 978-1-80162-989-8

Audio CD ISBN 978-1-80162-980-5

MP3 CD ISBN 978-1-80162-981-2

Digital audio download ISBN 978-1-80162-983-6

Boldwood Books Ltd
23 Bowerdean Street
London SW6 3TN
www.boldwoodbooks.com

For my brothers, Tony and Daniel. Thank you for lending me your names.

1

As usual, The Tavern, in Plaistow, East London, was crammed full of punters. The air was thick and heavy with expensive aftershave and curling cigarette smoke as men of varying age and status jostled to get served at the bar. A safe haven amongst the criminal underworld, The Tavern was the perfect venue for criminal activity and business to be planned out – albeit some very illegal business.

Strolling into the packed boozer with a confident air, Danny McKay smiled. He stopped and casually greeted the men he classed as business associates, before making his way towards his long-term friend and boss, who was holding court at the bar. Shaking hands with the more senior members of the firm Freddie Smith ran, he then ordered them a round of drinks.

He was a handsome man, with a tall, strong and muscular body, his thick dark hair and green eyes masking the fact that beneath the facade he was actually a hard bastard.

'Is it sorted?' Freddie Smith asked. Considering his fifty-five years, he was in good shape, his physique still a match for most twenty-year-olds. Only his lined face portrayed his true age.

Paying for the drinks, Danny looked over at his boss with a blank expression.

'Fucking hell, Earth to McKay. I said, is it sorted? The meet, is it on?'

Amid laughter, Danny nodded. 'Yeah, sorry, mate. I was miles away.'

Freddie took out his cigarettes and lit one before answering, 'You're in a world of your fucking own. It's about time you started pulling your weight around here ain't it; every time I look at you you've got a face like a smacked arse.' It was a sly dig. Something he had been doing a lot of recently.

As expected, banter followed, only, instead of joining in, Danny found that it rankled. Just lately, he'd begun questioning his role within the firm.

At the age of thirty-eight, the fact that he still took orders from Freddie, even down to which doors he worked, had started to bother him. It wasn't as though he even needed the money. Thanks to a job he'd done years ago with his pal Tommy Carter, he happened to be loaded. The job, which had entailed melting down a considerable amount of gold bars so they could be sold back on to the market, had made him a rich man. Not only that but he was a face in his own right; without him, Freddie's firm would crumble down around him, and as for pulling his weight, he did a damn sight more than anyone else who worked for Freddie did. Look at the Greeks; it'd been him who'd sorted out the meet and it'd been him who'd put his neck on the line by even making contact with them.

'What the fuck are you laughing at?' Danny snapped, turning his attention to Matty Payne, one of the firm's younger hangers-on. He'd detested the lad on sight. He was one of those kids whose mother should have swallowed the night he was conceived.

As far as Danny was concerned, the kid should crawl back to

the council estate he came from. Payne had even had the cheek once to ask him if he wanted to buy a gun. Why the fuck would he need some spotty kid to source a gun for him? He was more than capable of sourcing them himself. In fact, when he'd been in his early twenties, he'd once ran a successful side line dealing firearms, and still had plenty of contacts in the business who he could buy from. Not that they were his choice of weapon; he was old school and wasn't averse to getting his hands dirty. He would rather use his fists, boots or even a blade, than pull a trigger; where was the satisfaction in that?

'I said, what are you laughing at?'

'Nothing.' Matty looked down at his feet, his cheeks flushed pink.

Danny took a sip of his brandy. All the while, his eyes remained firmly focused on the boy. Everything about this kid, from his close-cropped hair to the ill-fitting cheap clothes that hung off his thin frame, irritated him.

He could feel the hatred seep from his pores and would have liked nothing better than to obliterate the little rat. He couldn't put his finger on it, but there was something about Payne that had got underneath his skin from the moment he'd laid his eyes upon him. Maybe it was because he could see something of himself in Matty; the kid was a stark reminder of his past. They'd both come from the same council estate, both been latchkey kids, and both been dragged up rather than brought up. But it was Matty's eyes that unnerved him the most; there was a sadness there, a vulnerability that Danny recognised only too well, a sense of hopelessness, a desperate need for help.

'Leave the boy alone. Who's rattled your cage, eh?' Freddie grabbed hold of Danny's elbow and yanked him close. 'We need numbers today. Don't fuck this up all because you've got a personal beef with the lad. Do you hear me?' he said, leaning into Danny's ear, his voice suddenly menacing.

Danny nodded, but inside he was seething. His eyes were hard as he swallowed down the irritation. For more than twenty years, he'd stood alongside Freddie Smith, and only now, as he looked around him, did he realise what he had to do.

After all this time, it had finally sunk in. He would always have to toe the line. Freddie would never allow it to be any other way, and with the likes of Matty Payne joining the ranks, thinking he was one of them, Danny decided he needed out. He gulped down his brandy and immediately ordered another. This would be the last job he did. Once today was over with, he would tell Freddie exactly where he could stick his firm.

Freddie could almost taste the excitement in the air, the thrill of the unknown. His body felt like a tightly coiled spring, ready to release at any moment, and he knew from experience the feeling would stay with him until his fists had thrown that first punch.

As per usual, he was the focal point of the firm, a role in which he thrived. Only today, he felt more uneasy than usual. From the corner of his eye, he watched Danny.

The man whom he had watched grow from a young lad to the man he was today, now stood at the same height as him. Over the years, there had been many men who had tried to take over, but he'd always remained the Top Dog. They had neither the power nor knowledge to push him from the ranks.

Danny, on the other hand, was a different kettle of fish. If it were to come down to it, McKay could easily overpower him. The sheer strength of the man was enough to tell him that.

Standing at just over six feet tall, McKay was a force to be reckoned with. Fighting was second nature to him. He'd always been more than happy to steam in with his fists or size eleven boots. It had made him stand out as a young lad and was what had made him climb the ranks and become a well-respected member of the firm so quickly.

More than once, Freddie had been glad that Danny was one of theirs; only now, that fact felt threatening. Danny didn't only have the power to take over, he also had the knowledge of how the firm ran. He was too clever for his own good, and if he'd been anything other than a heavy, a thug, he would have made a bloody good copper.

Freddie was worried, not that anyone would be able to tell that by looking at him.

He had a sinking feeling he just couldn't shake off when it came to his number two, and he decided, there and then, he would keep a close eye on him. He would bide his time and if, and only if, the time came, he would deal with it, as quickly and as quietly as he could.

* * *

They drained their remaining drinks, and in single file, they left The Tavern. Once out on the street, they made their way to the car park. From there, they would drive towards Barking, on the outskirts of East London.

The atmosphere in Danny's car was almost tangible.

'I still think we should have steamed into that Greek ponce's restaurant, instead of arranging this meet,' Danny said.

Freddie dismissed him. 'The place will be swarming with customers.'

'Element of surprise. We could have taken the lot of them out, and been on our toes within minutes,' Danny argued.

'Fucking hell, Danny, are you trying to get us all nicked?' This came from Tony, or Big Tone as he was more commonly known, due to his formidable size.

'I'm just saying, that's how I would have played this out. Now the bastard Greeks know that we're coming,' Danny answered with a shrug of his shoulders.

Freddie shot him a look. 'It's a good job that I'm running this firm then, eh? Fuck me lads, we would all be in the nick tonight if it was left to McKay.'

Despite himself, Danny allowed a small smile to cross his lips. It was a veiled threat, to remind him of who was in charge, not that he needed reminding. Freddie had never let any of them forget that fact.

'Sod that. I had enough trouble the last time I was nicked,' Lloydy said.

Big Tone laughed. 'He hasn't had a shower since then. He's still paranoid about dropping the soap.'

Danny laughed along with the rest of the occupants of his car. At some point over the years, the majority of them had all had their collars felt. It had almost become an initiation rite. But as for doing proper bird, it wasn't something he envisaged for his future, and he certainly wasn't prepared to do time for Freddie, hence why he'd taken over the day to day running of the firm. The less risk involved the better, in his eyes.

* * *

Pulling into a disused industrial area on the south side of Barking, Danny stepped his foot on the brake and switched off the engine. 'This is it,' he stated as he surveyed the barren wasteland. Abandoned warehouse units stood in the distance. The glass windows were shattered, and brightly coloured graffiti was scrawled across the walls. The area was well and truly out of sight from any passers-by.

The cold air hit him as he climbed out of his car, not that his brain registered this fact. Blood pumped through his veins. His firm body was taut, every muscle straining.

'You all know what to do?' Freddie asked as he looked around at the men beside him. 'This Greek bastard has taken liberties with me for too many years, and it ends today—'

The rumble of tyres from across the tarmac broke Freddie's speech. It was clear to see by the number of vehicles pulling into the once thriving area, that they were outnumbered.

'What did I fucking tell you?' Danny growled. 'Didn't I say we should have steamed in unannounced?'

'Just do what I pay you to do,' Freddie spat, his breath quickening with anger.

* * *

George Christos was a small, balding man, whose jovial face belied the vicious nature he'd been naturally graced with. Coming from a large family, he rarely travelled anywhere alone, which was just as well considering he'd made many enemies over the years. As he stepped out of the car, he adjusted the navy blue cashmere overcoat he had shrugged across his shoulders, then spread open his arms in a greeting.

'Freddie.' He smiled. 'A very strange place to do business,' he stated, his Greek accent heavily accentuated. 'I feel this is not to be a happy meeting.'

'Too right it's not. You're stepping on my toes, on my territory, trying to muscle in on my pubs and clubs, and it ends now... today,' Freddie roared.

George Christos looked around him at the vast number of

brothers, cousins and nephews who stood beside him. 'Your pubs and clubs?' he asked in mock surprise. 'I do not believe they belong to you, Freddie. Why, you only ran the doors, did you not? And now, I will be running them.'

Spittle gathered at the corner of Freddie's lips, so tangible was his anger. His face was pale and drained of all colour. 'I'll fucking kill you before this day is out.'

George Christos gave a small smirk and nodded towards his brother, Alexandros. 'Deal with this,' he ordered before hastily retreating back to the safety of his car. He'd not got to where he was today by getting his own hands dirty, and why should he, he argued, when he paid out a significant amount of money for others to do his dirty work for him.

* * *

Danny curled his fists into balls. Adrenalin coursed through his veins, and as far as he was concerned the charge couldn't come quick enough. He could feel the crack of a cheekbone as his fist connected with flesh. He had never felt more alive than he did right now. Testosterone raged through him. He loved the buzz of a good old tear up. He liked inflicting as much damage as he could and could think of nothing better he would rather be doing.

As his opponent fell to the ground, Danny grasped the man's head between his hands and smashed it repeatedly down onto the hard concrete. Swiftly, he moved on to the next Greek.

He knew he wouldn't stop until he was spent, until the very last member of George Christos's firm was either down on the floor or had run from the meet. He glanced up to watch Matty Payne go down, underneath a rain of blows. Any other man would have gone to his aid; after all, it was an unspoken rule. Instead,

Danny turned his back. The kid could fight his own battles as far as he was concerned.

After what seemed like hours, yet in reality was only minutes, it was all over. Danny helped members of the firm up from the floor, whilst using the back of his hand to wipe away blood from his own mouth. He breathed heavily, waiting for his heart to, once again, reach a steady rhythm. It was only now, as he watched George Christos and his men speed away from the scene, that he would allow his taut muscles to relax.

Aware of being watched, he glanced over his shoulder to see his Freddie staring at him. The older man lunged forward.

'What the fuck was that?' Freddie demanded.

'What?' Danny took a step backwards and held up his hands. He looked around him, genuinely puzzled by Freddie's outburst.

A vein pulsated at Freddie's temple and spittle gathered at the corners of his snarled lips. He jerked his thumb in the direction of Matty Payne, who at that precise moment, was being heaved up off the floor. 'We don't leave our own,' he spat.

'He isn't anything to me.' Danny gave a nonchalant shrug of his shoulders.

'He's one of the firm,' Freddie roared. Taking a step forward he stabbed his forefinger into Danny's cheek. 'And we don't leave one of our own to get a hammering.'

Pushing Freddie roughly away from him, Danny could feel his temper rising and he battled to keep it under control. 'That bastard is fuck all to do with me. He's nothing. So come on, you tell me, why the fuck do we want the likes of him hanging around? Can't you see what a fucking embarrassment we're becoming?'

Freddie moved closer; his voice was low, angry. 'The second that lad pulls a punch, he is one of us.'

'The fuck he is,' Danny yelled back. He looked around him at the men he had known for most of his adult life. The cold stares they gave in return were more than enough to tell him that not only were they on Freddie's side but that they also agreed with everything he said.

He could hardly believe what he was seeing and hearing. Since when did Matty Payne take precedence? Since when was Freddie more concerned with some spotty kid, rather than the fact that the Greeks had just hot footed it away on their toes, with the business in hand still unresolved?

'Do you know what? I'm done. Done with all this shit. Do what you want with the firm, I'm out!' He turned and walked away from the only life he'd known; all the while, he could hear Freddie shouting obscenities at his retreating back.

* * *

'I don't trust him.' Freddie rubbed at his temple before lighting a cigarette, his second in the last ten minutes.

Big Tone narrowed his eyes, confused. 'C'mon, Fred, this is Danny we're talking about. If they were to cut him open, the firm would run through his veins. I mean, come on, he's been around even longer than I have, and I'm practically a relic.'

Freddie shook his head. They were sitting in the garden of the Spotted Dog public house in Barking. 'He knows too much. He knows everything, mate.'

'Are you saying he's a grass?' Big Tone's mouth fell open.

Freddie shrugged. 'He knows too much, and we don't know what he might do with that information.'

Big Tone took a few moments to think about this. 'Look, do you want me to have a word? I might be able to knock some sense into him, and if I can't, then at least we'll know how the land lies.'

The men fell silent. The sound of people sitting at nearby

tables was suddenly loud to their ears. Finally, Freddie spoke.

'McKay's causing too much trouble. He's getting involved with things he shouldn't, he's interfering with how the firm runs, he's trying to take over. Every time I turn around, he's there trying to shove his opinion down my throat. And as for wanting out, I won't allow it. *We* can't allow it,' he said. He stubbed out his cigarette in the overfilled ceramic ashtray and continued. 'At least not until we know what he'll do with the information he has, not only on the firm's business dealings over the past twenty years, but also the information he has on us.' He watched as Big Tone raised his eyebrows at the last part of his sentence, and knew he had the man's attention. 'Exactly, mate. This is why we can't allow him to walk away. He knows too much, and some of the shit we've been involved in over the years will carry a hefty sentence should the Old Bill get wind of it.'

Freddie decided to leave out the part that was really worrying him. What bothered him more, much more, was the fact that Danny could now go on and start up his own firm, and Freddie was getting too old to be chasing rival firms off his manor, especially when that rival firm was run by his much younger, stronger, number two. He waited for Big Tone to digest what he'd just said, and when the big man nodded, Freddie gave a satisfied smile.

* * *

Danny lay back in the bath. The soapy suds covered his aching muscles and he glanced down at his bruised knuckles. A small chunk of skin was missing, more than likely caused by some Greek's tooth. He dropped his hand back into the warm water and closed his eyes.

In the kitchen below, he could hear his wife, Maxine, chattering away to their son, Logan. He tried desperately to drown out her voice, but he couldn't drive away the disappointment he'd seen in her face, when he had finally staggered home from the meet with blood staining his shirt.

Since then, Maxine had given him the cold shoulder. The rational part of his brain didn't blame her. It was the irrational part of him that wanted to shout, 'This is who I am, get over it!' He knew, though, that it would be difficult for her to comprehend any type of violence. As hard as he knew she would try, she would not be able to either rationalise or condone his behaviour if she were to find out just how much of a bastard he really was.

He climbed out of the bath, dried himself, and then sprayed a generous amount of deodorant underneath his arms. Once dressed, he made his way down the stairs. He pushed open the kitchen door and stood leaning against the wooden frame.

'You okay?' he asked Maxine.

When she didn't answer, he sighed, crossed over the kitchen, picked his son up out of his highchair and kissed the top of the little boy's head. 'I take it you're planning on ignoring me today then?'

Standing at the kitchen sink, Maxine turned her head to look at her husband.

He gave her a small smile to take the edge off his words. 'Come on, Max, enough now, eh?'

'No,' Maxine said as she held up her hand to cut him off. 'You promised me the last time that you wouldn't come home in that sort of state again. What's wrong with you? You're meant to be a father' – her gaze went to their son; Logan looked so much like Danny that it was frightening: same dark hair, same green eyes, same thick black lashes – 'you shouldn't be coming home covered in blood; what kind of a role model is that for him?'

Danny looked his wife in the eyes. As much as he loved her, at times, she aggravated the fuck out of him. As for Logan, if he had any say in it, his son wouldn't be following in his footsteps. In fact, he would do everything in his power to make sure he didn't. 'It's work.' He shrugged. 'You know what it's like working the doors,' he lied, 'I can't help it if someone takes a swing for me, can I? It's my job Max, what do you expect me to do, take a kicking?'

Maxine gave a sarcastic laugh. 'Just like the last time was work, I suppose, and the times before then?'

Danny rolled his eyes. 'It is what it is, babe.'

Maxine turned her head away and continued drying the dishes. Despite her anger, she loved this man with all her heart. But at times, even she had to admit he truly tested her patience. She felt him come behind her, and when his hand gently rubbed her shoulder, she sighed. 'I'm just scared that you won't come home one day, that's all.'

Leaning forward, Danny nuzzled his face in her dark hair. 'Of course I will, you silly mare.' The fact she was right to worry, lay heavy on his mind. Of late, Freddie was taking more and more risks; he was becoming sloppy. Take the meet for example: he was more concerned with Matty Payne than the fact the Greeks had had it away on their toes. Who knew what they were planning, or who they would target next. All Freddie had done was give George Christos the ammunition to start a war, a war that – unless Freddie stepped up to the plate – they were going to lose.

Tossing the tea towel onto the worktop, Maxine turned to face her husband. 'I mean it, Danny. I'm scared you'll end up getting yourself killed one day.' She pointed towards the small television set on the kitchen counter. 'You see it on the news all the time, someone's been stabbed or shot.'

'Leave it out, Max.' He laughed. 'As if that's ever gonna fucking happen; I know how to take care of myself babe, I've been in this game a long time.'

'Yeah but...' She pointed back to the television.

'No buts,' Danny said, kissing the top of her head. 'You don't need to worry about me.'

Inside his pocket his mobile phone began to ring. Fishing the device out he narrowed his eyes; Big Tone flashed up on the caller ID. He was in half a mind to cancel the call, only curiosity got the better of him.

'Sorry darling,' he said, handing over their son, 'I have to answer this, it's work.'

* * *

Big Tone took a sip from his pint of lager. A layer of white froth remained on the top of his lip, and he wiped it off with the back of his hand before giving Danny a wide smile. They were sitting at a corner table in The Tavern, far away from prying ears.

'I take it this is about Freddie?' Danny asked.

'Look, I don't know what's gone on between the two of you, but for the sake of the firm, it needs sorting out, and quick,' Big Tone answered. Eyeing the brandy glass in Danny's hand, he sat back in his seat as an extra precaution. He wouldn't put it past the man to smash it into his face. He certainly had the temperament to do just that.

The action was not lost on Danny, and he slowly swirled the brandy around his glass, before swallowing the liquid down.

When Danny remained silent, Big Tone changed tact. 'Look, mate. This trouble with the Greeks is getting out of hand. Something has to be done about them.'

Danny began to laugh. 'Is that what all this is about? You need numbers?'

Shaking his head, Big Tone leant forward. 'Look, I'm not going to lie. Freddie is not happy, mate. In fact, he's pissed off, big time, but at the end of the day, we need you. I'm here as a mate, and all this talk about you leaving the firm is madness. What are you going to do without work, eh?'

'Nah, I'll tell you what's madness. Having little pricks like Payne on the payroll. That was Freddie's call. That's how Freddie wants to run things now. What the fuck is it all about?'

Big Tone shrugged. 'Fair enough. The kid isn't the brightest bulb on the Christmas tree, but—'

'Don't tell me,' Danny interrupted. 'He makes up the numbers?'

Big Tone shrugged, as if to admit defeat. 'That's about the size of it, mate. Look, Freddie wants to go with your plan, and take out the Greeks at their restaurant in Barking on Saturday night.'

Faced with a dilemma, Danny sat back in his seat. A huge part of him wanted to cave in. He'd been looking forward to running the Greeks out of East London. The feud between the two firms wasn't something new. It went back years. The other part of him knew he would never make anything of himself without leaving Freddie.

He would always have to live in the man's shadow, doing as he was ordered to do. He knew he would easily find work elsewhere. He'd been head hunted more than once over the years. Only his loyalty had kept him working for Freddie.

'So, Freddie's finally admitted I was right all along, then?'

Big Tone threw Danny a look. How was he supposed to answer that? 'He's probably just covering all angles.'

Danny burst out laughing. 'Covering all angles? It's not a fucking snooker table, Tone.'

'C'mon, Danny. What do you want me to say? I'm trying to make things right between the two of yous.'

Getting up from his seat, Danny went to the bar to order them another round of drinks. He needed time to think. The feud with the Greeks wasn't solely to do with who ran the doors, it was personal. He'd barely been out of school when he'd had his first run in with one of the Christos brothers. Still to this day he felt ashamed of the circumstances that had led to him committing murder. Other than his best mate, Moray, no one else knew what they had done that fateful night, nor the reason why. Not Freddie, not even Maxine. How could he tell them? He didn't want to see pity in their eyes, let alone disgust. By the time he returned with the filled glasses in his hands, he already knew what his answer would be.

'Okay, I'll be there for the meet with the Greeks, but after that, I'm out. I'm already in the dog house with my missus, and this will just about push her over the edge.' Danny sighed. 'Oh, and before you even say it, I promise I'll keep my opinions about the kid to myself.'

Physically relaxing, Big Tone smiled. This had been easier than he'd expected. 'Nice one, mate.'

Danny raised his glass in a toast. 'To the firm.'

Mirroring the action, Big Tone repeated, 'To the firm.'

Downing his lager, Big Tone heaved his heavy body up out of the seat. 'One more for the road, mate?'

'Go on then, you've twisted my arm.'

An hour later, they left The Tavern. Once they were in their cars, Big Tone watched in the rear-view mirror as Danny drove out of the car park. He then pulled out his mobile phone, punched in a number and brought the phone to his ear.

After a few moments, he spoke. 'It's done.' He then switched off his phone and dropped it onto the passenger seat. With a heavy heart, he began to drive in the direction of his own home.

As unpredictable and as violent as Danny McKay was, Big Tone actually liked him. Not for the first time, he wondered if he'd done the right thing by coming here tonight. Freddie Smith's decision to permanently silence Danny lay heavy on his mind.

2

Of all the things that Danny was, stupid wasn't one of them. He'd almost laughed at the fact they had seemed to forget he knew Freddie Smith, probably better than his own mother did. And because of that, Danny also knew Freddie would never have allowed him to walk back into the firm with open arms quite as easily as he had. After all, he had practically mugged the man off in front of the entire firm. No, the Freddie he knew would have had a bit more to say about the situation than what Big Tone had indicated, and Danny's instincts were that the man would want revenge.

In his twisted mind, he would think of it as using Danny as a warning to other members of the firm who dared step out of line. At the same time, it would be the perfect opportunity to dispose of the one person who really could take over. He would be killing two birds with one stone, so to speak.

A few days after his meeting with Big Tone, Danny was lifting weights in Abdul's Gym. Sitting on the bench press, he grabbed a towel and wiped the sweat from his forehead whilst he took a few moments to rest. All the while, his mind was working overtime.

He had a plan, even though it was somewhat sketchy. He'd battled it out inside his mind, ever since his meeting with Big Tone, and the more he thought it through, the more he believed it could actually work.

Glancing up at the clock on the wall, he had just over an hour to decide whether or not to put his plan into action. The situation with the Greeks was only just starting to warm up, and time was ticking.

* * *

After leaving the gym, Danny drove towards Gascoigne Estate in Barking. Gascoigne was a typical concrete jungle council estate, dominated by rundown tower blocks. As he pulled into The Hope public house's car park, he could smell the pungent scent of decay around him. Signs of poverty were everywhere he looked. Supermarket trollies were flung alongside rusting cars, no doubt the pound coin deposits having been prised out first.

He watched as a mother, pushing a double pushchair laden down with shopping bags, screamed at a small dawdling child to hurry up before she beat his lazy arse.

Danny shook his head. Scum, pure scum, he thought to himself. He'd once been that child, his own parents' only waking thought had been where they could get money from to go out and score. All he'd ever been to them was an inconvenience, until of course he'd been old enough to go out and earn money for them. That was the only time they had ever given him praise or a kind word. It was no wonder he'd gone off the rails. And then along had come Adam Christos. By the time Danny had reached sixteen he was a law unto himself, uncontrollable. He closed his eyes in a bid to block out the sickening images that flashed before his eyes. Christos had deserved to die for the things he'd done, he'd deserved everything he'd had coming to him, he was only thankful it had been him and Moray who'd finally brought him down, that they'd had the justice they deserved.

His eyes scanned the pub and he found who he was looking for in the bar. It was going to take every ounce of his willpower just to control the pure hatred he felt for the younger man.

* * *

Matty Payne was somewhat of a legend amongst his friends. They listened in awe as he regaled them with stories about the firm. Somehow, he always became the hero of the story. The firm would be lost without him, he had them believing.

Standing at the bar, Matty gulped down half a pint of the cheapest lager he could buy. He wiped the back of his hand across his mouth and began counting out his change to buy another.

As the entrance door opened, Matty turned to look, as did most of the regulars –usually those who were either trying to avoid the local drug dealers due to debts, or those who were looking to score.

He felt the colour drain from his face when he saw Danny McKay standing in the doorway. The sheer size of the man was more than enough to make him look menacing. When the big man beckoned him over, Matty felt his insides instantly turn to mush.

Looking around him, he saw the barmaid, whom he had half-heartedly tried to chat up once, look Danny up and down appreciatively, an effect he had on most women, and Matty decided there and then that he had even more reason to hate the man. Danny McKay was everything he could never be.

For a brief moment, Matty contemplated pretending he hadn't

seen him. Until, that was, one of his friends nudged him in his ribs and he could no longer deny it.

'It's one of the firm... must need me for something important, innit,' he said. He was full of bravado; he couldn't show his fear.

Following Danny outside, Matty found his voice. 'How did you know I would be here?'

'Where else would a rat like you be?'

'Oh.' Matty felt his heart sink. This clearly wasn't a friendly visit.

They walked a short distance away from the pub, and Matty looked around him. Being somewhere secluded with Danny McKay scared the shit out of him, and he wasn't afraid to admit that.

When they were a safe distance away from prying ears, Danny stopped.

A bead of sweat formed across Matty's forehead, and he felt sick with fear. He was terrified that someone would find out his secret. It was becoming harder and harder to conceal it, and he'd started to become paranoid about it. Instinctively, he knew that if anyone was going to suss it out, it would be Danny McKay.

Finally, Danny spoke. 'You told me you could get hold of a gun,' he said, lowering his voice.

Relieved, Matty almost cried. He'd truly thought his number was up. Now that he knew what it was Danny was after, he was once again acting the gangster.

'Yeah, blud. That's my ting, innit.'

The punch to the face that followed was so hard, it knocked Matty off balance. Within seconds, Danny had lifted Matty up by the front of his T-shirt.

'Speak to me in fucking English, you little prick. Now, can you get me one or not?'

Despite barely being able to breathe, Matty managed to nod

his head. Once Danny had released him, he rubbed at his neck where the cotton T-shirt had chaffed his skin.

'How soon can you get it?'

Matty's voice quivered as he spoke. 'It's going to take me a few days.'

He watched Danny think this over. Finally, the big man spoke. 'Okay,' he said. 'I'll come back here Friday night to collect it. Make sure that you're here.'

Matty nodded.

'Oh, and one more thing, keep your mouth shut about this,' Danny warned, stabbing his finger into Matty's temple.

Matty nodded again. He watched as Danny walked back towards his car, then he wiped a stray tear away from his cheek, before hastily straightening out his clothes. He had no intention of telling anybody about this visit from Danny. He wanted to stay as invisible as he possibly could, and he knew, instinctively, that the moment he opened his mouth, all hell would break loose. Out of the two, the secret or Danny, it was Danny he was more scared of, even though, by rights, it should have been the other way around.

He waited for a few moments, then slowly made his way back to the pub.

Once back inside, the barmaid called out to him. 'Hey, who was your friend?'

Matty ignored her. He had enough on his mind. He was up to his eyes in something he had no idea how to get out of.

The barmaid shrugged and continued wiping down the bar.

* * *

Back in his car, Danny couldn't wait to get off the estate. The stench of Matty Payne surrounded him. He turned the key in the

ignition, switched on the CD player and waited for the sound of
U2 to fill the car. He turned up the volume, then sped out of the
car park.

In all fairness, he could have bought a firearm from any one of
his contacts, but Matty was the one who would be easier for him
to make disappear, should his plan go wrong and he need to cover
his tracks. Briefly he pondered over how he would dispose of the
gun, once the deed was done. The Old Bill would be crawling all
over the place, and he would need to have all loose ends tied up
before he fired a single bullet, as it would make the gun hot and
easily traceable. He wondered now if he should have loaned the
weapon, instead of buying it, and left the disposal to someone
who would make sure it was gone forever. No, he decided, the less
people involved the better.

One thing he did know was that he wasn't prepared to allow
Freddie to take him down without a fight, not now, not when he
was so close to leaving the criminal underworld behind him with
his life still intact, which, considering the shit he'd been involved
in over the years was a miracle in itself. Besides, he had Maxine
and Logan to think about. He didn't want to leave them; he
wanted to prove to his wife that he could go straight, that he could
be decent, that he could be someone she was proud of. He wanted
to be able to watch his son grow, he wanted to be there to see him
go to school, meet his first girlfriend, get married, have children of
his own.

With Maxine and Logan the driving force behind him, he
prayed that he could pull it off. If he didn't, he knew life would
become even more dangerous than it already was. He would have
one chance at this, and he couldn't miss his target. If he did, then
he was a dead man walking, because Freddie Smith certainly
wouldn't allow him a second chance.

Another thing he knew for certain, was that the shooting had to happen in the presence of the Greeks, so Freddie's murder could be pinned on the opposing firm.

* * *

Six miles away, Freddie Smith was at home, contemplating how he was going to do the exact same thing. Progressively, he was becoming more and more paranoid where McKay was concerned. He was convinced the man wanted his firm, and that he wanted to be the Top Dog.

All of his instincts told him that he needed to take Danny out before the war with the Greeks had even started. But the competitive side of him wanted to wait until afterwards. Danny was the best man he had, and if they were going to bring down George Christos, then he needed him there.

He and Big Tone had discussed the matter at length, for hours, and whichever way he looked at the situation, he could see no other alternative than to dispose of his number two. Danny McKay was a thorn in his side. In fact, he was sick to the back teeth of him. Just the mere mention of McKay's name was enough to make his blood pressure sky rocket.

Under no circumstances was he prepared to let McKay have the chance of poaching his men, and he knew, given the choice, they would go with him. McKay was a natural leader, he was well liked, and the men respected him. Danny's hatred of Matty Payne had also been playing on Freddie's mind, to the point he was becoming increasingly paranoid. Had Danny somehow sussed out that Matty was one of his boys? Had Matty opened his mouth and blurted out his deepest darkest secrets? He'd kill the kid stone dead if he had. There and then he decided for the umpteenth time to put the hard word on Matty and warn him that if he opened his trap he was a dead man. And it was no idle threat. He was fully

prepared to do whatever it took to keep his secret buried, and if
that meant Payne would need to be disposed of then so be it.

* * *

The general planning of the attack had been left to Big Tone. His
orders had been to put together the men who would carry out the
assault, which was proving to be a lot tougher than was expected.
The problem he had was that Danny was not only a face, he was
also well liked, and Big Tone knew senior members of the firm
would question the order to take him out. In other words, they
wouldn't like it any more than he did.

In all honesty, Big Tone wasn't at all happy with what Freddie
was asking of him. He was a heavy, not a murderer, and there was
no other way to describe what was being planned other than
plain and simple murder. There was no pussy-footing around that
fact.

As much as he'd tried to dissuade Freddie from this course of
action, he just couldn't get through to the man. He may as well
have been talking to a brick wall, and to be perfectly fair, it had
felt like just that.

Big Tone pulled into a car park beside Epping Forest.
Surrounded by woodland, it was a location they had used on
numerous occasions, and perfect for the firm to talk in private.

The area was already in darkness. Climbing out of his Range
Rover, he made his way towards two men standing at the far end
of the car park.

The men had no idea why they had been summoned. He had
refused to give them any details over the phone, and Big Tone
could sense their uneasiness from their body language.

He knew they would be questioning the reason only three of

them were at this meet, rather than the majority of the firm. And more importantly, they would question the fact that key members, such as Freddie and Danny, were missing.

Big Tone greeted the men and shook their hands. He cleared his throat and then spoke, not wanting to beat around the bush. 'We've got a situation, lads. Freddie has asked me to put together a small team. He wants something done when we meet with the Greeks.'

The men looked at each other, and Big Tone took this as his cue to continue. 'He wants McKay taken out, permanently.'

One of the men gave a low whistle, the other took a sharp intake of breath. Of all the reasons they had been summoned, neither of them had expected this.

'Are you having a fucking bubble?' This came from Lloydy.

Big Tone held up his hand to quiet them down. It was no joke; he only wished it was. 'I know this is a big ask,' he said. 'In fact, it's a really massive fucking ask.'

Big Tone let his words sink in for a few moments, before continuing. 'If you want no part in this, I hand-on-heart would understand,' he said, placing his hand on his chest to emphasise his words.

Terry Stevens, the quieter of the two men, then spoke. 'If that were the case, mate, you wouldn't have called us here. I'm guessing this is something you don't want anyone else knowing too much about either? And the fact that we now do has put us in an awkward position.'

The two men looked at Big Tone expectantly, and he instantly regretted taking these men for fools. He wasn't used to this side of the firm. This had always been Danny's speciality. It was what Freddie paid him a hefty wedge to do, and was what he excelled in.

'You're right. No one else is to know about this, not yet anyway.'

'So basically, we have no choice. We have to do as Freddie asks. And what if we refuse?'

Big Tone rubbed his hand across his dark cropped hair. 'To be honest, I don't know the what-ifs.' And he truly didn't know what the consequences would be if either of the men, himself included, refused. Would Freddie simply assemble a second team to take all of them out?

'Look, let me give you a day or two to think about this. It's a lot to take in, I know.'

He nodded at the men, shook their hands and walked back to his car. As he reversed out of the car park, he saw them huddled together, discussing what had been asked of them, and not for the first time did he feel sick to his stomach. A huge part of him wanted to give Danny a heads-up on the situation. Time was ticking for Danny McKay, and that time was running out fast.

3

'Have you said anything to his lordship yet?' Freya Jenkins asked.

Maxine McKay glanced up from her magazine to look at her mother. 'About what?'

'You know full well what about. The Greeks!'

'I can hardly say to him... my mum heard a rumour from old Mrs Jones, whose niece scrubs floors for Mr Christos, that there is trouble afoot.' Maxine laughed. 'C'mon, Mum, Danny would think I've lost my mind.'

Pointing her finger towards her daughter, Freya Jenkins was more than angry, she was incensed. 'That's right. You laugh, but you won't be laughing when he's doing a twenty stretch and you're trying to scrape a few pounds together to try and feed Logan, or keep a roof over his head, like I had to do when you were little and your dad, may God rest his soul, was away.'

'Dad went away for armed robbery, Mum; my Danny is nothing like that. He has a real job for a start.'

'Oh, do me a favour... your Danny has a real job! He's the biggest villain this side of the water, darling, and you mark my words, girl, there'll be trouble there.'

Annoyed herself, Maxine's cheeks were flushed pink. She sat forward in her seat. 'You don't know anything about my Danny. You won't even let him into the house. He's not a villain at all. You do come out with some nonsense, Mum.'

Freya sighed. She could see there was no point in arguing with her daughter. Her Maxine would defend her husband till the cows came home. 'I just worry about you and Logan, that's all,' she said, reaching over and clasping her daughter's hand. 'If he ends up doing a stretch, how would you cope?'

Maxine rolled her eyes. Admittedly, her Danny might not be perfect, and it would be fair to say he was a bit of a rogue, but he was a lovable rogue. He certainly wasn't the monster her mum portrayed him to be. Anyone would think he was the devil himself, the way she carried on about him.

She went back to her magazine and absentmindedly flicked through the pages. She had to admit, though, she was worried, only for a completely different set of reasons, not that she would ever let on to her mum. She didn't want to fuel the fire that was already there. Despite what her mother thought, Maxine had begun to take a lot more notice of her husband's comings and goings, and as much as she hated to admit it, she didn't like what she saw, not one little bit.

Two hours later, Maxine walked out of Tesco with a super-market trolley full of groceries. Logan sat snugly in the infant seat, and she smiled down at him as he sucked on a teething rusk.

She walked towards her car and clicked the fob on her keyring to operate the central locking system. Lifting her son out of the trolley, she placed him into his baby car seat, then set about the task of loading the boot with shopping bags, all the while unaware that she was being intently watched.

After slamming down the boot, Maxine ran the few short yards to return the trolley to the trolley park. She fumbled to release the pound coin deposit, then hurried back to her car.

As Maxine climbed into the driving seat, she glanced behind her and checked on Logan. She laughed as he gave her a gummy grin, then turned in her seat to start the ignition. It was at that moment that she noticed her husband's boss Freddie Smith, staring at her from across the carpark. She pulled down the sun visor, in a bid to take a better look at him. When he didn't break his gaze, she gave a little shudder and locked the doors before putting the car into gear and easing out of the parking space. As she drove away, Maxine checked in the rear-view mirror to make sure he wasn't following.

She couldn't put her finger on it precisely but seeing Freddie had unnerved her.

As she drove home, she found that she was more aware of her surroundings than usual, and on the lookout for anything out of the ordinary.

What with the spat of carjackings recently, she wanted to kick herself for leaving Logan in the car alone, even if it had been only for a few seconds. There and then, Maxine decided not to mention it to her husband. She knew Danny would only lecture her about leaving their son, and she already felt guilty enough. She could only hope and pray that Freddie didn't tell Danny she'd left Logan alone in the car.

* * *

'So,' Terry said, as he took a swig from his bottled beer, 'what are your thoughts on the situation Big Tone has kindly landed us in?'

Lloydy shook his head. 'Mate, I can't fucking believe it. I'm still in shock. This is Danny, for fuck's sake. How the fuck are we meant to turn on one of our own?'

Terry blew out his lips. 'The way I see it, we don't have much choice in the matter, not unless we want to end up supporting a flyover ourselves. So the question is, how are we going to play this out?'

Lloydy rested the cold bottle against his forehead. 'This is all wrong,' he muttered before gulping down his beer. He had a feeling he would need several alcoholic beverages over the course of the next few days just to get him through. 'Well, I don't fancy any of our chances taking him on, not single-handed anyway. The man is an animal. Even the Old Bill thinks twice before getting involved with him.'

Nodding his head, Terry answered, 'Then we steam in when he's least expecting it. Let's face it, that might be the only chance we have.'

The two men sat quietly with their own thoughts. Lloydy stared out of the patio doors to the garden beyond. He and his girlfriend had gone out for a meal with Danny and his wife once. They'd had a lovely evening and had made plans to do it again. Now, he realised, that time would never come, and he felt pained and heart sorry for what was to happen.

'Are we in agreement then? We take Danny down and keep going until the job's done?'

Lloydy looked across to Terry and reluctantly agreed. If truth were told, he just wanted to get out of this house and away from the madness that his life had suddenly spiralled towards.

* * *

Ending the phone call, Big Tone sighed with relief. He felt as though a weight had been lifted off his shoulders. A part of him had had a feeling of dread that the men he'd chosen would refuse Freddie's request. If that had been the case, then he didn't bear to think about the repercussions. He knew, instinctively, they would be harsh.

Big Tone was becoming increasingly concerned about the state of Freddie's mind. His long-time friend and boss had become obsessed with the situation with Danny. It wasn't healthy, and definitely wasn't warranted, as far as Big Tone could tell.

He had never heard any whispers about Danny wanting to take over the firm. As far as he was aware, the man had only ever been loyal, and he knew there would be gossip if that hadn't been the case. Someone, somewhere, would have let Freddie, or one of the other faces, know. If for no other reason than to cause hag or point score.

Closing his eyes, Big Tone took a deep breath before giving Freddie a call to give him what seemed like the tenth update on the situation that morning alone.

He felt mentally drained. How the fuck Danny had put up with Freddie's demands for all these years, he had no idea. As far as Big Tone was concerned, Danny McKay deserved a medal.

* * *

Freddie Smith switched off his phone and smiled. He felt happier now in the knowledge that his plan to extinguish Danny McKay's life was falling into place. There was nothing he would like better than to bring the fucker down, to plant a bullet in the man's skull, but the sick, twisted part of his brain wouldn't allow him to take that course of action.

More than anything, he wanted to see Danny suffer. He

wanted to see the man surrounded in pain. Not only did he want
him to know that he was about to take his last breath, but that it
was him who was responsible for the hit. No, shooting was too
quick, too easy... McKay was going to go down underneath a hail
of blows, all the while wishing he had never been born.

Momentarily, he felt sorry for McKay's pretty little wife. Still,
he thought to himself, once Danny was out of the picture, she
would be fair game. She would need a shoulder to cry on, and his
shoulders were big enough for her pretty little head to rest upon.

As for the little lad, well, he would need a father figure,
wouldn't he? Someone to show him the ropes, someone to show
him how the world worked. Yes, Freddie Smith was more than
happy to play the role of an uncle, or even daddy, if his luck was
in, and what a great role model he would make for the boy.

Feeling euphoric, Freddie dialled Matty Payne's mobile
phone. He was up for a party now, and he knew the lad would
oblige. He had no other choice in the matter.

* * *

Driving out to Essex, Danny flicked the indicator as he
approached the Southend turn-off. He had a contact there who
owned a small holding. He'd done the man a huge favour a few
years back concerning a piece of land adjacent to his farm, and
now it was time for him to call in his debt.

As he drove down the country lane, he checked the rear-view
mirror frequently. He wouldn't put it past Freddie to have him
followed. He knew how the man's mind worked. After all, it was
Danny who had dealt with the firm's business dealings for all of
these years.

Andrew Marsh was waiting at the gate as Danny drove in. He
waved at him in a greeting, and Danny lifted his hand in return.

Parking the car, he climbed out, and careful of where he stepped, he managed to navigate around the mud-splattered ground.

He shook Andrew's hand. 'Nice to see you, fella.' Danny smiled.

'And you. Come on into the house. I've got a nice brandy waiting for you.'

Danny followed Andrew inside. As promised, he saw a full brandy bottle and two glasses on the sideboard.

'Take a seat,' Andrew said as he collected the bottle and glasses.

Danny sat at the scrubbed pine table beside the kitchen AGA cooker, and warmed his hands.

'So, what is it I can do for you, Danny?' Andrew asked as he poured out their drinks.

'I've got a situation, mate,' Danny answered, turning in his seat. 'And I need you to repay the favour you owe me.'

'I thought as much. To be honest, I've been waiting for this day to come.'

Taking a sip of brandy, Danny got down to business. The fact that he trusted this man was at the forefront of his mind.

'I'm going to need a gun disposed of. You don't need to know the whys, and it's safer you don't know, to be honest, mate.'

Andrew listened intently. He showed no shock in what was being asked of him. Instinctively, he knew that if Danny McKay was coming to him for help, then it was something big. 'So, how do you want me to dispose of the gun?'

Danny smiled as he glanced out of the window towards the farm. 'I want it cut down, then distributed in various locations. You have the facilities here to do that.'

Andrew followed Danny's gaze and then nodded his balding head. 'When should I expect you?'

'Late Saturday evening, maybe early hours of Sunday morning.'

'I'll be here waiting. I'll clear the farm, so it's just you and me.'

Satisfied, Danny nodded, and drained his drink. Now that the business was over with, he was able to relax.

'Let me show you around the farm, so you can see what I've done with the place.' Andrew smiled.

Danny followed Andrew out of the house. He was impressed with what his friend had done, and he nodded as Andrew pointed towards the land that Danny had acquired for him.

'Look's the business, mate. You've done a good job.'

'Getting there, Danny. All thanks to you.'

An hour later, Danny left the farm and made his way back towards East London. He was eager to get back on familiar territory. He still had a lot of work to do.

* * *

Thirty-seven years ago, Danny's best friend, Moray Garner, had been born in South London to a Dominican father and a Romany mother. Moray went to great lengths to hide his accent. He was from the wrong side of London, according to the cockneys, and he knew for a fact that the South and East London divide was definitely alive and kicking. He had a six-inch scar that ran the length of his cheek to prove that very point.

Moray fingered his scar now as he thought through the proposition that had been put to him. He was sitting behind an oak desk, in his plush office suite, above Ritzy's Nightclub in Romford, Essex, and sitting opposite him, was Danny McKay.

He and Danny went back years, twenty-three of them to be precise. They'd worked the doors together, once, many moons ago, for Freddie Smith. As soon as Moray had earned enough capital, he'd left Freddie's firm, and started running his own doors. More than once, he'd tried to poach Danny. He'd always believed that he and Danny would make great business partners. After all, Danny's reputation preceded him, and he knew his own doormen would be wary of the man, let alone the punters.

Only it wasn't work Danny was after. What Danny wanted was going to cause an out and out war.

Sitting forward in his seat, Danny rested his arms on his knees. 'Business is business, mate.'

Moray blew out his cheeks. 'Fuck me, Danny. Taking over Freddie Smith's business dealings is not some small quest; this is fucking big time. Do you even realise what you're asking of me? You do know this is going to cause a fucking war, don't you?'

Moray watched as Danny nodded. He could see that his best mate had thought the situation through.

'I'm more than aware it's a big deal, Moray. C'mon, I wouldn't be here if I didn't know what I was doing. You know me. Let's face it, probably better than anyone else does. Would I even be here, if I hadn't thought this through? All I'm looking for is a business partner, someone else with capital, such as yourself.' Danny remained calm, his voice composed. He decided to leave out the fact that after Freddie's demise, his business would be up for grabs anyway.

All he needed was a business partner, someone with wedge and a vast workforce at his disposal, to be able to take over the contracts without himself needing to muscle in practically single-handed. The fact that he trusted Moray tenfold was an added bonus.

'Would this be an equal partnership?' Moray asked.

'Straight down the middle, fifty-fifty, mate.' Danny smiled, knowing full well that he had Moray's attention.

Moray sighed. He'd always known his best mate was ruthless,

but until now, he hadn't realised how brutal he actually was. 'Won't Freddie have something to say about this?' he asked through narrowed eyes.

Danny shrugged. 'Nothing that we can't handle, and combined, we would have enough man-power to take on whatever Freddie throws our way.'

Moray had worked hard to get to where he was today. He had been raised by the Romany side of his family, and he'd earned his money and reputation through bare-knuckle fights. Those days were far behind him. Now, he liked to concentrate on his business, but he had to admit, he missed being in the thick of the action, and Danny had definitely sparked his interest. Only, the fact that taking on Freddie Smith was going to bring untold grief niggled at him.

'Come on, out with it. Tell me, what has gone on between you and Freddie?' He stabbed his finger towards Danny, his eyebrows raised. 'And don't even think about giving me some bullshit story. I know you, remember, and the Danny I know and love, would never have breezed into my office wanting to take over Smith's businesses.'

Danny cleared his throat. He wasn't sure just how much information he should divulge. Fuck it, he decided. Moray was one of his oldest and closest mates, and if he couldn't tell him exactly what was going down, then who could he tell? 'Freddie's planning to kill me.' It was the first time he had uttered the words out loud, and suddenly, his potential fate seemed more real.

Visibly shocked, Moray whistled through his teeth and slumped back in his seat. 'I can't get my head around this,' he said, opening the drawer to his desk and taking out a silver flask filled with whiskey.

Drinking deeply from the flask, he then offered it across to Danny.

Danny shook his head, declining the offer. 'It's simple. I don't agree with how Freddie is running the firm, so he wants rid of me. It's been on the cards for a while.'

'But taking you out, that's...'

'A fucking liberty,' Danny offered.

'Yes, it is, and that's an understatement. I can't believe what I'm hearing.' Even though Moray had known that if Danny was sitting here in his office then there must be trouble afoot, he hadn't expected Freddie to resort to murder, especially not the murder of his number two – the man who many whispered actually held Freddie's firm together.

'How do you think I feel then?'

'Fuck me, Danny. What are you going to do?'

Danny shrugged. 'Get it sorted out.'

'Do you need help?' Moray asked, sincere. 'You only need to ask if you do. You know I'll be there at the drop of a hat.'

'Thanks for the offer, but I can take care of it, mate,' Danny answered, shaking his head.

Moray raised his eyebrows. He didn't doubt Danny for a second. After all, he'd seen the man in action, but taking on an entire firm that had a price on your head was something else entirely.

'I'm positive, I can handle this,' Danny reassured him. 'So, are you interested in my proposition?'

Moray didn't need asking twice. There was nothing he would like better than to see Freddie brought down. There was no love lost between the two men, and secretly, Moray had always wanted to get his hands on the contracts of the pubs and clubs that Freddie owned.

He stood up. Moray's Romany roots were more alive than ever as he spat on the palm of his hand and then held it out towards

Danny. Spitting on his own palm, Danny mirrored the action, before they shook on the deal.

It was done. There was no going back now. Danny felt as restless as he had as a kid on Christmas Eve. Only a few more days to go, then it would all be over. The sooner the better, as far as he was concerned.

4

Matty Payne was scared. He wanted to run away. Anywhere would do, as long as he was far away from both Danny McKay and Freddie Smith. Ever since Danny had turned up at the pub, he had felt sick with fear, and knowing he had to go and meet the man again was almost enough to make him want to cry. He had done a lot of that lately, crying. He just couldn't see any way out of the situation he was in, and he didn't like the way it made him feel one little bit.

To make matters even worse, Freddie Smith had threatened him that if Danny ever found out about their secret, then he would personally make sure he had a slow and painful death. If truth be known, Matty was more worried about what Danny would do, rather than Freddie. After all, the man wasn't well known for the violence he inflicted for no reason. There was no smoke without fire, as his old granny used to say.

Matty glanced up at the clock on the wall. It was time to go. He pulled on his tattered trainers, switched off the light, then, after turning the key in the lock to the front door of his tiny bedsit, he reluctantly made his way towards The Hope, where Danny would be waiting for him.

He felt choked up and could feel a hard lump form in his throat. He swiped away the tears, which already had begun to glisten his eyes. He needed to get a grip and fast, before he really gave the game away. Otherwise, all the crying in the world wouldn't be enough to help him.

* * *

Danny pulled into The Hope car park. He switched off the engine, then pulled down the glove box, taking out the 400 pounds he had placed there.

After looking around him, he glanced at his watch. The little rat better not have stood him up. He contemplated getting out of the motor to check that the kid wasn't in the pub. He was about to open the car door when he saw Matty running towards him. He was all arms and legs, like a lanky streak of piss.

'I'm here,' Matty shouted out.

'For fuck's sake, keep your fucking noise down,' Danny growled.

'Sorry,' Matty replied, leaning against Danny's car, clearly out of breath after running the short distance from his home to the car park.

'Do you mind?'

Matty leapt away from the car. 'Sorry,' he said for a second time.

Irritated, Danny rolled his eyes. 'Just go and see if your contact is here and then come back and collect the money.'

Danny watched as Matty ran around the side of the pub. He shook his head in disbelief. What a sorry state of affairs they were going to become, with the likes of Payne in the firm. They were going to become a laughing stock, and not for the first time was he relieved to be out. What the hell had been going through Freddie's mind to recruit this little mug? The kid was a nervous wreck and sending the likes of him up against a real firm was suicide. Danny was still shaking his head in disbelief when Matty ran back to him.

'He's there.'

Danny passed the money through the open window. 'Don't fucking drop it,' he called out as Matty sprinted off.

After a few minutes, the boy returned. He handed over a package and Danny carefully unwrapped it. He was impressed that Matty had actually come through with the goods.

'And this definitely works?' he asked, turning the hard, heavy, black firearm over in his hand.

'Yeah, of course.'

'Okay,' Danny said as he rewrapped the package and placed it underneath the passenger seat. He dropped the cartridges inside his coat pocket. 'Remember what I said. Don't breathe a single word about this to anyone, and I mean absolutely anyone.' Danny's voice was suddenly menacing.

He waited for the lad to nod his head, then started the ignition and drove out of the car park. He was eager to get home. He still needed to pack a small holdall of clothes that he could change into after the shooting. He planned on burning the clothes he would be wearing, alongside disposing of the gun. Absolutely no trace of the crime could come back to him.

* * *

Maxine was bathing Logan when she heard her husband's key turn in the lock.

'I'm upstairs,' she called out.

'Okay, babe.'

Maxine could hear Danny run up the stairs, then move around in their bedroom. She could hear drawers being opened.

'What are you looking for?' she asked.

'Just my gym stuff.'

Pushing a lock of dark hair behind her ear, away from Logan's grasping hands, Maxine swiftly wrapped their son in a towel, dried him, then dressed him ready for bed.

She walked through to the bedroom and placed the baby in his crib. 'Did you find what you were looking for?'

'Erm, yeah, all sorted,' Danny replied. He swiftly kissed her on the forehead and left the room with a small black holdall in his hand.

Standing in the middle of the room, Maxine immediately looked towards the freshly washed gym clothes she had placed on top of the chest of drawers earlier that afternoon. Her husband had blatantly lied to her. She took a seat on the edge of the bed and looked towards the bedroom door that Danny had exited, wondering how many other lies he had told. How many times had she believed him, without questioning the truth? It was a sobering thought.

* * *

Another or Freddie Smith's young firm members, seventeen-year-old Lewis Hart, was playing snooker in a snooker hall in Romford, Essex. With a mop of blonde hair, he was a good looking lad. He was also a good little player and had been something of a child prodigy. He could have made it as a professional one day, but that dream had been shattered when he'd discovered the opposite sex, alcohol and fighting.

These days, he only played for fun, even though he could wipe the floor with men twice his age. He was a wasted talent, and if only he'd knuckled down and continued practising, who knew just how far he could have gone.

Three years earlier, Lewis had come into contact with Freddie Smith, and ever since then, he'd been working for Freddie in some form or another. Just recently, he'd been given the task of collecting debts. Lewis loved the job, he loved the reputation it gave him, and he loved acting the big man.

Even if some of the special jobs he had to do for Freddie made him feel both ashamed and sick, he wouldn't change his life for anything. Chalking the cue stick, Lewis was about to take a shot, when his mobile phone rang. He saw Freddie's number flash up on the caller ID, and felt his stomach form an instant knot. He knew what the call would entail. Freddie would have a special job for him to do, one he didn't particularly like, but it was money at the end of the day. He threw down the cue stick, then walked out of the snooker hall. Little did he know, this was to be the last ever special job he was to do for Freddie.

* * *

Danny pulled out a bottle of bleach from underneath the kitchen sink and placed it inside the holdall, amongst his clothes. He was all set for the next day. Everything was in place to end Freddie's life. He took the holdall out to his car. This time tomorrow night, it would all be over. As he walked back to the house, he glanced up to see his wife watching him from the bedroom window. He felt his stomach lurch and he paused for a moment, unsure of what to do next.

She would never understand that he was doing all of this for her. He would do anything to keep both her and Logan safe, and he knew that if he didn't do something about the situation with Freddie, then he couldn't guarantee their safety.

He couldn't bear to think about what would happen if he was taken out and he was no longer around to protect them. She and their son would be left alone. Would Freddie come after them next? Just how far would Freddie be willing to go to destroy everything he loved? Danny wasn't prepared to take that chance. Freddie had to go.

* * *

'Do you fancy a cheeky line?'

Lloydy and Terry Stevens were in the Railway public house in Dagenham East. They had gone out for a drink with a group of friends. Despite this, for most of the evening, they'd found themselves huddled together at the bar, with their backs to the group. Neither of them were in the right frame of mind to be out partying.

All Lloydy wanted to do was get out of his nut, to forget his troubles. He'd downed pint after pint, even double shots of Sambuca, yet nothing was having the desired effect, even though, by rights, he should have been paralytic by now. He finally acknowledged the fact that tonight wasn't his night. He would stay sober whether he liked it or not. He looked across at Terry wearily.

'I said, are you up for a cheeky line?'

'Yeah, mate.'

Lloydy followed Terry into the men's toilets. He may as well. It wasn't as if he was going to get plastered.

He waited for Terry to come out of the cubicle, then walked in, closing the door firmly shut behind him. He used his bank card to expertly cut the coke on the top of the toilet roll holder. Making two thick lines of the white powder, Lloydy then swiftly rolled up a twenty-pound note.

He swallowed quickly, as the bitter aftertaste trickled down his nasal passage, and he waited for the numbing sensation to work its magic, savouring the moment. It was only after taking coke that he believed they could actually take Danny out. The coke made him feel invincible. Immediately afterwards, Lloydy snorted his second line. He had a feeling it would take quite a few lines to get him through the night.

* * *

Danny woke early. In all honesty, he had hardly slept. He'd tossed and turned until the morning light had begun to stream through the window blinds. Maxine slept soundly beside him, and he crept out of the bed, careful not to wake her.

In the kitchen below, Danny flicked the switch on the kettle. He needed coffee, and spooned a large spoonful of coffee granules into a mug. He liked his coffee black and strong.

Sitting down at the breakfast table, Danny sipped the scalding liquid, savouring the peace and quiet before Logan woke and screamed the house down. Once he'd finished his coffee, he would bring his son downstairs, he decided. He wanted to spend the morning with him, just in case anything went wrong today. He pushed the thought from his mind. Keep thinking positive, he told himself. Everything was going to go to plan.

By the time Maxine came down the stairs, her hair in disarray and with sleep still in the corner of her eyes, Danny had already given their son his breakfast.

'Hey, what's all this?' She smiled. It was a first for Danny to let her have a lie in.

'Just spending some quality time with my little man.'

Laughing, Maxine nodded towards their son. 'I think he has more porridge over his face than he's actually eaten.'

Danny smiled. 'You're okay, aren't you son?' he asked, as Logan gave him one of his heart-warming gummy smiles.

After wiping over Logan's face with a wet wipe, Maxine sat down at the breakfast table. Danny pushed a mug of coffee in front of her.

'Look, Max, I'm going to be out for most of the day and night.'

Maxine narrowed her eyes, immediately suspicious. 'Where are you going?'

'It's work,' Danny answered, the lie easily tripping off his tongue.

Maxine nodded. The lie about the gym clothes her husband had told her was still fresh in her mind. 'I see.'

Danny ignored the tone of her voice, determined not to leave the house on an argument.

'I know you're lying to me. So, where are you really going?' she demanded.

'I told you... work.' Danny shrugged.

'Really?' Maxine asked, raising her eyebrows.

Danny nodded to placate her. 'Of course. Where else would I go?'

When his wife didn't answer, Danny sipped at his coffee, the lie he'd told hanging heavy around his neck. Maxine would never understand; she didn't come from his world, however much she might think she did. She was decent, and far too good for him. She'd be horrified if she were to ever find out about the things he'd got up to over the years, the violence he'd been a part of, not to mention the murders he'd committed. Admittedly she knew he was no angel, that he was a rogue, but that was as much as she knew and more importantly as much as he ever wanted her to know.

An hour later, once he was showered and shaved, Danny left the house. He'd pushed the gun down the waistband of his jeans, the jacket he wore ensuring it was fully covered. He then drove towards Plaistow. The fact that there was a strong possibility this would be his last day on Earth was pushed from his mind.

* * *

Danny was one of the first to arrive in The Tavern. This was to be the meeting point, and he planned to be there before Freddie. More than anything, he wanted to watch the man's face as he walked in and saw him standing at the bar.

Within the hour, members of the firm began filling the pub. They greeted Danny as they always had in the past, and offered to buy him drinks, all the while unaware of Freddie's murderous plan.

It was Lloydy who eventually gave the game away. He couldn't look him in the eye, and the fact he was glued to Terry Stevens's side told Danny everything he needed to know. It was these two men he needed to watch.

He almost laughed, a huge belly laugh in fact, that Freddie actually believed they could take him out. Freddie had clearly underestimated him, but that was Freddie all over. He had never looked at the bigger picture.

* * *

Walking the short distance from where they had parked the car, towards the pub, Freddie and Big Tone were deep in conversation. It wasn't too late to call everything off as far as Big Tone was concerned.

'Why don't you just out him?' Big Tone asked for the third time that morning.

Freddie shook his head. 'I want the cunt dead.'

Big Tone's heart sank. None of this made sense to him. 'C'mon, Fred. The man's got a kid.'

'Who will more than likely turn out to be a bigger bastard than his father,' Freddie spat. 'I'm doing the world a favour in disposing of McKay.'

Big Tone threw Freddie a sidelong glance. The man actually believed what he was saying.

Pausing, Big Tone brought Freddie to a halt. 'It doesn't have to be this way.' His voice took on a pleading tone. 'Just out him. We can call this off. Let him go home to his wife and kid.'

Anger was clearly evident across Freddie's face, and spittle formed at the corner of his snarled lips. 'Are you not fucking listening to me? McKay is going down. I want him obliterated. I've told you, time and time again. How many more times do I need to say it? McKay knows too much.'

Big Tone swallowed deeply and nodded. He had done everything he could to help Danny. There was nothing else he could do. The man's fate was sealed.

* * *

When Freddie walked through the door with Big Tone close behind him, Danny wasn't disappointed. He took great pleasure in seeing the contempt for himself, spread across the older man's face. A part of him still couldn't believe that it had come to this, yet he knew the problem between Freddie and himself had been bubbling under the surface for a long time. It was always going to come to a head. That was how things worked in their world. He watched as Freddie leaned in close to speak privately in Big Tone's ear, and when that message was relayed to Lloydy and Terry Stevens, he saw the two men nod their heads.

Inside, Danny seethed with anger. Despite this, outwardly he appeared calm, giving away no tell-tale signs that he was aware of what was being planned.

They wouldn't be able to organise a piss up in a brewery, Danny thought to himself as he drank his brandy, all the while silently observing everything around him.

After ten or so minutes, Big Tone finally made his way towards him. 'You okay, mate?'

Danny nodded. At this precise moment in time, he didn't trust himself to speak. He was fuming that these muppets obviously doubted his intelligence. He wouldn't forget Big Tone's, Lloydy's, or Terry Stevens's involvement in the attempt on his life, and if he survived out the day, then at some point in the very near future, their time would come. If it was the last thing he did, it would be to make sure these three men paid the price.

* * *

As per usual, Freddie was calling the shots, and for once, Danny didn't argue the case on how he thought they should bring George Christos down. He silently let Freddie do the talking. When it was time to leave The Tavern, he kept himself towards the back of the crowd. He wanted the four men in front of him, so he could watch their every move. He wouldn't put it past them to try and take him out whilst he was unaware. After all, that would be the only chance they were going to get. It was the only way they would ever get him down onto the ground.

Danny was on edge, waiting for the attack on himself. He could feel the hard firearm inside his waistband, cold against his skin, and he resisted the urge to pat it. He knew Freddie would be watching him closely, and he couldn't let any of them know he was carrying.

'Hey Danny, jump in the motor and I'll give you a lift down there,' Big Tone shouted out once they were outside, ready for the off.

Danny shook his head. 'Nah, it's okay, mate. I'll take my car.' He wasn't that stupid, he thought to himself as he climbed into his car and started the ignition.

He waited for Big Tone's Range Rover to pull out of the car park, and then followed suit.

* * *

Against his better judgement, Freddie had decided to have Danny taken out after the visit to George Christos's restaurant.

As soon as they had run the Greeks out of East London, that smug bastard McKay would get what was coming to him, and Freddie wanted a front row seat. He didn't doubt the men Big Tone had recruited for the job in the slightest. In fact, he was looking forward to seeing the life battered out of McKay. He had even felt a moment of satisfaction to see that the man whom he had grown to despise, had finally learnt to keep that big trap of his shut. It was an even greater victory to have watched the younger man slip to the back of the crowd, with his tail between his legs, so to speak. It was where he should have kept him for all these years. He supposed it was his own fault, really. He had given the little bastard too much power.

Travelling the short distance towards Barking, Freddie was in high spirits. He had never felt prouder than he did at this very moment. Almost every member of his firm had turned up. A few had even come out of retirement, just for this meet.

Tonight was definitely going to be a night to remember – one that he would treasure for the remainder of his life.

They pulled up outside the restaurant, and once the firm had regrouped, Freddie gave them their orders. Under no circumstances was George Christos to leave without Freddie getting the message across to him that the doors belonged to him, and him alone. Old scores were to be settled here, tonight.

* * *

As they burst into the restaurant, startled shouts and screams could be heard as the last few remaining, terrified diners ran for cover. Waiting staff hid behind the wooden bar, which sat proudly in the far corner. Bottles of alcohol and glasses adorning the bar top glistened in the dimmed light, as the staff members' frantic calls for help were muffled by the crash of tables and chairs being overturned.

'Christos,' Freddie roared. 'Get your arse out here.'

Greek voices filled the air, and angry shouts bounced around the confines of the small restaurant. When the Greeks finally emerged from the kitchen area, with meat cleavers and knives clutched in their fists, Freddie laughed out loud.

'Get that ponce Christos out here, and I'll tell my boys to play nicely.'

Danny's heart thumped loudly in his chest as he navigated his way around the crowd, until Freddie was in his sights. He would have just one chance at this, and if he fucked up, he was a dead man.

Danny hung back slightly, his hand hovering above his waistband. On tenterhooks, he watched as the scene before him played out, waiting for the right moment to take out the gun. He couldn't be seen pulling out the weapon – it would be the equivalent of signing his own death warrant, and as it was his life was hanging precariously by a fine thread.

Each passing second seemed like an eternity. Come on, he wanted to scream. Someone make the move.

Finally, as the two firms surged forward, he took the firearm out and held it by his side, with one last surreptitious glance around him to make sure he wasn't being watched. He took aim, and without even giving the matter a second thought he squeezed the trigger. The gunshot was unexpected, sudden and loud to their ears. For a split second, there was a shocked silence, before pandemonium broke out.

5

Danny ran as if his life depended on it, which just so happened to be the case. He could feel his heart thumping wildly inside his chest. How the fuck had that happened? How the fuck had he missed? In his mind's eye, he replayed the events which had just taken place, and could feel the vomit rising up inside his throat. He swallowed deeply, taking deep breaths, as he desperately tried to compose himself.

Each time he closed his eyes, he could see the kid, and he was just a kid for that matter, dropping to the floor, a mop of blonde hair flying out behind him, his life's blood draining rapidly from the gaping hole in his chest.

Fumbling with his car keys, Danny finally managed to open the car door. Climbing inside, he hastily locked the door behind him and leant his head against the cool steering wheel. 'Shit, shit, shit,' he muttered.

Looking up at the rear-view mirror, Danny rubbed his hand over his face, his skin clammy and ashen. Stunned, he tried to contemplate what had just taken place.

What had gone so very wrong? Freddie was in his sights. It was Freddie he had aimed for.

How, he wanted to scream, was Freddie still alive, and that poor little bastard on the ground dead? The sound of police sirens stirred Danny into action, and starting the ignition, he drove as fast as was legally acceptable, out of East London towards Essex.

* * *

For once Freddie Smith was too shocked to speak. He could smell the sickly iron scent of blood on his clothes and skin. Wiping the kid's blood splatter from his face, he finally spoke.

'I want whoever is responsible for this, dead.'

Big Tone looked around him at the few firm members who had assembled at Freddie's house, and could see the same shock he, himself felt, echoed in their faces. Somehow, they had made it to Freddie's home in Hainault, Essex, without getting their collars felt, which was a miracle in itself, considering Freddie was covered in the kid's blood.

'Did anyone see anything?' Big Tone asked as he looked at the men one by one.

'Of course someone must have fucking seen something,' Freddie shouted. 'Whichever Greek did this, I want him brought to me.' He pulled the blood-stained shirt over his head and dropped it at his feet. 'Get on the blower and put the feelers out. Someone, somewhere, knows about this, and while you're at it, I want a meet, and I want everyone there,' he growled, pointing a finger in Big Tone's direction.

'What about...?' Big Tone asked, leaving the sentence unfinished.

'Especially that cunt. I wouldn't put it past him to know something about this,' Freddie spat. 'That bastard wants my firm, I can feel it in here,' he roared stabbing a stiff finger into his chest.

Feeling his heart sink, Big Tone took his mobile phone out of his pocket and scrolled through his contact list. Would this nightmare never end? he thought bitterly. Purposely, he decided to leave calling Danny until last.

* * *

Danny dropped the gun onto the scrubbed pine table. The clatter of metal on wood was loud and harsh in the otherwise quiet room. Sinking into the nearest chair, Danny then held his head in his hands. Andrew Marsh watched him warily, concerned.

In a state of shock, Danny had driven out to Essex on autopilot. How he had made it to Andrew's farm in one piece without crashing the car, he had no idea.

All the while, his mind was working overtime. He'd just killed a kid. He could barely recollect seeing the lad before, and didn't even know his name, yet the boy's face was burned into his memory.

Gulping at the brandy which had been placed in his hand, Danny shook his head in a bid to clear his thoughts. He just needed to think through the dilemma he now found himself in. He knew, instinctively, he had just made the situation ten times worse. It was highly unlikely Freddie would allow him to get away twice. The price on his head had been raised.

Andrew took the empty glass from Danny's hand and automatically refilled it. Handing it back, he watched the big man gulp it down as if his life depended on it.

'There's a price on my head, Andy,' Danny stated as he wiped his hand across his mouth.

Taking the empty glass out of his friend's hand, Andrew took a seat opposite him.

'Then you do what you do best. You sit and you think through your next move.'

Reluctantly, Danny nodded. If truth were told, he'd just used up his one and only move. There was no back-up plan, so sure was he that his plan to kill Freddie would be fool-proof. Now, he wanted to curse himself. Why had he not thought through the possibilities of the shooting going wrong? Why had he been so cocksure of himself?

'You need time to think, and you need to rest,' Andrew stated, nodding his head towards the sofa. 'You look done in, mate.'

'I don't think I could sleep, even if I wanted to.'

'Get some rest,' Andrew repeated, 'and things will look clearer.'

As his friend walked out of the room with the weapon carefully wrapped in a cloth, Danny wearily pulled his hand through his dark hair. He then poured out a generous measure of brandy and swallowed it in one large gulp, before hesitantly making his way across to the sofa. Sinking down, he closed his eyes for a few moments. Almost immediately, the boy's face flashed in his mind's eye. Bolting upright, Danny leapt up off the sofa, ran out to the yard, and emptied the contents of his stomach.

As he heaved, he could hear the whirl of machinery from inside the outhouse.

Straightening up, Danny walked over to the outbuilding. He wiped the back of his hand over his mouth while watching from the doorway, as Andrew cut the gun down into small pieces. Satisfied that Andrew was capable of the task he'd set him, Danny returned to the lounge. He sat gingerly on the edge of a chair and held his head in his hands as he tried to think.

No one had seen him fire the gun, he was pretty certain of

that, and with the weapon soon to be disposed of, it therefore ceased to exist. The only real problem he had was Freddie, and the price on his head. All he needed to do was keep his nut down for a few days, until he could put a plan of action into place. Happier now, Danny closed his eyes. Andy was right, he needed to sleep.

* * *

Four hours later, Danny woke with a start. For a brief moment, he felt disorientated.

He sat up, and swinging his legs around, he reached inside his jacket pocket for his mobile phone. Thirteen missed calls from Big Tone. He switched the device off and stretched out his arms. He couldn't deal with this, at least not yet anyway.

He needed food and a shower, in that precise order, and then the day's events could unfold.

Danny wandered through to the kitchen. The scent of eggs and bacon simmering on the stove had never smelt better. He gave a grin as Andrew glanced over his shoulder at him.

'Hungry?' Andrew asked.

'Marvin,' Danny replied, using the slang word for starving.

'There's tea in the pot,' Andrew stated as he gestured to the teapot. 'Help yourself.'

Danny poured out two cups and drank deeply, quenching his thirst. 'The gun?' he enquired.

'Cut down, and residing in a bucket of bleach as we speak. Later on this morning, I'll go and see my brother. He has a boat moored here in Southend. I'll make sure that whatever is left of the weapon is thrown overboard.'

Danny nodded. 'I need these clothes burned, too,' he said, looking down at the crumpled shirt he wore.

'Eat, and then we'll take care of that.' Andrew smiled. 'I already have a small fire burning over on the back field.'

Satisfied, Danny took the plate of food Andrew handed him, and sat down at the table. He ate heartily, mopping up the juices with thick slices of buttered bread.

With his stomach full, and now freshly showered and changed, Danny felt better in himself. His head felt much clearer, and now that he was over the initial shock of the events that had taken place the previous day, it was time to get back to business.

He shook Andrew's hand and thanked his friend for everything he'd done for him, then left the farm.

* * *

Maxine was going out of her mind. She hadn't heard from her husband in over twenty-four hours. She had repeatedly called his mobile phone, and was becoming more and more panic stricken each time she reached his answering machine.

What with the shocking story of a young lad being shot dead on the local news, she was beside herself with worry. A child prodigy, the news broadcaster had stated, his face solemn, could have been the next Ronnie O'Sullivan, apparently.

Tapping in Danny's phone number again, Maxine anxiously waited for him to pick up. She chewed on her fingernail, her eyes trained on the comings and goings of the road outside the lounge window, hoping, praying she would see her husband's car pull into the drive.

'I'm sorry,' she said as she switched off her phone. 'It's going straight to answering machine still.'

'I'm sure he will turn up soon. So I will wait for a while, if that's okay with you? And how about making that tea now?' Big Tone smiled.

Standing in Danny's kitchen, his large frame dominating the space, Big Tone watched as Maxine set two mugs out on the marble worktop. He smiled reassuringly at her, as she glanced nervously towards him.

'How did you say you knew Danny?' she asked.

'We've worked together for years,' Big Tone replied. 'I was in the area, so I thought I would pop in and see him.'

'Oh, I see.'

'Nice fella.'

'Yes, he is,' Maxine answered, realising she knew so little about the people Danny surrounded himself with.

She handed over a steaming mug of tea, then began wiping the worktop down. Within moments, she heard Danny's key turn in the lock. Throwing down the cloth, she ran out to the hallway to meet him, unsure if she wanted to hug him or hit him for scaring the life out of her.

'Where have you been?' she cried. 'I've been going out of my mind.'

'I was at a mate's,' Danny answered as he pulled his wife into his arms.

'Your friend is here. He's been waiting ages for you to get home.' Her voice a mere whisper, Maxine glanced over her shoulder towards the kitchen.

Danny narrowed his eyes, then walked along the hallway, his body suddenly taut.

'What are you doing here?' he hissed, as he came to enter the kitchen. His voice was low, so his wife couldn't hear.

Big Tone smiled to take the edge off his words. 'I've been calling you for hours. If you'd picked up, I wouldn't need to be here now, would I?'

Indicating for Big Tone to follow him out to the garden, Danny rounded on him.

'What the fuck do you want?'

They were standing on the patio, the vast lawn spread out before them, and towards the end of the garden was an open air swimming pool.

'Unless it's escaped your notice, someone tried to take Freddie out last night.'

'What are the Old Bill saying about it?'

Confusion flashed across Big Tone's face. 'Do I look like a fucking copper? How would I know what's being said?'

'I just thought maybe something had been mentioned?'

'No,' Big Tone answered, flicking his hand to dismiss the conversation. 'There's a meet tomorrow night. Freddie wants you there.'

Danny shook his head. 'I've already told you, once the meeting with the Greeks was over, I'm out.'

'Things have changed. The attempt on Freddie's life, and the kid being gunned down, changes everything.'

'Not to me it doesn't,' Danny said, shrugging.

'It's not a fucking request, mate. It's an order, and Freddie wants you there.'

Danny stared at the big man, a menacing expression creasing his face. His eyes were instantly hard, dangerous. 'You're forgetting who you're talking to, Tone. I'm not some muppet off the street. Now, you can run back to Freddie and you can tell him whatever the fuck you like. I'm done with the firm.'

Big Tone cleared his throat. 'Fair enough. I will tell Freddie, but you know it isn't going to go down well, you know he—'

'Piss off, Tone, before I end up lamping you one,' Danny interrupted.

Big Tone held up his hands. 'Okay, I'm going.'

Danny watched as the big man walked back through the

house, and he stifled the urge to kick the garden table across the lawn. He'd had a gutful of Freddie Smith and the poxy firm.

* * *

'For Christ's sake Danny, what is wrong with you?'

Danny ignored the rising panic in Maxine's voice as he resumed his position in front of the living room window. Immediately, his eyes strained to look inside the car, which had been parked outside his house for the past three hours. In any normal circumstance, a parked car outside his home wouldn't have bothered him in the slightest, but everything had changed. These were not normal circumstances any more.

He knew who the occupants were, and more importantly, he knew exactly why they were parked just yards from his front door. Any other day, he would have laughed at the sheer audacity of the two men Freddie had sent to intimidate him. They were hardly worth him worrying about. He could take them out in seconds, and they were just as much aware of that fact as he was.

It was the fact that they had been sent at all which was worrying him – rather than sending senior ranking members of the firm, these two men had been chosen to give him the cold stare. It was more of an insult than anything else. It had been done to wind him up him, and was Freddie's way of getting the point across that he thought he was nothing, a no one, a mug. Well, that point had been well and truly understood, and as a result, he was livid.

'Danny!' Her eyes wide, Maxine jiggled Logan on her hip as she stood in the doorway to the lounge. 'What is going on?'

Danny glanced back at his wife. He could see fear spread across her face, and knew, instinctively, that like most mothers, Maxine's first concern would be for their son.

'It's nothing for you to worry about, sweetheart. Why don't you go and bath Logan?'

He could see confusion spread across her face, and when she walked out of the room, he almost felt his body sag with relief.

This was more than a joke; it was an absolute fucking piss take. All he wanted was out of the firm, and Freddie was giving him this grief.

If it wasn't for the fact that Maxine and his son were in the house, he would have dragged the two muppets out of their car and battered them to within an inch of their sorry lives, just for the sheer fun of it.

Danny stood contemplating this. He was still a face in the firm, and he knew the two occupants would shit themselves if he did. It was only his Maxine who was stopping him from doing just that.

He had kept so much of himself a secret from his wife. She had no idea what he was actually capable of, or for that matter, just what he was really involved in. His gut instinct told him that she would leave, and would take Logan with her, if she were to ever find out just who and what he really was.

He fingered his mobile phone in his pocket. All he had to do was make one telephone call, tell Freddie he would be at the meet, and then he would call off the two pricks sitting outside his house.

Pulling out his phone, he sat down heavily on the sofa. He punched in a number, and his finger paused over the dial button.

The problem he had was that he knew revenge would be plotted, and damage would be done – some serious damage at that. His life was already in danger, and if Freddie and the firm ever found out he was behind the shooting, they would have him hung, drawn and quartered.

He took a deep breath and exhaled slowly. This would be the performance of a lifetime. He then pressed dial on the keypad.

* * *

Freddie specifically chose the disused industrial unit that he had recently purchased, due to the sheer volume of men he expected to turn up for the meet, and he wasn't disappointed. The fact that it was in a remote location was an added bonus.

He held up his hand to quiet the men down, knowing full well they would be eager to get down to business. The Greeks had taken a liberty by trying to take him out. Now, more than ever, the cheeky cunts needed sorting out.

'What's the low down on the street?' he asked.

The men looked around at each other before answering. Their voices were loud, each having their own theories as to who exactly was responsible for the shooting.

'I want the facts,' Freddie shouted. 'Not your fucking conspiracy theories. Who was responsible?'

'What does it matter?' Mick Johnson asked, his voice hoarse from years of smoking too many cigarettes. 'They took one of ours, so we take one of theirs.'

Freddie watched as the men nodded. His eyes fell upon Danny, and a bubble of irritation rose within him. 'You're fucking quiet for once. What are your thoughts on the matter?'

Danny looked Freddie in the eye. His voice was loud and confident, giving away no tell-tale signs of his involvement. 'As Mick said, what does it matter? They took one of ours, so we do the same. An eye for an eye, and all that bollocks.'

Freddie snarled as he watched the men he'd worked with for a number of years nod in agreement, clearly agreeing that this was the route they should take.

He lit a cigarette, thinking it through. Yes, taking one of the Greeks made sense, yet his pride wanted the man responsible. The cunt, whoever he was, had tried to kill him, and that was something he couldn't swallow.

'Look at it this way. We take one of the Greeks, and Christos will have one of two choices. He either hands over the cunt who did it, or he doesn't. Either way, he will be a man down. It's a no-win situation. We still get to take out one of his boys.'

Freddie nodded, realising this was the only option he had. He'd put enough feelers out over the last few days that even MI5 would be proud, and still, no one was talking.

'Okay, this is what we do then. I want Big Tone, and you, Mick,' Freddie said, as he turned to look at Mick Johnson, 'to nab one of the Greek bastards. And the rest of you, I want your eyes and ears to the ground. Report back to me, personally, if you hear of anything, no matter how small it is.'

He waited for the men to nod, then dismissed them. The meeting was over.

They walked out of the unit and the cold air hit them as they made their way to their own cars.

All the while, Freddie's beady eyes remained focused on Danny McKay. 'What has that cocky little bastard had to say about this?' he asked Big Tone, his voice low.

Big Tone shrugged. 'Fuck all. He knows as much about any of this as we do.'

Freddie's face was hard as he watched the man who had been his number two for more years than he could remember, climb into his car. He hadn't forgotten about McKay, and once the problem with the Greeks was done and dusted, he would have him taken out.

He watched as Matty Payne was about to climb into Danny's passenger seat, and called out to him.

'Matty, I'm giving you a lift.' Freddie's voice brooked no arguments. Matty paused, clearly unsure of what he should do. Freddie swallowed down his anger. He would need to have a serious word with the kid and remind him of exactly who it was in charge.

* * *

Danny was annoyed as he watched Matty Payne run across the car park to Freddie's car. He'd wanted to put the hard word on the lad about the firearm he'd helped him to acquire. More than anything, though, he knew it was only sheer luck that had allowed him to walk out of the warehouse in one piece. That, and the fact that, as of yet, Freddie hadn't pieced everything together.

Realising the moment was lost, he started the ignition and sped out of the industrial area, all the while cursing Freddie Smith, Matty Payne and the entire firm. He drove towards Romford, where he had a meeting set up with Moray Garner. It was time to put the second phase of his plan into action, and this time, there would be no mistakes.

* * *

Matty Payne's small frame seemed tiny in comparison to Freddie's muscular body as he sat in the passenger seat of Freddie's car. As usual, he was quieter than normal when he was in Freddie's company. This man scared him in more ways than one.

Staring out of the window as Freddie drove down the A13, Matty instantly realised that Freddie wasn't driving him back to his bedsit in Barking. Instead, Freddie was taking him to his own home in Hainault.

'I've got a nice bit of weed; thought we could have a smoke.' Freddie grinned as he turned up the volume on the radio.

Silently, Matty nodded, not liking this turn of events.

'What did McKay want with you?'

'Nothing.'

'What's wrong with you? You miserable little fucker, we're going to have a party, so cheer the fuck up,' Freddie snapped, as he roughly grabbed hold of Matty's chin and forced the boy to look at him.

'Nothing's wrong,' Matty answered, his voice small.

'Well, fucking smile then, you miserable sod.'

Matty swallowed deeply as he reverted to staring back out of the window, the passing view a blur of brightly lit lights from the headlights of oncoming traffic.

When he felt the big man's hand come to rest on his thigh, it took Matty all of his strength not to flinch. Freddie hadn't touched him like that in years, and he had to bite down on his lip, as a stray tear trickled down his cheek, at the horror he knew for certain was to come.

* * *

Moray Garner hastily shook Danny's hand before turning his attention back to his two sons as they stood on the doors of Ritzy's Nightclub.

'Problem?' Danny enquired.

'You know what it's like, mate. Two bob punters, thinking they own the town.'

Danny followed his friend's gaze as the customer in question gave Moray's two boys abuse.

It was a typical night in any drinking establishment, when a punter is either thrown out, or refused entry.

Danny walked over to the man. 'Go home, mate. You won't be getting in here tonight.'

The man staggered on his feet. Clearly, he'd had too much to drink. 'Who the fuck are you, telling me what to do?' he slurred.

'Go home,' Danny repeated.

'You can't tell me what to do. Do you know who I am?'

Having a short temper at the best of times, Danny was sick to the back teeth of hearing the geezer's nasally, whining voice. Pulling back his fist, he used his considerable strength to knock the man to the floor. 'Now, piss off home, before I really do you some damage,' he spat, standing over the semi-conscious man.

Moray turned to his boys. 'Now that is how it's done,' he said, ushering Danny inside the venue.

'I'm sorry about that,' Moray said once they were inside his office. 'The boys are young, but more than willing to learn.'

Danny took a seat and grinned. He knew Moray's sons well. They were good lads and he was particularly fond of them. 'We've all been there.'

It was a lie, and Moray smiled his gratitude. He knew for a fact that Danny McKay had always been more than capable.

'What's this trouble with Freddie?' Moray asked, swiftly changing the subject.

Danny shrugged. He wasn't surprised that Moray had heard about the shooting. In their world, the grapevine was small. Rumours and gossip were commonplace. At times, they were worse than women. 'The Greeks tried to take him out. One of the kids was gunned down in the process.'

Moray shook his head. 'Occupational hazard.'

'Too true, mate.' Danny shrugged. 'So, what's the plan?'

Running his thumb down the length of his scar, Moray raised his eyebrows. 'I'm thinking the easiest way to do this, is to put a team of our best men into each of the clubs, bang out the heavies and take over. It's simple and effective, if we have the right team.'

Danny gave a nod of his head. It was a well-known tactic, and as Moray had pointed out, it was effective. He'd even used it himself once or twice over the years, for Freddie. 'Sounds like a plan then. Give me a few days to get a team of men together, and we will put the plan into action.'

Moray smiled brightly, before pushing a sheet of paper across the table. 'I've been busy, mate. Here is the list of Freddie's clubs, and the names of the men I think would be best put in place to take over.'

Impressed, Danny smiled. 'You've done your homework.'

'As always.' Moray laughed. 'You know me, Danny. I don't do things by halves.'

Studying the lists, Danny grinned widely. Without a shadow of doubt, he knew that he and Moray were going to make a great team.

* * *

For the first time in over ten years, George Christos's restaurant was closed. Sitting at a table, he surveyed the damage around him. For most of the day, he had had police officers inside his restaurant, interviewing himself and his staff, whilst a team of forensic officers inspected every inch of his workplace. Not only was his pride dented, but it was bad for business. He wiped his hand wearily over his face, before giving a small smile of gratitude as his nephew pushed a glass of Ouzo towards him.

'Everything will be okay, uncle,' Nico said.

Smiling once again, George pulled out a chair, indicating for the young man to take a seat beside him.

Nico was such a good boy, a clever boy. He was the only child of George's younger sister, and he was studying law at the University of East London. George had high hopes for the lad, and he could once again feel pride swell inside his chest as Nico explained how the law worked to him.

After a while, George patted the boy's arm. 'Go home, Nico, and rest.'

'But what about the tidying up?' Nico asked. 'I can help,' he said sincerely.

George shook his head. 'It can keep until the morning. Now go home to your mother and rest.'

Hugging George to him, Nico smiled. 'Goodnight, uncle. I will be back tomorrow to help you.'

George nodded and watched as his nephew gathered up his jacket before walking out of the restaurant. Little did he know that it would be the last time he would ever see his favourite nephew alive.

* * *

Bleary eyed, Danny pressed answer on his mobile phone. The shrillness of Freddie's voice forced him to move the phone away from his ear. It was five-thirty in the morning, and Freddie had woken him with his persistent calling.

He could hear the excitement in Freddie's voice. 'We've got one of the Greek bastards. I want you at the industrial unit, now.'

Switching off the call, Danny rolled over and closed his eyes. Fuck you, Freddie, he thought to himself, as he desperately waited for sleep to envelop him once more.

Within seconds, the phone rang again and Danny hastily snatched it up. He swore to himself that if Freddie woke Maxine or Logan, he would happily choke the life out of the man with his bare hands.

'Okay, I'm coming,' he growled into the phone.

Swiftly, he washed and dressed, before creeping out of the house. He was in a foul mood, thanks to Freddie and lack of sleep. All he had wanted was a few extra hours of kip, and then a black coffee... in that order. It wasn't too much to ask for, was it?

* * *

The industrial unit was cold and bleak. As Danny walked through the door, he rubbed his hands together, breathing hot air over them in a bid for warmth.

The scene he walked into was like something out of a horror movie. Most people would have been horrified. In Danny's eyes, it was simply business as usual.

Strapped to a chair, in the middle of the vast empty space, was George Christos's nephew, Nico. Both of the young man's eyes were bloodied, bruised and swollen shut.

'You took your fucking time,' Freddie shouted out as Danny walked towards them.

'I was sleeping.'

An expression of contempt crossed Freddie's face. 'This bastard has said fuck all.'

Danny shrugged and leant against the wall. Meanwhile, terrified pain-filled groans came from the man strapped to the chair.

'Shut the fuck up before I cut that bastard tongue out of your head,' Freddie roared, as he gave Nico a swift kick to his legs.

'Well, he's hardly going to talk if you cut out his tongue, is he,' Danny said, stating the obvious.

'I already fucking know that.'

Danny smirked. 'I would never have guessed,' he answered sarcastically, stifling a yawn.

Looking up, Freddie caught Danny's eye. 'Oh, I am sorry, are we keeping you fucking awake? Are you planning on getting your hands dirty, or are you just going to stand there watching?'

Shrugging, Danny gestured across to Nico. 'You don't need me to do your dirty work. You're more than capable of doing the job yourself.'

Freddie lit a cigarette as he contemplated his next move. He would never have admitted it out loud, but he was out of his comfort zone. Danny had taken over this side of the business many years before, and it had been a very long time since Freddie had had to get his own hands dirty. He flicked the cigarette butt to the floor, then indicated for Big Tone to pass over a hack saw.

'Well, let's see if Christos is willing to hand over the cunt responsible now. Hold out his hand, Tone,' he said as he began the grisly task of sawing through the flesh and bone of Nico's fingers on his right hand.

Nico's blood-curdling screams filled the air, before he slumped unconscious. The ropes strapping him to the chair were the only thing keeping his body from slipping to the floor.

'Bastard is bleeding out like a pig,' Big Tone complained, as he wiped his blood-stained hands across his jeans.

Bending down, Mick Johnson picked up the bloody stumps. 'I'll get these sent to Christos.'

Bored now with the scene before him, Danny shifted his weight. 'Are we done here?'

The three men turned to face him. 'Are we done?' Freddie repeated back Danny's question, his voice taking on an incredulous tone. 'Do we look like we're fucking done?'

'I don't know,' Danny answered. 'I can't really see what else you can do, until you hear from Christos.'

Freddie thought this through, before reluctantly nodding his head. As much as he hated to admit it, Danny was right. There was nothing else they could do for the time being, other than keep questioning Nico.

* * *

In a house in Manor Park, East London, Elini Kallas was dabbing a sodden tissue at her red-rimmed eyes. She took no comfort from her elder brother George's kind words.

'Where is my boy? Why did Nico not come home?' she asked repeatedly.

George Christos was concerned. It was so out of character for his nephew to worry his mother like this. He had sent family members out searching for the boy, and so far, there had been no sightings. It was plain for everyone to see that Nico had simply vanished into thin air.

'He will return soon, Elini. I promise,' George said for the umpteenth time that morning. A wide smile was spread across his face, masking the fear he actually felt.

A constant wave of worry that foul play was somehow involved in the disappearance of his favourite nephew rippled through him – a constant feeling of dread that he just couldn't shrug off.

He watched as the women of his family fussed over his sister, and decided there was nothing else he could do to help while stuck in the house. Taking her pale face between his hands, George kissed Elini on both of her cheeks. He told her he would do everything within his power to find her son, then left the house.

On the journey back to Barking, George was quiet. His mind was working overtime. Instinctively, he knew that Freddie Smith was somehow involved, although, in truth, he had upset so many people over the years, the list of his enemies was endless.

The restaurant was still closed and in the process of being cleaned and redecorated. Begrudgingly, George had needed to buy new carpets, due to the amount of blood spilled. As he walked through the restaurant door, the scent of fresh paint was overpowering.

Shrugging off his coat, George surveyed the decorating, which he'd paid a small fortune for. Satisfied that everything was as it should be, he began to make his way towards the kitchen. Out of the corner of his eye, a small, brown bubble-wrapped envelope, propped up on the bar, caught his attention. Grabbing up the package, George hastily tore it open and tipped the contents out.

In horror, George recoiled. Severed fingers rolled off the counter onto the newly fitted carpet. Rust coloured flakes of dried blood dotted the wooden bar top, and the putrid scent of rotting flesh filled his nostrils, making him gag.

His face drained of all colour, George clutched at his chest. The room spinning was the last thing he could remember before passing out.

6

In a Wimpy bar in Romford, Essex, Maxine was sitting at a window seat. Absentmindedly, she stared out of the window. Beside her, Logan was in his buggy.

'There you go, mate,' Jaqueline Cliffe said as she placed a steaming mug of tea in front of her friend, before sliding into the seat opposite.

'Thanks, Jac.'

Making a fuss of Logan, Jaqueline laughed as he gave her a gummy grin.

'This boy of yours is a handsome little devil. He's gonna break a few hearts when he's older.'

Maxine glanced down at her son. 'He looks like Danny.'

Jaqueline rolled her eyes. She had never been a fan of Danny. She wouldn't go as far as to say she disliked him as such, but to put it mildly, she could see through his charm. Like most people, she knew of Danny McKay's reputation, and knew his good looks were nothing more than a mask, his friendly manner nothing more than a charade.

'What's he bleedin' well done now?'

'Nothing.'

Raising her eyebrows, Jaqueline studied her friend's face. Maxine's eyes looked so sad; it was clear to see that something was bothering her. 'C'mon, Max. This is me you're talking to, and that beautiful little smile of yours is not going to fool anyone, least of all me. What's he done this time?'

Tears glistened Maxine's eyes and she scrambled inside her handbag, looking for a tissue.

'Hey, what's all this?' Alarmed, Jaqueline leant forward and grasped her friend's arm.

'It's nothing.' Clearly embarrassed to be sitting in the middle of Wimpy crying, Maxine half cried and half laughed as she waved her hand in front of her face in a bid to dismiss her startling behaviour.

'Max!' Jaqueline scolded. 'What the hell is going on? What has he done? Has he hit you or something?' she asked, lowering her voice.

Shaking her head, Maxine dabbed at her eyes. 'No, of course not. He would never do anything like that.'

'Then what's wrong? I know that bastard has done something.'

'Oh Jac, I'm so worried.' She gave a little sob. 'He's been acting so strange lately, and he doesn't tell me anything any more. He won't even tell me where he's going, and the other night, he didn't come home at all.' She twisted the tissue in her hands, her eyes wide with fear. 'Do you think he could be having an affair?'

In Jaqueline's eyes, an affair was the least of Maxine's worries. How could her friend be so blind as to not see what was going on, right underneath her nose? From what she'd heard about Danny, he was a vicious bastard, who would stop at nothing to get what he wanted. He certainly wasn't the angel Maxine portrayed him to be. However, playing around with other women was the one and only thing she had never heard whispered about him.

May God strike me down for lying, she thought to herself as she held Maxine's hands in hers. 'Yes, I think you're right, he is,' she finally answered, after convincing herself she was doing the right thing. The quicker Maxine was away from Danny McKay the better, as far as she was concerned.

* * *

Overnight, George Christos had aged. The sight of Nico's severed fingers had both shocked and sickened him, but above all else, the bloody stumps had made him hell-bent on revenge. As a result, his wrath was explosive and his temper short.

Convinced his nephew was already dead, George's main priority was to find Nico's broken, lifeless body, and have him brought home to his mother for burial.

Sitting at a table with a bottle of Ouzo in front of him, George listened intently as his brother talked him through the day's events.

'This is Freddie Smith's doing. He is behind this, I can feel it,' George spat.

'Maybe we should go to the police?' Alexandros said. 'It's been four days since the fingers were sent here, and we are still no nearer to finding him. Where do we even start searching?'

'No police,' George snapped. 'What kind of man do you think I am?' He unravelled his tie, slid it from underneath his collar and thumped it down on the table. 'When have I ever involved the police in my personal business before?'

'You haven't...'

'And I never will,' George roared, picking up the glass bottle and throwing it in the direction of his brother.

Alexandros ducked down. The bottle missed his head by a hair's breadth, before smashing to smithereens against the wall.

'Fucking hell, George, that nearly hit me.'

'The next time, I won't miss.'

Hastily, Alexandros retreated. He knew better than anyone not to antagonise his brother when he was in this kind of mood.

His eyes hard, George was quietly brooding. The fate of Nico was eating away at him like a cancer, and as the head of the family, everything fell upon his shoulders. He stood up and slowly walked towards the bar. Taking a fresh bottle of Ouzo, he returned to his seat, twisted open the sealed cap, then poured out a large glass of the clear liquid, before drinking deeply.

'Me, go to the police,' he spat underneath his breath.

He was George Christos, and his name alone demanded respect. He was more than ready to personally bring down the next person who dared to question his tactics again.

He then poured out a second glass. He had no intention of stopping, not until the bottle was empty and the alcohol had dulled the ache inside his chest.

* * *

After returning home, Maxine placed Logan in his bouncer chair. She then proceeded to tear through the house. She needed to see the evidence with her own eyes that her husband was having an affair. Until then, her suspicions meant nothing.

In the bathroom, she rifled through the laundry basket and pulled out all of Danny's used shirts. One by one, she inspected them for tell-tale signs of makeup, before smelling them for any lingering traces of unfamiliar perfume.

When she found nothing, she moved on to the bedroom, and began looking through the drawers of the bedside cabinet. Pulling out all of the receipts that Danny kept there, she studied them, checking which items he'd bought and at which times. Her eyes were searching for anything out of the ordinary.

There was nothing at all to alarm her, and she didn't know whether to laugh at herself for being so ridiculous, or cry, because she could find nothing to support her suspicions.

After tidying everything away, Maxine was about to leave the room, when her husband's jeans, hanging on the outside of the wardrobe door, caught her attention. She was supposed to have taken them to the dry cleaners that morning, but had forgotten.

She pulled them off the hanger, slipped her hand inside the denim pockets, and pulled out a crumpled receipt. In horror, she noted it was for petrol that her husband had purchased in Southend. The date indicated it was on the afternoon after he had stayed out all night.

What the hell was he doing in Southend? Knowing that the bustling seaside town was full of cheap bed and breakfasts, Maxine's heart lurched, as realisation set in.

This was the proof she had been searching for. It was true, he really was sleeping around with other women. Fresh tears sprang to her eyes, and collapsing in a heap on the bed, Maxine sobbed her heart out.

* * *

The stench that came from Nico was overpowering. Green pus had begun to pool on the bloody stumps where his fingers had been crudely hacked off. Being left to sit in his own urine and faeces for the past five days hadn't helped the situation.

As a result, Freddie and Danny were at loggerheads. The fate of Nico was at the core of their conflict. Sweat poured out from the young man's body, whilst he mumbled in a delirious state, as fever took hold. There was no denying that Nico was in a bad way.

'Fuck him. He's said sod all anyway. This stinking bastard dies tonight.'

Danny glanced towards Nico before answering. His voice was low. 'If you kill him now, then the war with the Greeks is going to become ten times worse. It's far too soon to wipe him out. Christos will be hell-bent on retribution.'

'Fuck 'em all,' Freddie spat.

'And that's exactly the reason why I run this side of the business,' Danny growled, his tone exactly how he wanted it to come across: sarcastic.

'What did you just fucking say?' Freddie roared.

'You heard what I said. This is the reason why I run this side of things. You have to be two steps ahead, and charging in like a bull in a china shop is not how things get done.'

'He dies tonight.'

'No,' Danny answered forcefully. 'We wait until we hear from Christos.'

'I said—'

'I heard what you fucking said,' Danny interrupted. Standing only inches away from Freddie's face, his famous temper began to bubble to the surface. 'We wait.'

'Whoa.' Big Tone came between the two men and pushed them apart. 'Fighting amongst ourselves isn't going to solve anything, is it?'

'That cunt dies,' Freddie said, stabbing his finger towards Nico.

Standing protectively in front of the young man, Danny waited for Freddie to turn and walk away. He knew from experience exactly what would happen if the Greek was taken out too soon. The backlash would be huge, and the last thing Danny needed was for the Greeks to open up a can of worms about the shooting. The longer he could keep Nico alive, the better.

* * *

'Listen,' Mick Johnson said. 'Freddie is right, we can't go on like this. Look at him, he's half dead anyway. It would be kinder to put the bleeder out of his misery.'

Danny glanced across to Nico. Mick was right. The Greek was in a bad way, but he'd seen a lot worse over the years, and at his own hands.

For over an hour, Freddie, Mick and Big Tone argued their case.

'It's got to be done. Someone needs to kill him, and the sooner, the better,' Big Tone added.

'Well, don't look at me,' Danny hissed. 'I'm not doing it. And, I'm warning you now, if you kill him, then this is going to bring all of us untold grief.'

Big Tone cleared his throat and looked across at Freddie and Mick. 'Looks like it's one of us then.'

The three men averted their gaze, each of them not wanting to get their own hands dirty.

Silently, Danny watched them. He couldn't help but feel a tiny bit smug. Without him there to do the dirty work for them, they were useless.

'Well,' Danny said, as he leant against the wall, his arms folded across his chest. 'Who's going to do it?' There was a hint of sarcasm in his voice, just enough to make Freddie see red.

Freddie's expression was twisted with contempt as he glared across the unit. 'You are one cocky cunt,' he snarled.

Danny shrugged. 'Sticks and stones, Freddie.' He grinned.

Purposely not taking his eyes off his number two, Freddie grabbed a six-inch knife. He wasn't prepared to let the cocky little bastard mug him off twice in as many weeks. In quick succession, he thrust the blade three times into Nico's chest, then threw the bloodied weapon to the floor. The stainless steel was loud as it scrapped across the concrete.

'Are you happy now?' Freddie spat.

'No, I told you not to do it,' Danny reminded him.

'What do we do with him now?' Big Tone asked.

Freddie heaved up a can of petrol and splashed it over Nico's body. 'We get rid of him, and any evidence.'

* * *

Crouching down beside Nico, Danny brought his ear closer to the man's face.

The scent of petrol was overpowering, stinging his eyes. 'He's still alive,' he stated, looking across at the three men.

'He won't be for much longer,' Freddie growled as he set about igniting a discarded newspaper.

'You can't fucking do that. Finish him off first.'

'Fuck him.'

'Finish him off,' Danny roared, his famous temper reaching boiling point. This was the exact reason he wanted to walk away from the firm; Freddie was becoming a liability, his behaviour erratic. If they weren't careful, sooner or later he was going to drag them all down with him. And as for the Greek, since when did they kill innocent kids? And other than bearing the Christos surname, the boy was innocent.

Danny stood up in a bid to block Freddie's way. 'You can't just burn the fucker alive,' he said, tapping his finger against his temple. 'What the fuck is wrong with you?'

'Get out of the way.'

'Give me the knife and I'll do it myself,' Danny implored, looking around him for a weapon he could use. Under the circumstances, anything would do: a Stanley blade, a box cutter.

He patted down his pockets as though he could miraculously conjure up a tool. 'I won't let you do this,' he shouted.

'Get out of my fucking way.'

Danny stood his ground. If Freddie wanted to burn the Greek alive, then he was going to have to go through him first.

It took all three men to physically remove Danny, and with a smirk of victory, Freddie threw the flaming newspaper towards Nico's broken body.

The petrol ignited with a whoosh, and a long guttural, animalistic groan came from the man strapped to the chair. His face twisted in agony as his body contorted.

The flames continued to lick and dance across the burning body as the dying muscles twitched. The heat was unbearable. The sickly scent of burning flesh tainted the air and stuck to the back of their throats, making them cough and gag.

Danny's eyes were murderous. He shrugged both Big Tone and Mick Johnson away from him. 'I'll fucking kill you over this.'

Shrugging, Freddie grinned. 'What are you so bothered about him for? He's fuck all to do with you, unless you're worried you might be next?'

'You cunt.' Lunging forward, Danny managed to crack his knuckles against the older man's jaw bone. Incensed, he rained blows down upon him, his heavy clenched fists going to town as he pummelled.

Pent up rage came to the fore. 'You no good fucking cunt,' he spat as he punched and kicked the living daylights out of the older man.

He had no recollection of being dragged outside, away from Freddie, so intense was the white hot fury that consumed him.

* * *

'You need to calm down.' Apprehension was clearly evident across Big Tone's face. He blew out his cheeks as he struggled to catch his breath. It had taken every ounce of his and Mick's strength to remove McKay, and he didn't believe they were capable of the same brute force, should the man charge back inside.

'I'm gonna fucking kill him.'

Big Tone held up his hands, desperately trying to calm the situation down. He was more than wary of the man in front of him. He had never seen such ferocity before. 'Come on, mate, that's not going to help the situation, is it?'

'I'm not your fucking mate,' Danny roared. He squared up to the big man, his fists clenched, ready to attack again.

Big Tone took a step backwards. 'Calm down, Danny,' he repeated, his voice wavering.

Pacing backwards and forwards, Danny clenched and unclenched his fists. He felt as though he could explode at any moment, as if the slightest wrong word from Big Tone or Mick would push him over the edge.

Nervously, Big Tone glanced inside the unit, before looking back towards the pacing man. He'd always known for a fact that McKay's notoriety was warranted, but he had never seen the man so vicious, so brutal, before. He gave a shudder as he remembered how he'd once believed that Lloydy and Terry Stevens could have taken him out.

After what he had just witnessed, he knew for certain the end result would have been carnage, in Danny's favour.

He watched Danny like a hawk. He reminded him of a caged animal and he wasn't afraid to admit that he actually felt more than a little bit scared of this crazed version of Danny McKay in front of him.

Danny continued to pace. When he felt his fury slowly begin to ebb away, he stopped, placed his palms upon the wall and leant his weight against them. The muscles in his forearms strained and his head bowed downwards.

After what seemed like an age, he finally looked up at Big Tone. 'I'm going to kill you for this, all of you,' he said, his voice chillingly calm.

Big Tone couldn't help but shudder. Danny's calmness was even more terrifying than his temper. Instinctively, he didn't doubt the man for a second.

* * *

Once he was seated inside his car, Danny looked over at the industrial unit and had to fight the urge to not get back out of the motor and drag all three men outside and finish his murderous rampage. He'd never been so livid, so angry before. The kid hadn't deserved such a brutal death, and he felt sickened to the core.

He took deep breaths in an attempt to get his anger under control, the stench of burning flesh staining his clothes and skin. His hands gripped the steering wheel tightly, his knuckles deathly white. This was the last straw, as far as he was concerned.

He picked up his mobile phone and scrolled through his contact list. He stopped when he came to Moray's telephone number, and without pausing, pressed dial.

'We put the plan into action tomorrow night,' he growled into the phone. 'I want Freddie brought down.'

He waited for Moray's agreement, then snapped off the call.

With one last glance towards the unit, Danny tossed his mobile phone onto the passenger seat, started the ignition, then sped away.

Enough was enough. As far as he was concerned, Freddie was finished.

* * *

Returning home, Danny turned his key in the lock. The house was in darkness and he was thankful for that. He felt drained and all he wanted to do was to fall into bed and sleep, if that was even possible after the night he'd had. Quietly, he closed the front door behind him and shrugged off his jacket, before making his way across the hallway towards the stairs. Careful of where he stepped, he managed to dodge the creaking floorboards. He didn't want to wake his wife or son. He couldn't deal with them, on top of everything else, at this precise moment in time.

'Where have you been?'

Startled, Danny turned towards the living room. 'For fuck's sake, Max, what are you doing standing there in the dark?'

Maxine repeated the question, her voice rising. 'Where have you been?'

'Where do you think I've fucking been?' Danny barked. He pushed past her into the living room and snapped on the light switch.

Blinking rapidly as the sudden light momentarily blinded her eyes, Maxine stood with her arms folded across her chest. 'I don't know, that's why I'm asking.'

Danny dragged his hand through his hair. 'You know where I've been, where I always fucking am... at work.'

'Really,' she answered, her eyebrows raised.

He gave her a cold stare. 'What is that supposed to mean?'

'It means, I don't believe you. What's this?'

Danny glanced down at the crumpled receipt his wife held in her hand and shrugged. 'What's your problem, Max?'

'My problem, Danny, is this receipt for petrol.'

'And?'

'What were you doing in Southend?'

'I'm really not in the mood for this, Max. I've had a bastard of a night.'

'Well, that's tough, because I am in the mood. What were you doing in Southend?'

Danny battled to remain calm. He took deep breaths. 'I don't know, you tell me. You seem to know it all.'

Determined not to cry, Maxine held her head high. 'Who is she?'

'Who is who?' Danny rounded on his wife. 'Come on, Max. You're the one who wants to accuse me of shit, so you tell me?'

'Who is she?' Maxine repeated, her voice taking on a hysterical tone.

'You're not right in the fucking head,' Danny snapped, pointing a finger to his temple to emphasise his point.

'Well, I hope she was worth it.' Maxine gave a sarcastic laugh, hiding the fact that all she wanted to do was break down in tears.

Ignoring his wife, Danny walked through to the kitchen. He opened the fridge door and peered inside, before slamming it closed again.

'I said—'

'Yeah, I heard what you said,' Danny snapped, cutting her off, his eyes hard.

Standing in the kitchen doorway with her hands on her hips, Maxine bristled.

'What the fuck is all of this about? I've done fuck all wrong.'

'This,' Maxine shouted, slamming the receipt onto the breakfast bar. 'You taking your tarts to Southend and staying in cheap bed and breakfasts, while I'm here with our son. Or have you forgotten all about that little boy upstairs?'

Danny stabbed his finger forward. 'Keep my son out of your twisted accusations. You're really pushing your luck now Max.'

'Our son,' Maxine corrected.

'I'm warning you, Max, I'm this close to losing my rag,' Danny said, holding his thumb and forefinger inches apart.

'Why, because I've caught you out?' Maxine cried. 'I can't believe you could do this to me.'

'I've done fuck all wrong.'

Tears sprang to her eyes. 'This is the proof,' she said jerking her head towards the receipt.

'You need to get a grip, Max, and fast. You sound like you've lost the fucking plot.'

'Who is she?' Maxine screamed back in frustration, as tears rolled down her cheeks. 'Who's the tart that you've been sleeping with?'

Danny shook his head. He picked up his car keys and headed for the front door.

'Where are you going? Are you going to her?' Panic was evident in Maxine's voice.

'There is no her. What the fuck is wrong with you?' he shouted, throwing up his hands. 'Don't you think I've got enough to deal with, without coming home and you accusing me of all this shit?'

His words stung her. In a romanticised way, she'd expected him to cry and beg for her forgiveness, even if there had only been a few tears.

As the front door slammed shut behind her husband, Maxine sank to her knees and wept. Her marriage was falling apart.

* * *

'You okay, Fred?'

Freddie winced and slowly nodded. Just that one simple action sent shards of pain shooting down his neck and back. He could barely breathe and he would put money on it that he had more than one broken rib. He gingerly touched his face. He could feel the swelling already forming, as his fingers came into contact with sticky blood.

Grey smoke billowed out from the smouldering, charred remains of Nico, and Big Tone averted his eyes. All the while, Danny's words echoed through his mind. He knew, without a doubt, the man meant every word, when he said he would kill them.

Big Tone was worried. He would speak to Lloydy and Terry Stevens, he decided. With them on board, just maybe, they could salvage the friendship they had once had with McKay. Maybe they could even make amends and smooth things over. He just hoped and prayed it would be enough in Danny's eyes. Somehow, he doubted it. It was not only a depressing thought, but also a terrifying one.

* * *

Danny lay back on the couch in Moray's office. All thanks to his wife, he was wide awake; he doubted he would be able to sleep even if he wanted to. He was still stunned that she was accusing him of having an affair. Where the fuck would he find the time to shag other birds? It was hard enough trying to keep himself alive.

The situation with Freddie was all consuming, and even if he wanted to, which he didn't, there was no room for other women in his life at this precise moment in time, or in the foreseeable future, for that matter.

He took out his mobile phone and contemplated giving his wife a call. Instead, he tossed the phone beside him. Fuck her, he thought bitterly. He had enough going on, without her hysterics adding to his problems.

He turned over onto his side and picked up a sheet of paper

from the floor that had the list of Freddie's clubs written on it. Studying them, he took out a pen and made his own notes beside each of the clubs. The men they chose would need to be as clued up as possible for the plan to work. If it was the last thing he did, it would be to make sure that everything went to plan.

7

The next morning, Danny woke early. Today was to be the day he blew apart Freddie's world, and as far as Danny was concerned, it couldn't happen to a nicer bloke. He stood up and stretched his arms above his head, shaking out the tension and easing his aching muscles. He was actually looking forward to tonight. He only wished he could be there to see Freddie's face when he discovered the empire he'd built up over the past twenty years, was gone.

'You all right, mate? Did you sleep okay?'

Turning to see Moray standing in the doorway, he nodded. 'Yeah, mate, all good. I've made some notes. Here, take a look.'

Moray took the sheet of paper. 'Everything's gonna go like clockwork, mate.'

'It better had.' Danny grinned. 'I need to go home and change. I should be back around four, and then we can put the teams together.'

'Off to see the enemy, eh?'

Danny shook his head. 'Women, mate. I swear they're not from the same fucking planet.'

'Can't live with 'em and can't live without 'em.'

'True.' Danny laughed. 'Right, mate, I'll be back soon. The sooner I get it over and done with, the better.'

'If you're not back by four, I'll send out a search party. You never know, she could have you tied up somewhere.'

'I'm not that lucky.' Danny winked, before leaving the room. He was in high spirits. He just hoped his Maxine didn't bring his mood crashing down.

* * *

Matty Payne was exhausted. He'd been at Freddie's beck and call all night, and he'd just about had enough, not that he would ever complain to Freddie about it. In the big man's company, he did as he was told.

He spooned sugar into Freddie's tea, and careful not to splash any of the liquid over the sides of the mug, he gave it a stir. He then took the steaming mug through to the lounge and placed it on the small nest of tables beside Freddie's chair.

With Lewis now dead, everything fell upon his shoulders, and he couldn't help but feel resentful. Out of the two of them, Lewis had always been stronger. Somehow, he had been able to cope with Freddie and the others demands, a whole lot better than he himself ever could.

He thought of Lewis now, and remembered the good times. There hadn't been many of them, admittedly, and the ones they had had, were few and far between. On the rare occasions they had been allowed to be the young boys they actually were, they'd had fun.

He missed Lewis and couldn't help but feel partly responsible for his death. It was him who had given Danny the gun, and it was Danny who had shot and killed his one and only true friend. He carried the guilt around with him like a lead weight hanging from around his neck.

Matty stood beside the doorway, watching Freddie as he slept. For a brief moment, he contemplated running away, but he knew there was no point. Freddie would find him, just like he had the last time. Only this time, he knew the man would kill him. He knew too much about them, about all of the men, and it was this knowledge that would sign his death warrant.

He returned to the kitchen, rolled up his sleeves, and began to wash up the few items in the sink. Looking out of the window, Matty imagined how different his life could have been, if he and Lewis had never met Freddie that fateful night. Imagining his life in a parallel universe was one of his favourite pastimes, and was one of the only things that got him through his day.

* * *

Big Tone climbed out of his car. He had been sitting inside it, with the engine switched off, for the past ten minutes, still unsure of how exactly he could get out of the precarious situation he found himself in.

He took a deep breath before banging his fist on Freddie's front door. It was his duty to check up on his boss, and he planned on being in and out within minutes.

Matty opened the door, and he waited for the lad to move out of the way before walking through to the lounge. 'How is he?'

Matty's voice was low. 'Okay, I think. He's been asleep for most of the day.'

'You doing okay today, Fred?' Big Tone asked in a loud voice as he nudged Freddie awake.

'I'm not deaf,' Freddie growled.

'Course you're not, mate. Look, I've brought you some grapes.'

Freddie looked from Big Tone, then to the bag of grapes clutched in his fist. 'I'm not a fucking invalid. What have you bought me those for?'

Big Tone shifted his weight, feeling somewhat foolish. 'I don't know. It's what people do, isn't it?' he asked, putting the bag down on the table beside his boss.

'Get Tone a cup of tea,' Freddie ordered, clicking his fingers towards Matty.

Big Tone held up his hand. 'Freddie, mate, I can't stop. This is just a flying visit.'

'Get Tone a cup of tea. We've got things to discuss... mainly that cunt McKay.'

Reluctantly, Big Tone took a seat. 'I haven't heard from Danny, and as far as I know, no one else has either.'

'Keeping his head down low, most likely. Look at what he's done to me. If he thinks he is gonna get away with this, then he can think again.'

'How are you feeling? You look in a bad way, if I'm being honest, mate.'

'I feel like I'm in a bad way.' Freddie winced as he made himself more comfortable. 'Bastard has broken more than one of my ribs, I can feel it.'

Big Tone grimaced. He would never say it out loud, but Freddie looked as though he had been in a car accident. He would put money on the fact that McKay had also broken his boss's nose, and unless he was very much mistaken, his cheekbones, too, if the bruising to Freddie's face was anything to go by. He decided to keep that little titbit to himself, though.

'I could kill him for what he's done.'

Big Tone nodded. From what he had seen of Danny's famous temper, he highly doubted it. 'So, it's business as usual tonight, is it? Do you want me to go around all of the pubs and clubs, checking that everything's okay?'

'Well, I can hardly go out looking like this, can I?'

'No, of course not.' Big Tone had to bite his tongue to stop himself from adding that the sight of Freddie would scare off the punters. Somehow, he didn't think he would appreciate his humour.

Gulping down his tea, he placed the mug on the floor, and then rubbed his hands together. 'Well, mate, I best shoot off.'

Freddie nodded. 'If McKay turns up for work tonight, tell him to fuck off. In fact, put him on the phone to me, and I will tell him to fuck off, personally.'

'Yeah, of course I will.' Somehow, Big Tone couldn't imagine Danny McKay turning up at the club as if nothing had ever happened.

* * *

'So, he just walked out?'

Maxine nodded. 'He said I was mad, and that he hadn't done anything wrong.'

'You don't believe him, do you?' Jacqueline frowned.

'I don't know what to believe any more.'

'Well, you've seen the evidence with your own two eyes, and he can't crawl his way out of that.'

'I know. It's just... he looked as though he was telling the truth. Oh, I don't know, Jac. Maybe I'm wrong?'

'And maybe you're right, and he is having an affair.'

They were sitting on the leather chesterfield sofa in Maxine's lounge. For the past hour, Maxine had poured her heart out.

'It's just... he actually looked shocked, you know?'

Flicking her blonde hair from her eyes, Jacqueline raised her eyebrows. 'Of course he looked shocked, he was bound to. You've caught him out.'

'I suppose so,' Maxine answered. Her mind was going ten to the dozen, and she didn't know what the truth was. All she knew for certain, was that something wasn't quite right. Something was going on.

As they heard the front door open, the two women looked towards each other. 'Keep strong,' Jacqueline whispered.

Easing her body up from the sofa, Maxine took a deep breath, then walked through to the hallway. 'You came home then?' she asked her husband.

'I do still live here, Max.'

'Jacqueline is here.'

He rolled his eyes and groaned, then poked his head around the living room door. 'Jac.'

'Danny,' Jaqueline replied frostily.

'I need to shower and change before work,' he said, making his way up the stairs.

Maxine followed him up. Once they were in the bedroom, she closed the door firmly shut behind them.

'If you're going to start, I'm gonna walk straight back out of that door,' he said, stabbing his finger towards his wife. 'I'm warning you, Max, I'm really not in the mood for this.'

Maxine shook her head. Her voice took on a pleading tone. 'I just want to know the truth, please. I deserve to know.'

Pausing, Danny looked his wife in the eyes. 'There are no other women. I don't know what else you want me to say,' he answered with a shrug of his shoulders.

'But...'

'There are no buts. I stayed at my mate's in Southend, and on the way home, I bought petrol. That's it.' He gave a bitter laugh.

'How the fuck you came up with me shagging other women, I'll never know.'

Maxine rubbed at her temples, her mind going into overdrive 'You're never here lately, and when I saw the receipt, I just put two and two together.'

'I've done sod all wrong.'

Tears sprang to Maxine's eyes, and she swiped them away, determined not to cry. As Jacqueline kept reminding her, she was stronger than that. 'You don't tell me anything any more. What am I supposed to think?'

'I've got a lot going on, Max. Stuff I can't talk to you about. It's work.'

'Am I supposed to just believe that?'

'Well, yeah. It's the truth.'

Moving forward, Danny pulled Maxine into his arms. 'Come here,' he said. 'I swear to you, babe, I've done nothing wrong.'

Maxine gave a nod, as he hugged her to him. She just wished the niggling thought in the back of her mind also believed her husband.

* * *

Lloydy listened intently to what Big Tone had to say. He had to admit, he wasn't entirely shocked to hear what had gone on between Freddie and Danny, and he certainly wasn't shocked to hear about the damage Danny had caused. They all knew to be wary of him, and he himself had learnt early on that the man was unpredictable.

'What did I tell you? He's like an animal. Only someone, either stupid or with a death wish, would cause hag with him.'

Big Tone shook his head. 'Well, it shocked me. Don't get me

wrong, we all know he's a lump. And I've seen him in action before, of course I have, but this was something else entirely.'

'He's a law unto himself, mate, and always has been,' Terry Stevens said as he lounged back on his sofa.

'The thing is,' Big Tone said, clearing his throat, 'I really don't think it's a good idea to go ahead with what Freddie wants any more.'

Lloydy and Terry Stevens looked towards each other, waiting for Big Tone to continue.

'Someone's going to get hurt.'

'Well, correct me if I'm wrong, but wasn't that the general plan?' Terry asked.

'Yeah, I know it was, but...'

'Has Freddie called everything off? Only he can make that call.'

'No he hasn't, and that's the other thing I wanted to talk to you both about. Freddie is losing his reign. This thing with Danny proves it. If he can't control one of his own, then what will happen out on the street?'

Lloydy shook his head. Remaining silent, he let Terry do the talking.

'Listen, mate, we work for Freddie, and only he can call this off. Until Freddie tells us otherwise, we still go ahead and end McKay.'

With a sigh, Big Tone nodded. He had expected this, and in any other circumstances, he would have had the exact same attitude. He chewed on the inside of his cheek, clearly concerned. 'Don't say I didn't warn you when all of this backfires in our faces, which I can guarantee you it will,' he warned.

* * *

Danny was greeted like a celebrity as he walked into Ritzy's Night-club. The men on Moray's payroll craned their necks to get a better view of him, the majority of them thrilled to be in the company of the man they only knew by reputation.

'Listen up,' Moray said. 'I'm sure most of you will know of Danny McKay. As of now, you are working for him, as well as myself.'

Hushed conversations went around the room, and Danny held up his hand to quiet them down. 'Tonight, we're taking over a number of pubs and clubs. All of you need to be tooled up, so take whatever you want with you. Just make sure it's something you can actually smuggle into a club. Then, you wait until Moray and myself arrive, for us to take over.'

This time, an excited buzz went around, and both Danny and Moray gave the men a few moments to talk amongst themselves.

'I'm Callum Riley,' one of the men said, coming forward and shaking Danny's hand, his Irish accent strong. 'But you can call me Cal, that's what me friends call me, so they do.'

Danny nodded. 'Okay, Cal. You know what to do tonight?'

'Sure I do, Mr McKay. And can I just say, it's a privilege to be working for you. I'm going to be one of your best men.'

Danny nodded and smiled. As Callum walked away, he leaned into Moray. 'He's got some front, hasn't he? But I like him. Put him down for the first club on the list.'

Moray laughed. He knew Callum well, and the cheeky Irishman was, indeed, one of his best men.

Once the men were put into teams, Danny ran through the plan for a second time, making sure there were no mistakes. It was vital they all knew what to do.

'There are two of you to each of the doormen inside, and two of you ready and waiting, outside. When you're given the signal, you bring down the men you are covering. I don't care how you get it done, just make sure they're on the ground and unlikely to get back up.'

'Is that clear?' Moray asked. 'Any questions?'

The men shook their heads and Moray dismissed them. Turning to Danny, he raised his eyebrows. 'This is it, mate. How are you feeling?'

'We can't fuck this up.'

'And we won't. Relax, Danny. Everything will go to plan. We've worked hard on this, and it's fool-proof. Not to mention, we have the added bonus of you knowing these clubs like the back of your hand.'

Danny nodded. He knew, without a doubt, that he wouldn't fully relax, until they had taken over the very last club on their list.

* * *

The first club they planned to target was The Belgrave in Stratford, East London. It also happened to be a venue where Danny often worked.

Danny and Moray pulled up outside the club. Climbing out of the car, they strolled across the road. There was no urgency in their manner, nothing at all to alarm Freddie's two men stood on the doors.

'Evening, Danny. You not working tonight?'

Danny smiled. 'Yeah, mate, I am working.' He then gave the nod to two of Moray's men stood waiting outside the club, and watched as they steamed in, heavy-handed, expertly knocking both doormen to the floor.

'Consider yourselves made redundant, as from now.' Danny grinned as he stepped over the semi-conscious men. He then walked through the doors of the club, giving a second signal.

The club was barely a quarter full. The night was still early, and Danny and Moray easily navigated their way around the venue.

'Throw these bastards out,' Moray said, looking down at the dazed doormen, as they lay in crumpled heaps on the floor. 'They're making the place look untidy.'

Laughing, Danny watched as Moray's men dragged Freddie's dazed and bleeding doormen towards the fire escape. 'Make sure they don't try to get back in,' he called after them.

The two men then made their way through the back doors, where the offices were located.

Danny barged open a door, his large frame dominating the small doorway.

The manager of the club, Warren Lewis, looked up from a mound of paperwork on his desk. His eyes were wide. 'Can I help you?' he asked, looking from Danny to Moray.

Danny pulled out a chair and sat down. 'As from now, you pay myself and Mr Garner each week for the services of our men on your doors.'

'But I already pay Mr Smith,' Warren began to stutter.

Danny laughed. 'No, mate, you pay us now. Freddie Smith is out of business, as from tonight.'

'I don't quite understand.'

His patience was being tested, and Danny leant across the desk. 'Do I need to bang it into your thick skull? We now run your doors.'

'Therefore, you now pay us for the service of our men,' Moray added.

Warren Lewis nodded. A bead of sweat formed across his forehead and upper lip. He was clearly terrified. 'Yes, yes, I understand.'

Danny rubbed his hands together and looked across to Moray

with a wide grin spread across his face. 'Good, well, our men are already on the doors, so payment starts from today.'

Warren gave a nod. With bated breath, he waited until the big men had left his office, before running towards the toilet and emptying his bowels.

Danny and Moray made their way back through the club.

'Well, that was easy.'

Moray smiled. 'Like taking candy from a fucking baby.'

They laughed together, before pushing their way out of the heavy club doors, both of them eager to get to the second club on the list.

* * *

Big Tone had heard some alarming rumours, and driving at break-neck speed, he drove towards Stratford. Although he didn't quite believe what he was hearing, he also knew that if it involved Danny McKay, then anything was possible.

He brought the car to a halt outside The Belgrave, and peered through the car window towards the club. He didn't recognise the men on the door, and his stomach lurched.

'Fuck,' he swore to himself. He was unsure of which way to turn. Should he drive to all of the clubs, hoping he could stop McKay's takeover? Or should he go straight to Freddie, and inform him of what was going on?

Faced with a dilemma, he leant back in his seat for a moment, before putting the gear into first, and screeching away from the kerb. He had to try and stop the takeover, before it was too late.

Bringing his mobile phone to his ear, Big Tone shouted into the receiver. 'Do not let Danny McKay inside the club, under any circumstances.' He could hear the confusion in Lloydy's voice, and roared, 'Just do as I fucking tell you to do,' before throwing the phone down beside him.

* * *

Lloydy was confused. He stared at the phone in his hand before slipping it back inside his jacket pocket. What the hell was going on? He looked around, concerned. His mind was all over the place. His eyes were on the lookout for Danny.

He absentmindedly nodded at the punters as they walked through the doors to the club, barely even frisking them. That was to be his biggest mistake. Without even realising it, he had allowed Danny and Moray's men to slip through the doors tooled up.

It wasn't long before he spotted Danny walking towards him. He held up his hands. 'I don't want any aggro, mate.'

Danny began to laugh. 'You don't want any aggro? Are you taking the piss? It's too late for that.' He pulled back his fist and knocked Lloydy to the ground. 'That's just for starters. I've got personal issues with you, you cunt, and at some point in the very near future, I will end you,' he said, giving Lloydy a swift hard kick to the groin.

As Lloydy rolled around on the ground in pain, Danny gave a signal for the takeover to begin inside the venue.

Crouching down, Danny pulled Lloydy's head towards him, a handful of his hair clutched in his fist. 'You actually thought you were going to take me out, that I didn't have the nous to suss you muppets out?' he growled as Lloydy squirmed in front of him. 'Well, son, here I am, so do your best. Go on, take a shot.'

'Come on, Danny, don't do this,' Lloydy whimpered.

'Don't fucking do this?' Danny growled. 'Don't you remember

you and Terry Stevens were going to try and kill me? Where is he?' Danny asked, looking up.

Lloydy remained silent.

'I said, where is he?' Danny roared, pulling Lloydy's face closer towards him.

'He's not here. I don't know where he is.'

Danny smashed his fist into Lloydy's face a second time, then straightened up. 'Come on,' he said, now to Moray. 'Let's take over this shithole.'

* * *

Writhing around on the floor, Lloydy brought his hand up towards his face. Blood trickled out from his nose. He rolled over onto his side, grimacing, as pain shot through his groin.

He could hear sniggering from the newly appointed doormen standing on the doors. They were big men, and even from his position he could tell that they weren't there just for show. They looked more than capable of taking care of business, and with Danny out of the equation, it was a lot more than could be said for Freddie's so called firm, the majority of them barely out of their teens. Spitting out a mouthful of blood-stained spit, Lloydy slowly staggered to his feet.

Unsteadily, he managed to walk a few yards away from the club, before Big Tone brought his car skidding to a halt beside him.

Jumping out of the motor, Big Tone raised his hands up to his head.

'He's already been and gone,' Lloydy groaned.

'Fuck, fuck, fuck,' Big Tone bellowed. This had to be some kind of a nightmare. He looked around him, stunned, with no idea of which club or pub Danny would turn up at next. It was a case of playing a game of cat and mouse.

'I think he's looking for Terry.'

'No.' Big Tone shook his head. 'He isn't purposely looking for him, or anyone else for that matter. If he comes across him, then he'll more than likely batter him to within an inch of his life, but until then, he is solely taking over the doors.'

'All of them?' There was shock in Lloydy's voice.

'Yes, fucking all of them. He's already taken over The Belgrave and this club. Fuck knows how many more he's taken over by now. Get in the car. We have to try and stop him.'

'Tone, I can barely walk. I think I need to go to the hospital.'

'Just get in the motor,' Big Tone snapped.

With great difficulty, Lloydy did as he was told, yelping in pain while he did so.

'I can't believe this is happening,' Big Tone stated once they had set off.

'I feel like I'm going to be pissing blood for the next week,' Lloydy cried.

Big Tone glanced across at his friend before sighing. 'I'll take you to hospital before the end of the night, okay? But right now, we have to find Danny.'

Lloydy nodded before taking a quick peek inside the waistband of his trousers. 'Bloody hell, Tone,' he cried, the colour draining from his face. 'It's bad.'

Big Tone rubbed his hand across his head. He stepped his foot on the brake and executed a three-point turn. 'Okay, okay. I'll drop you off there now, but,' he said, pointing his finger towards Lloydy, 'you're on your own, all right?'

Reluctantly, Big Tone drove as fast as he could towards Newham Hospital. God knew how many clubs Danny would have taken over by the time he returned.

* * *

Danny and Moray were celebrating. They had just successfully taken over all of Freddie's pubs and clubs.

'What did I fucking tell you? I said everything would go to plan.'

Danny nodded, feeling euphoric. 'Yep, we did it, mate.'

Lighting a cigar, Moray puffed on it, and grinned widely. 'I would love to be a fly on the wall when Freddie finds out.'

Danny burst out laughing. 'It's not going to be pretty, but fuck him. This is about us now.'

'Too fucking true, Danny, mate. To us, the new kings of the East End,' Moray said, raising his glass in a toast.

Danny grinned. 'To us,' he replied, raising his own glass. He had finally broken free from Freddie and the firm, and he couldn't feel any happier than he did right now. In fact, he wished he'd done it years ago.

* * *

The irate screams that came from Freddie were beginning to give Big Tone a headache. He couldn't, for the life of him, understand why he was getting the blame for everything. It wasn't as if he, himself, had personally taken over Freddie's clubs.

'And where were you, when all of this was happening? Oh yeah, that's right... you were taking Lloydy to the fucking hospital. Did it not cross your mind that stopping McKay from getting my doors was just that little bit more important?'

'Hold on, Fred. Lloydy was in a bad way. I couldn't just leave him.'

'I couldn't just leave him,' Freddie mimicked. 'You should have kicked him to the fucking kerb and sorted out McKay. What do you think I pay you for?'

'Sorry, Fred.'

'I'll give you fucking sorry,' Freddie growled, as he attempted to get out of his chair. His heavy fists were clenched as he tried to swing a punch towards the big man. In defeat, he sunk down heavily, gasping to catch his breath. The pain from his broken ribs clearly getting the better of him.

'I tried to stop him, Fred, but you know what he's like. He was always one step ahead of me.'

'Do you know how much damage you've caused?' Freddie wheezed. 'Twenty years it's taken me to build up this business, and it's all gone down the fucking drain now, thanks to you.'

'It wasn't exactly me, was it?'

'Well, you didn't try hard to stop him, did you? One fucking day, I left you in charge for, and now it's all gone.'

'I'm sorry, Fred. I did my best.'

'Fuck off, Tone. You're lucky I can't get up and knock seven bells of shit out of you, because trust me, other than killing McKay, there is nothing I would like to do better right now.'

Big Tone took this as his cue to leave. Once outside on the street, he walked as fast as he could towards his car, looking around nervously as he did so. The situation with Danny was beginning to make him feel paranoid. He had a feeling Danny McKay was capable of just about anything right now.

8

Ray Chambers loved being outdoors. A bit of fresh air never did anyone any harm, and it was certainly better than being cooped up inside the house all day.

He walked his border collie, Jack, every day, over at Barking Riverside. It had become an integral part of their routine, ever since Ray's wife had died suddenly four years earlier. The sound of seagulls circling above this stretch of the Thames was as familiar as the landscape itself, and he breathed in lungfuls of crisp air as he and Jack began their three-mile daily hike.

He picked up a tennis ball and threw it as far as he could, watching as Jack ran into the wind, his black and white coat flying out behind him.

'Here, boy,' he shouted, as Jack ran full pelt back towards him, the ball clenched between his teeth. 'Drop,' Ray ordered. He swooped down to pick the ball up and throw it again.

He watched as Jack disappeared amongst the overgrown weeds, and waited for a few seconds, before calling him back. 'Jack!' When the dog didn't appear, Ray put his fingers to his lips and let out a high pitched whistle.

'What the hell?' he muttered as Jack appeared into view with a long stick between his jaws. 'Come here, boy,' he called out.

Grabbing hold of Jack's collar, Ray brought the border collie to a halt. 'What's that you've got, eh? Drop.' In horror, Ray staggered backwards as he came to realise that Jack hadn't brought him a stick, but in fact, a charred bone, and judging by the blackened trainer dangling precariously from the end of it, most likely a human one.

He hastily clipped the lead to Jack's collar and dragged the dog away. He needed to get to a phone box, and quickly.

* * *

Detective Inspector Ronnie Dellow climbed out of his car. The cold wind whipped bitterly around him, and he pulled his thin jacket tightly against his wiry body. 'What have we got?' he called out.

'Looks like a body, Gov.'

'Looks like?' Ronnie muttered to himself. 'Either it is, or it isn't,' he snapped.

'It is. Well, what's left of one.'

Ronnie strode farther into the weeds. 'And who found it?'

Police Constable Stephen Hibbs looked down at his notebook. 'A Raymond Chambers. This gentleman,' he said, pointing across to a visibly shaken Ray.

'And what was he doing out here?'

'Walking his dog, Gov,' Stephen said as he hurried to keep up with the inspector.

'Make sure you take a statement from him,' Ronnie said, coming to a halt in front of a half-buried black bin bag. It had been dug up and torn apart, more than likely by foxes. He could see soot-covered bones and what looked like charred flesh protruding out from the thin plastic bag. 'I want this whole area cordoned off,' he demanded. His coarse greying hair blew in the wind, giving him the appearance of a mad professor. 'And get forensics down here,' he added as an afterthought.

Stephen nodded before rushing off.

Ronnie crouched down. He twisted his head this way and that way in order to look at the discovered remains from every angle. He then looked up at the at the barren wasteland. There were no houses for miles around, just a stretch of the Thames and Thamesmead directly opposite – only the lapping water separating the two areas.

He wondered briefly if there was a connection between the body and Belmarsh prison, situated across the river. Or was it solely a coincidence? There is no such thing as coincidence when it comes to crime. He could remember someone saying that once. He couldn't remember who it was now, but at the time, he'd agreed it was true. He looked across the water in the general direction of the prison. Somehow, he had a feeling this wasn't going to be an open and shut case.

* * *

Maxine hated herself for what she was doing, yet she couldn't stop the compulsion inside of her. She waited until she could hear water flowing from the en suite shower, then snatched her husband's jeans up off the floor and rifled through the pockets.

She found nothing. He'd obviously learnt from his mistake and was now hiding his deceit. She stood chewing on her thumbnail, thinking. Finally, she looked around the bedroom. As always, her home looked like a show house, with not so much as a plumped pillow out of place. A thick ivory bedspread draped down onto a plush cream carpet, a carpet that was so thick, she could curl her toes into it. Matching ivory drapes at the double windows fell to the floor in folds.

On an antique cream dressing table were two bowls of fresh pink roses, placed there to give the cream and ivory room a splash of colour. Her eyes fell upon her husband's wallet on the bedside table, and without even thinking, she snatched it up, flipped it open and quickly scanned through the contents.

'What are you doing?'

In shock, Maxine dropped the wallet. She hadn't heard her husband walk into the room. 'Nothing.'

Walking forward, Danny scooped his wallet up from the floor. 'What are you doing, Max?' His tone was loud and harsh, a lot harsher than he'd intended.

Her cheeks flushed pink. Maxine attempted to run past her husband but he grasped hold of her wrist, stopping her from escaping.

Water droplets sprayed over her as she struggled to break free. 'Ow, you're hurting me. Let go.'

He loosened his grip. 'What were you doing looking through my wallet?'

Maxine lowered her eyes. She wanted to kick herself for not being more careful. Now he knew she'd been snooping. Realising her husband wasn't going to let her leave without an explanation, she spoke quickly. 'I don't know.'

'Seriously, Max, what the fuck is wrong with you? Why are you looking through my wallet? Don't you trust me?'

Maxine bit down on her lip. 'I don't know.'

'Will you stop saying, "I don't know" and just answer the fucking question?'

'No, obviously I don't.'

Stunned, he released her and watched helplessly as his wife ran from the room. Stood half naked with just a towel tied around his waist, he wondered briefly how life could go from being fantastic one minute, to an all-time low the next. He would never understand women, he decided.

* * *

Ronnie Dellow watched from behind a strip of blue and white police tape as the crime scene manager took photographs of the remains. 'How soon can we get the PM done?' he called out to the appointed pathologist.

Judith Maine walked towards him. She pulled off her protective over-suit and dropped it into a polythene bag. 'We should have the go ahead to remove the remains soon. I'm hoping to schedule the PM sometime early evening. Obviously, it depends on the workload at the mortuary,' she said, glancing down at her watch.

'Can you tell me anything yet?'

Judith smiled. 'Other than that your victim is definitely deceased, you will have to wait until the PM. You should know that already, inspector.'

'You can't blame me for trying.' Ronnie grinned back.

As Judith laughed, her heavy jowls wobbled. 'They do say everyone loves a trier. Will you be attending?'

Ronnie nodded.

'Good. I should be able to give you something then.'

Ronnie watched as the pathologist walked away. He blew out his cheeks and looked back towards the crime scene. He had a feeling this was going to be a long night.

* * *

After he had dried and dressed, Danny walked down the stairs. He walked through to the kitchen and stood watching Maxine as she spooned pureed food into Logan's open mouth.

'Maxine, what the hell is going on?'

When his wife didn't answer, Danny came to stand in front of her. 'This isn't good, babe,' he said, his voice gentle.

Maxine looked up at her husband. She could feel her cheeks blush and hastily averted her eyes.

'If you don't trust me, then what does that say about our marriage?'

'I don't know.'

'I just don't understand where all of this is coming from. Is it that Jaqueline, putting ideas into your head?'

'No, of course not,' Maxine snapped, defending her friend.

'Then help me out here, Max,' Danny cried, 'because, for the life of me, I don't understand what I'm supposed to have done wrong.' Exasperated, he threw up his arms. 'Well, say something.'

When his wife didn't answer, he sat down heavily at the breakfast bar and massaged his closed eyes. 'Please, Max, will you just talk to me and tell me what's going on? Do you want me to leave, is that what this is all about?'

Maxine took her time in wiping over Logan's face with a wet wipe, before looking up at her husband. 'I don't trust you.' There, she had finally said it out loud. 'Every time you walk out of that door, I feel sick to my stomach, and it's eating away at me, driving me out of my mind.'

Shocked, Danny's mouth fell open. He hadn't realised the situation was so bad. 'Tell me what I can do to put this right.'

Maxine shook her head sadly. 'I don't think there is anything you can do. The problem is already here,' she said, pointing to her temple. 'It's in my head, and I don't think anything you say or do is ever going to change that.'

Danny felt his heart lurch, and he closed his eyes for a moment. Swallowing deeply, he nodded. As his wife left the room, he sat staring into the empty space she had vacated. His marriage was clearly over.

* * *

Moray was looking through his paperwork, when he glanced up to see Danny walking towards his office. He could tell by his stance that something was wrong. He waited until the big man had entered the room and was sitting down opposite him, before speaking. 'You okay, mate?'

Danny nodded. 'Is everything here all right? No comebacks or anything?'

Moray raised his eyebrows before speaking. 'Not a thing, mate.' He watched as Danny continuously turned a gold lighter over in his hand. There was clearly something on his friend's mind.

Standing up, Moray walked towards the office door, pushed it shut, then leaned against the glass panel, his arms folded across his chest. 'What's going on, mate?'

Without looking up he said, 'I need to be working. I need to keep busy.'

Moray nodded. 'When you say work, do you mean going around the clubs, checking that there aren't any problems? Or do you mean finding someone to have a row with, so you can tear him apart?'

Danny looked up. There was no emotion in his green eyes. 'Whichever comes first.'

At least Danny was being honest, and Moray had a feeling this was something to do with his mate's marital problems. He knew from experience the quicker Danny got it out of his system, the better. 'Okay,' he said. 'I'll get Callum to go around with you tonight.'

'I don't need babysitting.'

'I know. I know you're more than capable, and let's be honest here, that's half the fucking problem.' He smiled to take the edge off his words.

Danny gave a small smile in return. The smile didn't quite reach his eyes. 'Right, mate. I'd better be off.'

Moray moved aside and watched as he walked from his office, then beckoned Callum Riley over to him. 'I'm putting you with Danny tonight. Keep an eye on him,' he said, pointing a finger towards his own eyes, then across to Danny, to emphasise his request.

Thrilled to be working with Danny McKay, the Irishman nodded. 'Of course, boss.'

Moray watched as Callum ran across the empty dance floor, and then sighed. Maybe he should have gone himself. He knew for a fact that if Danny did kick off, Callum would have no chance in stopping him.

'Wait,' he called out, grabbing his overcoat as he did so. 'Change of plan. Callum, you're at The Belgrave tonight. I'll go with Danny myself.'

* * *

Lloydy grinned widely as he hobbled out of Newham Hospital towards Big Tone's Range Rover. 'Cheers, Tone, for picking me up.'

'No problem, mate.'

Once he was seated in the car, Lloydy asked, 'So, what happened with the clubs?'

Big Tone shook his head and sighed. 'They're all gone, mate.'

'Fucking hell.' Lloydy's eyes widened. 'I bet Freddie is screwing.'

Big Tone gave a bitter laugh. 'That's an understatement.'

'So, what's the plan now?'

'There's a meeting tomorrow night. Somehow, Freddie needs to salvage something from the situation. It's not going to be easy though, mate.'

Lloydy a gave a low whistle. 'You were right, Tone... what you said about Danny. We should have listened. I mean Terry and me.'

Big Tone glanced sideways. 'Yeah, well, I did try to warn you. We should have gone straight to Danny from the start.'

Lloydy shifted his weight. The ache in his groin was a reminder of what Danny McKay was capable of, yet he knew without hesitation, that the beating Danny had dished out was mild in comparison to the damage he could have caused. 'There's nothing we can do about it now though, mate. We're up to our necks in this, and I can't see any way out, if I'm being honest.'

'I was thinking maybe we should try and speak to him.'

'Are you mad?' There was alarm in Lloydy's voice. 'I'm not going anywhere near that nutter, not if I can help it.'

'So, you're planning on hiding from him for the rest of your life, then, are you? Because you know he won't let this drop.'

Lloydy thought about this for a few moments, before speaking. 'I've been thinking about just fucking off, if I'm honest, mate. All of this is getting too much for me. No matter which way we turn, we're going to have someone after us. If it's not McKay, it's Freddie.'

Big Tone sighed. 'Why don't we talk to Terry first, then decide on a plan of action?'

Lloydy sat quietly, then nodded. If truth were told, he just wanted to pack a small bag and get as far away as he could. If that made him a coward, then so be it, because it had to be a lot better than the alternative.

* * *

Terry Stevens was a worried man. He knew, without a doubt, that he was lucky Danny McKay hadn't caught up with him yet. Every car that passed by his house had him jumping up from his seat. He'd convinced himself that the big man was going to turn up and batter down his front door, just to get to him.

In his mind's eye, Danny's large frame became even larger, with each passing second, and if he wasn't so scared, he would have laughed at himself for how ridiculous and paranoid he was becoming. Just the mere thought of being in Danny McKay's presence did that to a man.

The screech of tyres outside his house had Terry leaping out of his seat. His heart was in his mouth as he peered through the net curtains. He wanted to curse the broken street light, because he couldn't see a damn thing.

Heavy banging on the front door made him jump out of his skin. It had to be McKay. He felt his stomach lurch and could feel beads of cold sweat break out across his already clammy forehead. He knew, only too well, what was to come.

Panic-stricken, Terry looked around him for an escape route. He crept out of the lounge and began to make his way through the dining room, towards the patio doors leading out to the back garden. If he could scale over the fence into his neighbour's back garden, he may have a chance of escaping.

'Terry, open up.'

Recognising Big Tone's voice, Terry's body sagged with relief. He walked towards the front door and paused before he pulled back the locked bolts. 'Who's with you?'

'Lloydy. Come on, mate, open up. We're freezing our fucking nuts off out here.'

'Is anyone else with you?'

'It's just me and Tone,' Lloydy shouted out.

Relieved, Terry unlocked the door and let the men walk through, then, just as quickly, slid the heavy bolts back into position once again.

'Are you all right, mate?' Big Tone asked, his forehead furrowed.

'Do I look all right? You know he's going to come for me as well, don't you?'

Big Tone nodded. 'That's why we're here. We need to talk through our options. We need a plan of action. I've got an idea, and it could be the only thing that's going to save our skin.'

'Go on.' Terry was all ears. He was willing to do just about anything to get McKay off his back.

Taking a deep breath, Big Tone spoke. 'Well, this is what I'm thinking.'

* * *

The sterile, unmistakable scent of disinfectant, which could only be found in a hospital, hit Ronnie's nose as he walked through a maze of corridors towards the mortuary. He glanced at his watch and cursed out loud before picking up his pace. He knew full well that Judith Maine would start the post mortem without him if he was late.

He made it into the morgue just in time to watch the remains being lifted onto a stainless steel table.

'Evening, inspector,' Judith called out from behind a surgical mask as she set about cutting away the black plastic bin bag wrapped around the body.

Once the black bag had been removed, Judith slowly walked around the table, her eyes observing everything. 'Okay then, my lovely, let's see what happened to you, shall we?' she said, speaking to the body. 'First thing's first... we need an X-ray.'

Ronnie watched with morbid fascination as Judith set to work. He was more than eager to hear her results.

Finally, Judith pulled off her mask and disrobed. 'Your victim has told us quite a lot.' She smiled.

Ronnie raised his eyebrows. 'So, what can you tell me?'

'First of all, we have a male. I would put a rough estimate to being early twenties. Do you see here?' Judith asked, pointing towards the body's raised wrists. 'This is called pugilistic attitude. It resembles a boxer's stance when a body is subjected to extreme heat, or at least it should do. All upper limbs, for example, elbows, wrists and fingers, should be flexed upwards in a defensive pose. In your victim, only the wrists and the left knee are flexed. On the X-ray, we can see the right leg is fractured, hence why that leg is not in the expected stance. Same goes for the fingers here, on the left hand. We would expect to see them curled into a fist, but again, fractures explain the lack of a fist. What I can't explain, is why the forearms are not flexed. There are no breaks from the wrist to elbow, so there should be nothing stopping them from flexing upwards.'

Ronnie stood quietly, taking everything in. 'Could it be possible he was restrained across his forearms?'

'That could explain the lack of a flex, yes,' Judith replied.

'And what about the missing fingers?'

Judith tapped the X-ray. 'You can see a number of marks across the finger bones. These were false starts. Your perpetrator more than likely found it was a lot tougher to cut through bone than they first thought, hence why it took a few attempts. I would say the weapon was a small hand saw, possibly a hack saw.'

'How certain are you of that?'

'Very certain. The spacing between the saw teeth is quite small, so it's very likely to have been a small type of saw used.'

Ronnie nodded. 'Anything else?'

'Yes, your victim was also stabbed twice in the sternum. This V-shape here, on the X-ray, would have been the knife hitting the bone.'

Ronnie shook his head. 'He went through it then?'

Judith smiled sadly. 'That isn't the worst, I'm afraid. I found soot in the throat. Soot was also present below the airways. This indicates your victim was alive when the attempt to burn him took place.'

Ronnie blew out his cheeks. 'Any idea on an ID, time of death?'

Judith shook her head. 'We've taken dental X-rays. There is no hope for fingerprints, I'm afraid. As for time of death, I would say you're looking at approximately two days, but I can't tell you if the injuries were made around the exact time of death, or in the days before.'

It was what Ronnie had been expecting. With one last look towards the victim's remains, he thanked Judith and left the mortuary.

* * *

'No fucking way.'

Big Tone rolled his eyes, agitated. 'It's the only thing we can do to get out of the shit we're in.'

'So, let me see if I've got this right. You actually want us to go and talk to the man, who is more than likely going to batter us to death? Am I hearing this right?' Terry asked. There was genuine confusion in his voice.

'Well, do you have a better plan?'

'Why don't we all just fuck off somewhere?'

Terry rounded on Lloydy. 'And what do I tell my Hayley, eh? I've had to pack her off to her mum's for the night, as it is. And the amount of grief that caused me, you wouldn't believe.'

Lloydy shook his head. 'If we go and see Danny, I seriously don't think we will come out alive.'

'Listen,' Big Tone said, 'unless the two of you can come up with something better, then the only thing we can do is speak to him – grovel on our knees, if we fucking have to. It's got to be better than living in fear for our lives, or looking over our shoulder, every fucking day, just waiting.'

Terry and Lloydy remained silent. They could see Big Tone had a point, but to put themselves in front of the big man, willingly, still sounded like suicide to them.

'Why hasn't Freddie taken control of this?'

'I told you days ago, in my opinion, Freddie has lost his reign. He's definitely lost control of Danny. Something is not right up here,' he said, pointing to his head. 'Freddie's losing the plot.'

'Brilliant,' Lloydy said in a sarcastic tone. 'So, we now have two nutters to deal with?'

'When have either of them ever been completely sane? We've got Freddie, a coke head who's paranoid as fuck, and Danny, who would kill his own granny if she got in his way,' Big Tone said bitterly.

'Do you think this could work then?' Terry asked.

Big Tone turned his head. 'What other alternative is there? If we can get Danny to just hear us out, then I think we have a good chance.'

Terry nodded. He couldn't see what else they could do. 'Okay, I'm willing to give it a try.'

Big Tone looked to Lloydy. 'Are you in, mate?'

Lloydy took a few moments to think. Reluctantly, he agreed. As Big Tone had not-so-kindly pointed out, they had no other choice.

* * *

Danny drove towards East London. Moray was sitting beside him.

'I don't want to pry, mate, but clearly something is on your mind.'

Danny stared straight ahead. The muscles in his forearms were taut as he turned the steering wheel. 'Women, mate. I just don't understand them.'

Moray nodded. He'd been right after all. It was marital problems causing Danny's foul mood.

'She thinks I'm having an affair,' Danny said, without being prompted. He needed to get it off his chest.

'And are you?'

Danny shot Moray a sideways glance. 'No, of course I'm fucking not.'

'So, what are you going to do?'

'I don't know. She wants me out of the house.' He rubbed his hand over his face, the enormity of the situation finally sinking in. 'She wants a divorce.'

Moray screwed up his face. 'Bit drastic ain't it? What, and you can't try and work things out with her?'

Danny shook his head. 'I've tried, mate, until I'm blue in the face. She doesn't want to listen. Until all of this happened, I was happy.' He gave a sad laugh. 'I should have known something would go wrong, it always fucking does, just about sums up my life.'

'You know, you're always welcome to stay at my place. I've got a spare bedroom.'

Danny pulled the car over to the kerb outside one of the clubs. 'Thanks, mate, but if I'm being honest, I just need to be by myself. No offence, pal, but I need to process all of this.'

Moray understood where Danny was coming from. He'd felt the same when he and his wife had divorced.

The two men climbed out of the car and strode towards the club. The music was loud, the heavy beat vibrating underneath their feet. The queue of punters waiting to be admitted inside the venue, stretched the length of the club. Business was obviously booming.

They walked through the doors, checking that everything was as it should be, all the while unaware of a black Mercedes which had been following them for the past hour. The occupants of the car making notes of each of the clubs they visited.

9

Freddie wasn't happy. He'd been expecting a good turnout for the meeting, and although the majority of the firm had turned up, he couldn't help but notice that a few were missing. He looked around him. Where the fuck were Big Tone, Lloydy and Terry Stevens? He was sure they'd been made aware of the meet. He'd ordered Matty to tell them personally.

He grabbed hold of Matty's elbow and pulled the lad towards him. 'Did you tell Big Tone and the others about this meeting?'

Matty paused for a moment. He was pretty certain he had, but with all of the running about Freddie had him doing, it could well have slipped his mind.

'Think hard, boy,' Freddie growled.

'Yeah, of course I did, Fred.'

Freddie narrowed his eyes. Then where the fuck were they? 'Get on the blower, now, and see where they are.'

'I haven't got any phone credit.'

'Do you know what, you're beyond fucking useless,' he said, throwing Matty away from him. 'I pay you more than enough, and you can't even top up your phone credit?'

Matty's cheeks flushed. In truth, Freddie paid him peanuts, considering all that he did for him.

Freddie pulled out his own mobile phone and tapped in Big Tone's telephone number. It went straight to his answering machine. A familiar knot of anger churned in his gut, and his mind went into overdrive. Paranoia was beginning to set in, and he chewed on the inside of his cheek while he thought the situation through. He would put money on it that the reason for them not being here somehow involved Danny McKay. Hadn't that cunt caused him enough grief?

'Maybe they forgot,' Matty said.

'No.' Freddie shook his head. 'Something's going on. There's definitely something not right about all of this.' There was no other explanation for their absence. He tried to think back to the conversations he'd had with Big Tone over the last couple of days. There had to be something he'd missed, some sort of clue, proving that the big man was swaying towards Danny. 'Did you definitely tell them about this meet?'

Matty nodded sheepishly.

'Are we gonna start this meeting or not, Fred?' Mick Johnson asked.

Annoyed, Freddie turned to face the men. 'You all probably know by now, that that no good bastard, McKay, has taken over all of the doors.'

Mick blew out his cheeks. He couldn't understand how Danny had managed to do it single-handedly. 'He must have had help, Fred. I mean, come on, where did all the men come from? They must work for someone. So, who else is involved in all of this?'

Freddie nodded. He'd heard rumours that Moray Garner was involved. 'Of course he fucking did.'

He'd never liked Moray. To put it mildly, he despised him. He'd always been suspicious of the pikey bastard's motives. The man had always been there, in the background, hanging around, just waiting to poach his number two, and now he finally had.

Conveniently, Freddie let it slip from his mind the fact that he, himself, had ordered McKay's death. The truth of the matter was, he'd always been jealous of Moray and Danny's friendship, their closeness. In fact, it wouldn't surprise him if Moray had been the one who'd put Danny up to the takeover. After all, the idea had to come from somewhere. 'Moray Garner is the other man behind this.'

Mick stood quietly. He was more than concerned. After seeing Danny in action, he really didn't want to get involved. And hearing that Moray Garner and Danny had formed a partnership only made matters ten times worse.

He looked around him and listened as the men, most of them young enough to be his grandsons, told Freddie exactly what he wanted to hear. Telling him how they were personally going to bring McKay down, all of them acting the Billy Big Bollocks in front of their boss. It was laughable.

The truth was, they hadn't seen the real Danny McKay in action, but he had, and if he was being honest, it had scared him shitless. In all of his years, he had never seen anything so brutal, and he doubted he ever would again. Besides, he was getting too old to be scrapping with the likes of McKay and Garner, and after what he'd witnessed, he knew he wouldn't stand a chance against the younger man, if it ever came to blows.

'So, what do you want us to do about it then, Fred?' Mick asked.

'What do you think I want you to do? Invite that cunt McKay to a fucking tea party? I want my doors back,' Freddie answered, looking around him. 'And I want McKay's head brought to me on a plate.'

Mick had just about heard enough. Most of these kids didn't

have a clue what they were up against. 'I'm not being funny, Fred, but how do you expect us to do that? It's not as though we can just turn up and take them back, is it? McKay's gonna expect comebacks, and he'll be ready and waiting for it to happen.'

'I don't fucking know, or care, for that matter, how you're going to do it. Just get it done,' Freddie snapped. His patience was being truly tested, and he felt as though he may as well be surrounded by imbeciles.

'All right, fucking hell. Calm down, Fred.'

'Calm down?' Freddie roared. 'No, I won't calm down. I'm finished because of that little cunt.' He threw his arms up in the air and gave a bitter laugh. 'And you seriously expect me to be calm?'

'No, I expect you to have a plan. Something proactive we can actually do, instead of telling all of this lot here, to just go out there and get your doors. They don't know what he's actually like, and it's gonna be a suicide mission, sending them out unaware.'

Freddie narrowed his eyes. He stared hard at Mick. 'Shut your mouth,' he growled. 'You're going too far now.'

'They need to know what they're up against.'

'I said, shut your fucking mouth,' Freddie spat. He took a step closer towards the older man, his fists clenched at his sides.

Mick stood his ground. 'I can see why McKay left now. This is no way to run a firm. And as for all of you,' he said, pointing his finger towards each of the kids who made up Freddie's firm, 'if you follow this through, and attempt to take those doors unprepared, or try getting lairy with McKay, then so help you all, because you're going to need every bit of luck on your side that you can get.'

Freddie lunged forward, his broken ribs slowing him down. He needed to shut the older man up before he let slip about the hammering he'd received from McKay. The last thing he needed was for the last few remaining men he had, to think he'd lost control.

With ease, Mick pushed the man away from him. 'I'm going,' he said. He turned to walk away, and then coming to an abrupt halt, he spun around and moved closer to Freddie's ear. 'Let me give you some advice, son. I've been in this game a long time, and I swallowed what happened to that Greek kid, but you were bang out of order with what you did. You should have finished the lad off first, before burning him. You need to get a grip on this firm before it all goes tits up, which trust me, the way you're going, it will. And you need to lay off the coke and sort your nut out, before you end up getting another kid killed.'

Stunned, Freddie watched as Mick walked away. He stood for a few moments, just thinking. Fuck him, he thought bitterly. Fuck them all. He didn't need any of them. One way or another, he would get his doors back, even if it was the last thing he ever did.

* * *

'You've got a good one there, girl. That man loves the bones of you.'

Hayley Stevens rolled her eyes. She opened up the jewellery gift box, pulled out a diamond bracelet, and turned it over in her hand. It was the latest in a long line of gifts from her husband, Terry, and was his way of apologising for making her stay at her mum's the night before.

She hated this shithole. It was cramped, old-fashioned and stank of mould. It was nothing like her beautiful house in Brentwood. In her opinion, she was too good for the Dagenham Council Estate she'd grown up on, and always had been.

She dropped the bracelet down beside her, uninterested. If Terry had bought her the Mercedes A-class, which she had her eye on, instead, she may have been able to raise a smile.

'You're one ungrateful moody cow. What's wrong with you?' Hayley's mum asked.

'Oh just fuck off, Mum,' Hayley snapped. She sat staring at the television set which dominated the tiny front room, bored out of her mind. She couldn't spend another evening stuck indoors with her mum, whose sole purpose in life was to gossip about the neighbours.

She stood up and admired her reflection in the gilt mirror above the mantelpiece. A night out on the town was exactly what she needed, she decided.

* * *

'I'm still not sure about all of this,' Lloydy said, sitting forward in Big Tone's car.

Terry Stevens turned in his seat. 'Other than all of us fucking off, have you got a better plan?'

Lloydy shook his head. 'You know I haven't,' he groaned, flopping backwards in his seat, defeated.

Big Tone tapped his fingers on the steering wheel. To say he was nervous was an understatement. If they could just make Danny listen to what they had to say, he had a feeling this could work out in their favour. Surely, the man would understand the predicament Freddie had put them all in. Freddie was, after all, their boss.

He had a little speech prepared, and he'd rehearsed it over and over in his mind, only each time, it became shallower and more meaningless. He cleared his throat.

'This is it, lads,' he stated as they spotted Danny pull into the car park of Ritzy's Nightclub. 'Are you ready?'

'As I'll ever be.' Terry sighed as he opened the car door and climbed out.

They walked across the car park, quickening their pace, before Danny disappeared inside the building.

'Danny, hold up a minute,' Big Tone called out.

Danny turned his head, immediately suspicious of the three men's intentions. 'What the fuck do you want?'

Big Tone held up his hand. 'We just want to talk, mate. I swear.'

Danny's body was taut as he went into defence mode. His fists were clenched, ready to defend himself. He'd been expecting something like this to happen, and was more than ready for the three men, should they attack.

'Do we have a problem here, boss?' Callum asked.

'I don't know yet,' Danny answered.

Coming to a halt, the three men stood a safe distance away from their former colleague. 'Just five minutes of your time is all we're asking for.'

Danny watched them warily. They'd not only been work colleagues, but friends, until they'd betrayed him, that was. Now, they were nothing to him, in fact he wouldn't piss on them if they were on fire.

A part of him was actually intrigued to hear what they wanted. Obviously, it was Freddie who'd sent them, and he wanted to hear what his former boss had to say about the takeover. He thought it through for a moment, then nodded. He might as well get the inevitable over with. After all, he had more than one bone to pick with them, and seeing as all three were on his hit list, it made sense.

'You'd better come in then, but make it quick.' His body remained taut, his muscles straining, as he walked inside the club.

The three men looked towards each other, then followed Danny inside. Flanked on either side by Moray's men, they knew if this went pear-shaped, they were in big trouble.

Making his way up the stairs to Moray's office, Danny took a seat behind the oak desk. He stared at the three men, his expression giving away no tell-tale signs of what he was actually thinking. It was unnerving.

'Well?' he finally asked. 'What the fuck do you want, and you'd better have a good explanation for being here, because right now, I'm doing everything I can to not tear the three of you apart.'

'We just want to apologise for everything,' Big Tone said, his voice wavering.

Danny nodded, his expression devoid of any emotion. 'Let me see if I've got this right,' he said, his voice calm. 'You planned to have me taken out, and now you have the audacity to come in here and apologise?'

Lloydy looked down at his feet. He was more than terrified. Danny McKay was unpredictable. You never knew which mood you would catch him in, and as Big Tone had pointed out more than once, that famous temper of his was always there, ready and waiting to explode. He'd known coming here was a bad idea from the start.

'We had orders from Freddie. It wasn't as if we wanted to actually do it.'

'So that makes it all right then, does it? If that was the case, then why didn't any of you useless cunts come to me and tell me what was going down?'

Big Tone looked across at Terry for support. 'We had no choice, mate.'

'What are you looking at him for? He's not going to help you out, and believe me, Terry here is in enough shit as it is.'

Big Tone swallowed deeply. The speech he'd rehearsed over and over again was gone from his mind now. 'We're sorry. There's nothing else we can say.'

'What about my wife and my boy? Did they not cross your minds in all of this?'

Big Tone nodded furiously. 'Of course they did, and I begged Freddie to let you go home to them. I told him from the off that this was all wrong.'

Danny gave a hollow laugh. 'Oh well, that's all right then, isn't it? Thanks for that. The fact of the matter is that you were still going to try and take me out,' he roared, banging his fist down on the table, making the three men physically jump.

Terry could feel his heart thumping wildly in his chest. His throat was dry. He needed to say something, and fast, to help the situation. 'We had no choice. If we didn't do as Freddie ordered, then he would have taken us out as well.'

Danny turned his head towards Terry. The anger he felt was clearly evident across his face. 'So basically, you all decided to save your own skins. What about me, eh? Didn't I matter in all of this?' he asked with a sarcastic tone.

Terry looked down at the floor. There was nothing else he could say. Danny had hit the nail on the head, and the truth of the matter was, they had only looked out for themselves.

'Well?' Danny demanded. When Terry didn't answer, he stood up and moved forward. 'You were next on my list,' he said, giving the man a cold stare. 'Did you honestly think I was going to let you get away scot-free, for your part in all of this?'

Terry jumped back in his haste to put himself at arm's length from the big man.

Moving cautiously forward, Big Tone held out his hands in a

bid to ward Danny off. 'Please, Danny,' he said. 'We don't want any trouble. We only came here to talk. We're done with Freddie. We've walked out on him and the firm. All we want to do is smooth things over with you, so we don't have to look over our shoulders any more. What more can we do to put this right? We'll even get on our hands and knees and beg, if we have to.'

Danny listened intently to what Big Tone had to say. From the sound of it, Freddie's men were dropping away like flies. His so-called firm was disintegrating in front of his very eyes. He felt a flicker of satisfaction spread through his veins. Leaning back against the desk he wondered briefly how he could put these three men to use for his own gain.

He had a plan. 'Okay, let bygones be bygones,' he said, looking at each of them in turn. 'From now on, you work for me person-ally. That means, you report to me and no one else, is that understood?'

Stunned, Big Tone glanced across to Terry and Lloydy. He couldn't believe what he was hearing. How on earth had they managed to get Danny onside so easily and so quickly? What a turn around. 'Yeah, of course, and thank you,' he said, grinning from ear to ear. He felt as though the weight of the world had lifted off his shoulders, so immense was the relief.

'I want you all back here by six tonight, okay? I'll put you back on the doors.'

The three men nodded, shook his hand and then left the office. As they walked out, Danny stared after them. The contempt he felt for them was at the forefront of his mind. They were a means to an end, as far as he was concerned, and nothing more.

* * *

Hayley Stevens lay back on the bed. She was naked and had positioned herself in a manner to show off her best assets. She watched as her Greek lover emerged from the shower, towel drying himself as he did so.

'Come back to bed,' she purred.

Giorgio Christos smiled, showing perfect bleached white teeth. 'Tell me more about your husband first.'

Annoyed, Hayley pulled the sheet around her. 'Why do you always want to talk about that old bastard?' she sulked.

Giorgio sat down on the edge of the bed. 'I need to know everything about my competition, my beautiful lady.'

'He doesn't compare to you.'

When Giorgio raised his eyebrows, Hayley sighed. 'Okay, I don't know exactly what is going on, but there's trouble.'

'What sort of trouble?'

'I don't know,' Hayley said. She let the sheet drop from around her for a second time.

'Well, how do you know there is trouble?'

Sitting up, Hayley wrapped her arms around him and pushed her ample breasts against his back. 'He told me. He's always whining about something or other, though, so it's probably nothing.'

'You need to find out exactly what is going on,' Giorgio said as he turned and prised her arms from around his waist.

'I will do.' Hayley smiled. It didn't occur to her to seriously question why this man, who'd come out of nowhere and pursued her, never wanted to talk about anything other than her husband and the men he worked for.

* * *

Moray was furious. 'Have you actually lost your fucking mind?'

'I know what I'm doing.' Danny sighed. Moray was one of the only people who could get away with speaking to him in this manner, bringing further proof to just how close they were.

'Seriously, Danny, do you? Because from where I'm standing, this is fucking bizarre, even for you. Have you actually forgotten that they were going to try and kill you?'

'Of course I haven't.'

'Then why the fuck have you recruited them to work for us?'

'As I've already said, I know what I'm doing. Besides, what's that saying? Keep your friends close and your enemies closer, or some old bollocks.'

Moray threw up his arms. 'This is fucking unbelievable.' For the life of him, he couldn't work out what was going through his best mate's mind.

'Look,' Danny said as he leant forward in his seat, 'let's just put them to work and see how it goes.'

'Put them to work? Do you actually trust them to work on the doors? The very same ones that we took from Freddie, might I add.' He blew out his cheeks. 'What's stopping them from trying to take them back?'

Laughing, Danny shook his head. 'They're not going to try and take them back.'

'And how do you know that?'

'Because they're as thick as two short planks, for starters. And plus, they wouldn't dare to.'

Moray raised his eyebrows. 'Well, I hope you're right about this.'

'I am,' Danny replied confidently.

Moray sighed. Against his better judgement, he had to trust Danny on this one. He supposed his mate knew the three men a lot better than he, himself did. But one thing he knew for a fact, was that he wouldn't trust them, and if the situation ended up going south, just as he predicted it would, then he would be ready and waiting to come down on his mate like a ton of bricks. To put it in simple terms, Danny wasn't going to know what had hit him once he was finished unleashing his wrath upon him.

* * *

Terry was over the moon with the outcome regarding Danny. The grin on his face couldn't be any wider. He climbed out of his car and strolled into the Mercedes showroom. Now that everything was sorted out, he couldn't wait to have his Hayley back home, where she belonged. As a surprise and an apology for making her stay at her mum's, he'd decided to buy her the A-class. She'd dropped enough hints over the past few weeks that she wanted one, and he couldn't wait to see her face, when he collected her from her mum's with it.

He paid in cash and arranged to have the car dropped off in Dagenham. Walking back to his own car, he smiled. He had just one more thing to do, and that was to buy his wife the biggest bouquet of flowers she had ever seen. His Hayley meant the world to him, and as far as he was concerned, she was worth every penny he spent on her.

* * *

Giorgio Christos walked out of the hotel and climbed into his black Mercedes. He could still smell Hayley on himself, and he squirted a generous measure of aftershave over him, in a bid to rid himself of the stench of her over-powering perfume.

He couldn't stand the woman and her self-importance. She wasn't even that attractive, once she was stripped of all her makeup, and as for her personality, well, it was non-existent.

The situation had got to the point where it was starting to become difficult for him to pretend he even liked her, let alone that he was interested in her and her droll conversation. He had never met a more stupid woman before in all of his life. How the hell she believed he could actually want someone like her, he had no idea.

With a quick glance back at the hotel, he started the ignition and drove towards East London. It was becoming harder and harder to get information out of her, and he decided there and then he would tell his uncle tonight that the plan wasn't working any more.

He would reluctantly have just one more meeting with her, and if there wasn't any information coming forward, then he would cease all contact. He'd had enough, and Hayley had served her purpose.

* * *

For the first time in her life, Hayley Stevens was in love. She felt her cheeks blush pink at the mere thought of Giorgio and the things he could do with his tongue. Everything about her Greek lover was amazing. There was just no comparison, when she compared him to her husband.

She turned the key in the lock of her mum's front door and walked through to the front room.

'And where have you been, young lady?' her mum asked, her shrill voice loud.

'Out,' Hayley replied, flopping down on the sofa.

Her mum bristled. 'And what would I have told Terry if he'd turned up looking for you?'

'Did he turn up?'

'No.'

'Well then, why do you always have to start, eh? If you must know, I didn't want to be stuck in this poxy house with you.'

Sucking in her cheeks, her mum folded her arms underneath her ample breasts. She wasn't offended by her daughter's words. Her Hayley had always been the same – a cold heart was what she had. 'You better not be playing around on that husband of yours,' she said, looking slyly across at Hayley. 'Remember, I know you, girl.'

Hayley threw up her arms. 'Will you just leave me the fuck alone and mind your own business?'

The sound of a car horn beeping outside stopped her mum's comeback. She jumped out of her seat and her mouth fell open as she peered through the net curtains. 'Well, I never.'

'What is it?' Hayley asked, making her way over to the window. Letting out a loud squeal, she ran outside the house. She couldn't believe it. Terry had bought her the car she had her eye on. She leapt into his arms and kissed him on the lips.

'Do you like it, babe?' Terry asked.

'I love it,' Hayley replied, climbing inside the car. She felt a tiny bit guilty now for cheating on him, but she couldn't say she would never do it again, because she knew, without a shadow of a doubt, that she would. She wasn't prepared to give up her Greek lover for anyone.

* * *

Maxine was folding the last of Danny's shirts, ready to be packed into boxes for when he moved out. He hadn't asked her to pack for him, but she felt the quicker it was done, the easier it would be for the both of them.

Late into the night, they had talked things over and decided to go their separate ways. That morning, she'd seen a tear in his eyes as he'd cuddled Logan to him, knowing this would be the final night he would spend underneath the same roof as his boy. As from tomorrow morning, everything would change

She knew she would never be fully free of her husband. The fact that she had his son would ensure that would never happen. Danny would always have a hold over her, in some form or another. She just hoped he didn't intend to make her life any more difficult than it already was.

She heard him come into the house and felt her heart sink. As hard as this was, she had to do it. If not for her sake, then for Logan's. It wasn't fair for him to be brought up in a home with warring parents who could barely tolerate being in each other's company.

As Danny came into the bedroom, she watched him pause. She knew this was going to be difficult for him, and she kept her tone neutral as she spoke.

'This is the last of your clothes to be packed away.'

Danny nodded.

'I was thinking that maybe we should get the divorce started as soon—'

'I'm not even out the door yet. At least give me a bit of time to get used to the idea,' Danny interrupted.

Maxine could hear the hurt in his voice and she nodded. 'I just think the quicker we get this over with, the better.'

'Where's my son?'

He was changing the subject and Maxine sighed. 'He's at my mum's for the night.'

'What do you mean, he's at your fucking mum's? This is my last night with him.'

'I just think it's going to be a lot easier if he's not here when you leave in the morning.'

'I don't give a fuck about what you think. That wasn't your choice to make.'

'Danny, this is exactly what I'm talking about. You getting angry isn't good for Logan, is it?'

'I can't believe you've done this,' he said, wiping his hand over his face. 'My last night, Max, and you've taken him away from me. Do you hate me that much, is that what this is all about? What have I done that's so bad that you would do this to me, eh?'

'Don't be so ridiculous. It's just better for our son this way. It's better for all of us.'

'It's better for you, you mean,' Danny spat. He shook his head, unable to understand this turn of events.

Maxine could see the anger flicker across her husband's face, and knew she'd made the right decision in sending their son away to her mum's for the night. The last thing she needed was for Danny to start kicking up a fuss when it was time to leave and say goodbye to their little boy in the morning. She wanted him out of her life, as quickly and as quietly as possible.

'Go to your mum's now and bring him home.'

'No, my mum has taken him out for the day and she won't be back until late,' Maxine lied.

'You had all of this planned out, didn't you?' He stabbed his finger towards her. 'Even when we talked this through last night, you never had any intention of it being any other way.'

Maxine didn't answer. It was true.

'I'll never forgive you for this,' Danny said. His eyes flashed dangerously and he had to fight the urge not to destroy everything around him. It was only the fact that he didn't want to give his wife even more ammunition to keep him away from his son that he kept his cool.

Maxine watched as he bounded from the room, and her body

shook as she heard him slam out of the house, almost taking the front door off its hinges with him as he did so. She wondered how love could turn to hate so quickly. Once upon a time she'd been so blinded by Danny that she would have given her all to keep him by her side; she would never have been able to envisage a life without him. That time seemed like a lifetime ago, now she couldn't wait to see the back of him. She didn't trust him, and no matter what he said or did she knew she would never rest easy by his side again. There would always be a doubt in her mind, would always be a niggle eating away at her wondering who he was with, what he was getting up to. She'd seen her own mother almost drive herself crazy, believing that her father was having an affair, and didn't want her son to witness or go through the same trauma she had as a child. Taking deep breaths to quash the fear inside of her, she returned to the task of packing away her husband's shirts. Just a few more hours, and then it would all be over. He would be out of her life for good.

* * *

Danny was absolutely furious. He still couldn't get his head around how, seemingly overnight, his wife had become such a cold heartless bitch. His last night with his boy, and even that, she had taken away from him. She had to hate him, he decided. There was no other explanation for her cruel mind games.

He could happily wring her neck right now, even though, deep down, he knew he would never lay a finger on her. He'd never raised his hand to a woman and didn't intend to start now, no matter how much she provoked him to want to do just that.

As he drove towards Romford, he dared someone to try and cut him up. His vicious temper, coupled with the pent-up rage inside him, was definitely not a good combination. His expression was menacing, his blood was boiling, and he could practically feel the fury seep out of his pores.

He had to physically stop himself from driving to his mother in-law's house, grabbing Logan and then just fucking off some place with him. It wasn't as if Freya would be able to stop him; Logan was his son, he had rights, didn't he? Freya had never liked him, right from the start; before he and Maxine had even married she'd shown her displeasure and looked down her nose at him. She even refused to let him into her house. She didn't trust him not to pinch the silver, apparently. It was laughable; he could buy her house ten times over, and she was worried he might steal the silver cutlery set she'd received as a wedding present, and considering Maxine's father went down for armed robbery he wouldn't be surprised if the gift hadn't fallen off the back of a lorry to begin with. He contemplated actually going through with it and snatching Logan, but knew, deep down in his heart, it wasn't the right thing to do. No matter how much his wife had hurt him, Logan needed his mother, and he couldn't take her away from him, he couldn't do that to his son.

Tapping his thumb impatiently on the steering wheel, he waited for the traffic lights to turn green. 'Come on,' he shouted.

When the car in front didn't move, he banged his fist on the horn. 'For fuck's sake, what are you waiting for? Go.'

Danny watched as the passenger door opened, and shook his head. He really wasn't in the mood for this. God help this stupid prick, whoever he was, because he was about to feel the full strength of his wrath.

He unbuckled his seat belt. His hand was on the door handle, ready to jump out.

Before he could even climb out of the car, there was a loud pop, shattering the windscreen. It all happened so fast. Danny didn't stand a chance of moving out of the way, once he'd realised, far too late, that the man was pointing a gun towards him.

Dressed in black, with a makeshift balaclava pulled over his head, the assailant jumped back into the waiting car and within seconds it had sped away from the scene.

Danny brought his hand up towards his chest. His white shirt was already turning crimson. A searing pain, and blood trickling through his fingers, were the last things he could recall before slumping across the steering wheel.

10

Moray raced through the entrance of the Accident and Emergency Department at Oldchurch Hospital in Romford, Essex. 'I need to know where someone is. Danny McKay, he was brought in an hour ago,' he shouted out to the receptionist.

Julie Buckle's head bobbed up and she adjusted her glasses as she looked up from the desk at him. 'I'm sorry, sir. There's a queue. You will need to wait your turn.'

'For fuck's sake,' Moray yelled, 'just tell me where he is.'

Julie's expression became stern. She was used to dealing with situations like this. They were a daily occurrence. In a monotone voice, she spoke. 'Sir, as I've already told you, you need to wait your turn. Otherwise, I will have to call security to escort you out of the building.'

Moray gave her a cold stare and moved towards the back of the queue. He could see there was no point in arguing. She was a jobsworth, and would probably get a kick out of having him thrown out. He'd met her type before.

Finally, he reached the front of the queue.

'Name?' Julie snapped.

'Danny McKay. He was brought in an hour ago. He was shot, that's all I know.'

Julie held up her hand. 'Please, sir, all I need is the name for the moment.'

Moray was losing patience and his voice was low as he answered. 'I've just told you. Danny McKay.'

'Date of birth?'

'I don't fucking know. What does it matter? You've got his name, and he was shot.'

Julie arched her eyebrows and her tone was harsh as she spoke. 'I need to know, because there could be more than one patient with that name.'

Moray snarled. 'Are you for fucking real? How many Danny McKays who've been shot do you actually have in here? I'm warning you now, lady, tell me where the fuck he is, otherwise, I'm going to tear this fucking hospital apart looking for him.'

Julie swallowed deeply. She looked back down at her computer screen. 'He was taken to theatre,' she said, as a pink flush spread up from her neck to her cheeks.

'See, that wasn't so difficult, was it? Why couldn't you have just said that from the start? Fucking jobsworth,' Moray shouted.

He ran through the department, following the signs pointing towards the theatre. Racing through the corridors, Moray's heart was in his mouth. He prayed Danny could pull through this. He knew his friend was physically strong, but he wasn't invincible. A little thought niggled in the back of his mind. What if Danny died, or was already dead? He felt sick with fear.

He had absolutely no idea of what could have happened, or for that matter, who could be responsible. Who would've been able to get that close to him? Immediately, his mind went to the three men Danny had recruited just that morning. He would put money on Freddie having an involvement somehow. It had to be him. No one else would have been able to get that close.

'Excuse me, wait,' he called out to a nurse about to enter the theatre doors. 'I'm looking for my relative, Danny McKay,' he lied. 'He's in theatre now.'

He followed the nurse through to the relatives' room. 'Wait here and I'll see what I can find out,' she said with a soft Irish lilt.

Moray took a seat. Quickly, he stood up again and looked through the glass panel towards the theatre reception. He was on edge and couldn't relax. The nurse walked back to him. 'He's still in theatre. I've asked for the surgeon to come and speak to you, once he's out.'

'Thank you,' Moray said. He sat back down and rested his forearms on his knees. He knew he should try and get hold of Maxine, but he had no contact details for her, and he didn't even know if Danny would want her here.

Finally, a surgeon dressed in theatre scrubs appeared at the door. Moray jumped up from his seat. 'How is he doing?'

The doctor closed the door behind him and pulled off his theatre cap, leaving his thick dark hair to stand up on end. 'He's lost a lot of blood, but fortunately, he was shot just below his shoulder, missing his vital organs. We've removed the bullet and I'm optimistic. However, the next twenty-four hours will be critical.'

Moray nodded, barely taking it all in. 'Can I see him?'

'Let's get him settled into intensive care first, and then you can see him.'

'Intensive care?' Moray was alarmed. This didn't sound good at all.

'It's protocol. Danny has lost a lot of blood, and as I stated, he is in a critical condition.'

Moray nodded. 'Thank you.'

'Oh, one more thing. Do you have contact details for his next of kin?'

Moray shook his head. 'I'm trying to contact them now.'

He wandered out of the theatre area and stood just thinking. What the fuck was he meant to do now? He moved aside so the porters could wheel a patient out of the double doors, on a bed surrounded by machines and tubes. It took him a few moments to realise it was actually Danny. Jesus, this wasn't good at all. He brought his hands up to his head, as the reality of the situation sank in.

Walking fast, Moray followed the porters towards the Intensive Care Unit. 'I'm his cousin,' Moray lied again, to the nurse walking beside Danny's bed.

'Wait here, please. I'll tell the staff you're here, once they have him settled.'

Moray watched, helplessly, as they wheeled Danny inside the ward. He needed to contact Maxine. He would deal with the consequences of his decision once his mate was awake.

* * *

George Christos beckoned his nephew over to him. 'Well?' he asked.

Sitting down at the table beside his uncle, Giorgio shook his head. 'It's getting harder and harder to get her to talk.'

'Keep at it. She must know more than she is letting on.'

'I really don't think she does. She said there was some trouble, but when I asked what it was, she didn't have a clue what was going on.'

George looked his nephew over. He was a good looking boy, who had no problems attracting the ladies, which was the main reason why he'd used him to extract information from this woman. 'You need to try harder. Do whatever you have to do to make her talk.'

Giorgio felt his heart sink. This wasn't what he wanted to hear. He couldn't bear the thought of weeks or months even, stuck with Hayley. 'I was thinking maybe just one more meeting, and if she doesn't give me anything useful, then I should cut ties with her.'

George held up his hand to quiet Giorgio down, as his brother, Alexandros, leaned forward to speak privately in his ear. Nodding his head, George smiled and he returned his attention back to his nephew. He'd just heard the most wonderful news. Freddie Smith's number two had been gunned down. 'Yes, yes, you do what you feel is best, Giorgio.'

Surprised, Giorgio gave a wide smile, feeling somewhat happier. 'Thank you, uncle.'

'Come,' George said, placing his arm around his nephew's shoulders. 'Let's wait for your cousins to return, and then we will celebrate the good news.'

* * *

'You can see him now.'

Moray followed the nurse, Sophie Nolan, through the ward. When he reached Danny's bedside, he shook his head sadly. His closest friend was covered in tubes and drips, and surrounded by lifesaving equipment. He glanced up at the beeping machines. He had no idea what the beeps meant, or what any of the equipment was used for. The only thing he knew for certain, was that if he was being totally honest, they scared the life out of him.

'How is he?'

Sophie smiled. 'He's doing okay. Hopefully, we should be able to bring him around in the next few hours.'

Moray nodded. He waited for the nurse to leave the bedside,

then rifled through the grey plastic patient's property bag, containing the belongings Danny had been brought into the hospital with. He needed Danny's mobile phone. He had to get a hold of Maxine, and fast.

With the phone grasped in his fist, he left the ward. Once outside, he scrolled through Danny's contact list, pressing dial when he found Maxine's phone number. He quickly explained the situation. In utter disbelief, he listened open mouthed, as Maxine refused to come to the hospital.

'He's in a bad way,' he said, interrupting her several times, hoping she would change her mind.

When he realised Maxine wasn't going to budge on the matter, he switched off the call. He couldn't believe it. No matter what had gone on between them, Danny was still her husband and the father of her child. He walked back to the ward and slipped Danny's phone back inside the plastic bag. He then sat on the edge of the chair beside the bed, his eyes nervously darting towards the beeping machines.

'You can talk to him if you want to,' Sophie said gently.

Moray looked up at her in disbelief. He glanced towards Danny. He was confused. His friend wasn't even awake.

'He can still hear.' She smiled.

Nodding his head, Moray waited for the nurse to leave Danny's bedside. 'All right, mate?' he began. He could feel his cheeks blush and he looked around him, to check that no one else was within earshot. He was feeling more than a little bit foolish, and didn't want anyone else to hear the words he was about to say. 'I promise you, I'm gonna find out who did this, and as soon as you're better, mate, we'll sort them out, together. So, you just do what you have to do to get out of here.'

He didn't know if Danny could really hear him or not, but he certainly felt better for pledging his allegiance to catch whoever it was responsible for the shooting.

* * *

Big Tone was enjoying an ice cold beer. He was sitting with Mick Johnson, and between them, they were putting the world to rights. Finally, they came to the subject of why they were really sitting in The Bull public house in Romford.

'Freddie's a loose cannon,' Mick stated.

Big Tone nodded. He already knew this. 'Why do you think me and the lads walked out on him?'

'He's gonna get one or more of those kids killed.'

'A lot more went on in the firm, than you, or any of the others, knew about.'

Taking a sip from his pint, Mick raised his eyebrows, waiting for Big Tone to continue.

'He ordered Danny's death. Terry Stevens and Lloydy were meant to have taken him out, only the kid was gunned down in the restaurant, before they had the chance to carry it through.'

Mick blew out his cheeks. To say he was stunned was an understatement. He'd had no idea things were so bad. 'Fucking hell, mate. What the fuck is going on? I take it Danny found out, or at least he knows now.'

Big Tone nodded. 'Apparently, he'd sussed it out straight away. To be honest, there is so much bad blood between them, this is only going to end up going one way. It'll be a case of the best man wins, and I know who I've got my money on.'

'I told Freddie he needs to get a grip on himself. Something's not right up here,' Mick said, pointing to his temple. 'It's the coke, mate. It's fucking him up. I'm sure it is. To be honest, I'm done with him. He's becoming too reckless for my liking, and as for those kids, they haven't got a clue what they're walking into.'

'Do you remember when all of this trouble first started? We were at the meet with the Greeks, and Danny kept asking why Freddie had these kids on the payroll. Makes you wonder, doesn't it?' Big Tone asked, raising his eyebrows.

Silently, Mick nodded in agreement. Just lately, he'd begun asking himself the exact same thing. Why was Freddie surrounding himself with kids? 'They're impressionable, mate. They hear Freddie's name, and want to jump on the bandwagon. What they don't realise, is that this isn't a game. One of them will end up getting hurt or killed. Let's face it, in this game, you're not guaranteed a long life. If we manage to reach old age, then we've been more than lucky. Either that, or we haven't stepped on the wrong toes.'

'True. You live by the sword, you die by the sword.'

'Exactly,' Mick answered. 'That's what these kids don't understand.' He took a sip of his lager and quickly swallowed it down. 'So, you're working with Danny now?'

'It's got to be a lot safer than working for Freddie.'

Mick shook his head. 'I don't know about that, mate. We've both seen the real Danny McKay, haven't we? And let's face it, it isn't pretty.'

Big Tone couldn't help but agree. 'I'll be keeping my head down, mate. I don't intend to get on his bad side. Why don't you think about getting in contact with him, and see if he'll take you on?'

Mick thought about it for a moment. 'I may do, mate. Either that, or I'll just retire. I'm getting on in age now, and wouldn't mind spending a bit more time with my grandkids.'

Big Tone laughed. 'There's still some life in you, mate.'

'Tell that to my knees.' Mick grinned. 'But yeah, I will think about it.'

They continued supping their pints, each of them quiet with their own thoughts. The last few months had been a roller coaster. Surely, things couldn't get any worse.

* * *

A sliver of guilt ran through Maxine for refusing to go and see her husband. She looked up at their wedding photo on the wall. That day had been one of the happiest days of her life. The other being when she had given birth to Logan. The truth was, she was scared that she would fall to pieces if she saw him.

Deep down, she did still love him. How could she not? He'd given her their son. But she had to get tough now. Enough was enough, and she couldn't go on living with the constant knot of worry, each time he went out, or received a telephone call. She didn't trust him any more, and there was nothing either of them could do about that.

She didn't know what to do for the best. Should she go to the hospital or not? Maybe she should telephone them and see how he was. She was so confused. She'd put on a brave face for so long when it came to her husband, she really didn't know what to feel any more. The only thing she knew for certain, was that for her own sanity, she couldn't live with him a day longer.

She chewed on her fingernail as she thought it through. She would wait and see how things went. He couldn't be that bad. It was more than likely just a ruse to get her to go and talk to him about Logan. If he was that seriously injured, surely the hospital would have phoned her themselves.

* * *

After leaving the hospital, Moray drove back to the club. He wanted to call a meeting with his men. He wondered, briefly, if any of them had noticed anything unusual in the last couple of days. Although, he was pretty certain he or Danny would've been informed, if they had. He glanced down at his watch. He would call the men in an hour early tonight, including the three men Danny had recruited.

He still had a feeling Freddie's men were involved. It was too much of a coincidence that they should turn up, and the next day, Danny was gunned down. He would suss them out later on, at the meeting, that was, if they even turned up. So help them if he found out they had played a part in any of this, because if they had, he would tear them apart with his own bare hands.

Moray turned into the car park. He spotted more than a few cars he recognised, already parked up. Word had more than likely got out about the shooting, and he knew they would be eager to find out the facts. He climbed out of his car, locked up, then walked inside the club.

'What's happened, boss? How's Danny doing?'

Moray was met with a barrage of questions. 'Let me get everyone here first, and then I'll explain everything,' he said, walking towards his office.

* * *

DCI Ronnie Dellow was sitting behind his desk at Dagenham Police Station. There had been no breakthroughs in the case whatsoever. As of yet, he didn't even have a positive ID. He'd personally looked through every single missing person's file he could get his hands on, hoping it would relate to his murder victim. Each lead had led to a dead end. They were still no nearer to finding out who he was.

Someone, somewhere, must be missing this man, he thought to himself, as he absentmindedly tapped his Biro pen on the desk.

'It's confirmed. The case will be on the six o'clock news.'

Ronnie looked up. 'Let's hope we get something, then. Have you chased up forensics?'

Detective Constable Josie Morgan sat down at her desk. 'Just about to do it now,' she replied, picking up the phone.

Ronnie turned back to his computer screen. He had to be missing something. He looked across at the mountain of paperwork surrounding him, then to the yellow Post-It notes he'd stuck randomly around the screen. According to many of the colleagues he worked with, his desk was a cluttered mess. Ronnie liked to think of it as organised chaos. Somewhere, amongst this lot, there was a clue. He just had to sift through and find it.

He glanced up at the clock on the wall. Just an hour to go, and then the case would be broadcast on the local news. He only hoped it would bring him a lead. He was hedging his bets that once they found out who their victim was, everything else would slot into place.

* * *

Moray stood in front of his men. He still couldn't get his head around this turn of events. They were gathered around the bar area, and he could see disbelief, coupled with anger, in their expressions. Danny wasn't just their boss; in a short space of time, he'd become one of their own, and like a family, they looked out for one another.

'So what happened, boss?' Callum asked.

'Someone shot him, and from what I can gather, he was in his car at traffic lights. At least that's where he was found, anyway. For all we know, he could have been shot earlier, and then collapsed at the lights.'

'Is he gonna make it?' It was the one question on all of their minds.

Moray sighed. 'I don't know yet. They said he's critical and he's lost a lot of blood. We know he's strong, though, and if anyone can pull through this, then it will be him. They said they would start waking him up soon, so until then, it's a waiting game.'

'So he must have been followed then?'

Moray turned back to look at Callum and shrugged. 'To be honest, I really don't know, but I don't think it was random. Someone either knew he would be there, or had to have followed him. Or,' he said, looking across to Big Tone, Lloydy and Terry Stevens, 'it was someone he knew. How else did they get so close to him?'

All eyes went to the three men, and Big Tone shifted his weight, feeling uncomfortable. The shooting had nothing to do with them.

'What do you know about this?' Callum asked the men, his tone accusatory.

Big Tone shrugged. 'The same as you. Fuck all.'

Moray watched their reactions carefully. He still didn't trust them.

'It's a bit strange, though. You three come along, out of fucking nowhere, and all of a sudden, he's been shot,' Callum stated.

'What are you trying to say?' Big Tone asked. 'If you're accusing us, then come out and actually say it.'

'That's right. I am accusing you,' Callum said as he stared hard towards the men. In his opinion, this was no random attack. Danny wasn't stupid. He wouldn't have let some hood rat get the better of him like this. Whoever was responsible knew Danny, and also knew what they were doing.

Big Tone bristled. 'Listen here,' he said, stabbing his finger in Callum's direction. 'You know fuck all about any of this, and we know fuck all about what happened, because we weren't there. We wouldn't have come to Danny, putting our lives on the line, if we planned all along to kill him. Where's the logic in that?'

Callum shrugged. 'Well, what I do know is, you three turn up out of nowhere, and now our boss has been gunned down. Seems a bit strange to me, that's all I'm saying. I think Moray's right. We should be looking closer to home.'

'We've done fuck all wrong,' Terry said, his voice rising. Just like Big Tone, he didn't like how the conversation was turning towards them.

'Got alibis, have you?'

'Who are you, a fucking copper?'

Moray held up his hand to quiet the situation down, before it escalated. Tempers were beginning to flare. 'Until Danny wakes up, we won't know the full story, but until then, we need to try and find out what happened. Someone will be talking about this. Most of you gossip more than women do anyway, so it goes without saying that someone will talk, and unless someone claims responsibility, that's going to be our best chance of finding out whoever did this.'

Reluctantly, the men agreed. Moray then dismissed them before turning towards Big Tone. 'I want to talk to the three of you in my office.'

They followed Moray and waited for him to close the office door before speaking.

'We don't know anything about this.'

Moray shook his head. 'First of all, let's get something straight. I'm not happy about the three of you being here. I didn't employ you. That was Danny's call, and I've swallowed the situation, solely for that reason. But let me tell you now, if I find out any of you had a hand in this, I will personally tear the three of you apart.'

Lloydy looked Moray in the eye. 'We didn't do this.'

'Okay, for the time being, I'll have to take your word on that. So who else, other than Freddie, would have a reason to do this?'

Big Tone blew out his cheeks. How long did they have? Danny had upset more than one person over the years.

'Well, come on. You three worked with Danny for a lot of years. So, who are the big players? Who could've held a grudge against him?'

'Well, Freddie has had a lot of problems with the Greeks. It was Danny who personally arranged the meetings, so they would know him.' Big Tone looked across to Terry and Lloydy. 'Who else has Danny had to deal with?' he asked them.

'Ron Page. You remember him, that bloke from North London. He had a problem with Freddie. Something or other that went back years. Things got pretty heated between him and Danny.'

Big Tone shook his head. 'He's in the scrubs.'

'The Carters, didn't Danny have some trouble with the eldest one, Tommy?' Lloydy asked.

Screwing up his face Moray shook his head. 'You're thinking of Jonny Carter. He owes Danny money, but not enough to need to kill him, besides, Tommy would kill his brother stone dead if he had even the tiniest inkling that Jonny was involved.'

'Dougie Chambers?'

'Mad Dougie, from Newcastle? I thought he died last year,' Moray stated.

Big Tone shrugged. 'I don't know, and to be honest, we could be here all night. Let's face it, Danny isn't scared to have a pop at anyone, but of late, the Greeks were causing the biggest problems.'

'Okay.' Moray nodded as he thought over their theories. 'Well, keep your ears to the ground, and make sure you give me the nod personally, if you hear anything.'

The three men nodded. 'So, where do you want us tonight? Danny said it would be on the doors.'

Moray thought for a few moments. He still didn't agree with Danny's plans of putting them on the doors. He didn't trust these men, not when they could so easily try and take the doors back for Freddie. At the same time, he had no idea of what else he was supposed to do with them. The understanding he and Danny had finally come to, had been to let Danny deal directly with the men. He, himself, had wanted no part in it. 'Go down to the Becton Arms. If I need to shuffle you around, I'll let you know later on, once I'm back from the hospital.'

Moray watched the three men leave his office. As much as he distrusted them, he had to admit, for all intent and purposes, they did come across as sincere.

* * *

George's celebrations were short lived. The six o'clock news broadcast had brought some worrying news for his family. The body found amongst wasteland in Barking, had to be Nico. He could feel it in his gut.

'What should we do?' Alexandros asked, his voice raised so he could be heard above the furious shouts from his family members.

George stood quietly, brooding. He could feel the ache once again beginning to build up inside his chest, and he sat down at the table heavily. He wasn't a well man. Ever since Nico had gone missing, the constant ache inside of him had been there. Some days, he could feel a tight vice-like grip around his chest. It felt as though it was squeezing the life out of him. He dabbed at his clammy forehead and loosened his tie. He needed air.

'Are you okay, George?' Alexandros asked. There was more than a hint of concern in his voice.

George shook his head. 'Water,' he gasped.

Alexandros snapped his fingers together. 'Giorgio, get some water, now,' he shouted.

Passing over the glass of water, he watched as his brother took a sip before taking a bottle of aspirin from his jacket pocket.

'Here, let me help you,' Alexandros said, taking the bottle from George and opening it. He passed over a tiny white pill and watched as George swallowed it down. 'What's going on?' he asked, concerned. 'Are you ill, brother?'

George remained silent. He suspected his heart was giving out. What else could be causing the pain?

'You need to go to the hospital.'

'No,' George answered. The truth was, he was scared. All he had to do was resolve the situation with Nico, and then he would be fine. He was in denial.

Alexandros watched his brother warily. He sat down beside him, unsure of what he could do to help. George had always been the head of their family. Without his orders, they were lost.

Finally, George spoke. 'Pass me a telephone, and give me the phone number for the incident room.' He was going to do what he should have done weeks ago. He was going to bring Nico home.

* * *

Josie Morgan pulled her blonde hair up into a ponytail. The news broadcast had just gone live, and now they were waiting patiently to catch the lead they so desperately needed to solve this case.

When the phone rang, she hastily picked it up. 'Detective Constable Morgan,' she said into the receiver. She listened intently, before waving her hand towards the DCI in a bid to gain his attention.

Ronnie immediately got to his feet. Josie's eyes were wide as she mouthed, 'I've got something.' He watched as she took down some particulars, then put down the phone.

'Gov, a young male, same age as our victim, has been missing two weeks,' she said.

Ronnie's heart leapt. Snatching up Josie's notebook he studied the details she'd written down. 'Come on,' he said. 'This could be exactly what we've been waiting for.'

* * *

Moray was about to buzz the intercom to the Intensive Care Unit, when he spotted police officers through the glass door panels. 'Fuck it,' he thought to himself. He knew, instinctively, they were there about Danny and the shooting. It was only a matter of time before they turned up to investigate.

He would need to get his story straight. As far as they needed to know, he and Danny were not only distant cousins, but business partners. He was only thankful his business was legit, and that he had the paperwork to prove that fact.

Walking towards Danny's bedside, he pretended to be oblivious to the police presence.

'Excuse me, sir, can we have a word?'

Moray turned to look at the officers. His eyebrows were arched in mock surprise. 'How can I help you, officers?' he asked. He knew how to play the game, and he quickly answered their questions without faltering.

Once they were finished questioning him, he watched as the

officers left the ward, hoping it was the last he would see of them. He then turned his attention back to Danny.

'How is he doing?' he asked Sophie.

'He's doing well. He's started to come around.'

'When will he fully wake up?'

'It varies from patient to patient, but all of the signs are good.'

Satisfied, Moray sat at Danny's bedside. Come on, mate, he silently willed.

* * *

Danny was feeling groggy. He opened his eyes gingerly. His head felt as though he'd spent the past week out on the piss. He gave a small cough and brought his hand up to his chest, grimacing, as pain shot through him just below his shoulder.

'How are you doing, mate? It's good to have you back.'

Danny slowly turned his head to see Moray sitting beside him. 'What happened?' he asked. Everything was hazy.

Sophie had warned Moray that this could happen. 'You were shot, mate.'

Danny was confused. He couldn't remember. The only thing he knew for certain was that he felt tired, so very tired. He closed his eyes and drifted off to sleep again.

* * *

Sophie stopped by Danny's bed. 'See, I told you. He's doing well.' She smiled. 'It's perfectly normal for him to be feeling tired. It's the sedation he was given causing that.'

'So he's on the mend?' Moray asked.

'Yes, we should be able to move him to the general ward soon.'

Moray was feeling happier. He couldn't wait to tell their men that Danny was doing okay. He knew they would be as relieved as he was.

* * *

The restaurant had been cleared. Only George and Alexandros remained. They were sitting at the staff table, and opposite them were the two detectives.

'My nephew, Nico, has been missing for two weeks. This body you found, we believe it could be him,' George explained.

Ronnie was gentle as he spoke. Dealing with relatives and loved ones was always tough. 'There is a good chance that this isn't Nico. Until we can confirm either way, please don't presume that it is him. There is still a high possibility that your nephew is alive and well. Once we've accessed Nico's dental records, we can determine if it is or isn't him.'

'We can identify him now, if you want us to.'

Ronnie shook his head sadly. 'I'm afraid that won't be possible.'

George and Alexandros looked towards each other. They were confused. How would they be able to identify Nico, if they couldn't see the body?

'I don't understand. Why can't we see him?' Alexandros asked.

Ronnie cleared his throat. 'I'm afraid viewing the remains is not a viable option.' He could see their confusion, and explained himself further. 'The body isn't in very good condition, I'm afraid.'

'Oh.' George wearily wiped his hand across his face and made the sign of the cross in front of his chest. Poor Nico, he hadn't deserved this to happen to him.

'What can you tell me about Nico? Does he have any enemies?'

'No, Nico is a good boy. He's a law student, at the University of East London.'

Ronnie could hear the pride in the older man's voice. He smiled gently. All the while, his mind was racing. He wondered, briefly, if there was a link between the law student and the prison situated across the water in Thamesmead. He couldn't help but feel there was a connection. Law and prison... they went hand in hand, after all, and it had been his gut instinct from day one.

'When will we know if it is Nico?'

'As soon as we can have access to Nico's dental records. Then we will get the process underway. It shouldn't take too long for us to get the results back.'

'Is there anything else we can help you with?' George asked.

Ronnie looked around him. He surveyed the recent decorating, and the plush, newly fitted carpet. 'You had a shooting in here a few weeks ago. Could there be any link to Nico's disappearance?'

George shook his head vigorously. 'A random attack, nothing whatsoever to do with Nico. He wasn't even here when the shooting happened.'

'And where were you at the time of the shooting?'

'At home. I told the investigating officers this when they interviewed me. I have no idea who was responsible, or why the shooting took place.'

'Why have you waited two weeks before reporting your nephew as missing?' Josie Morgan asked.

It was Alexandros who answered, and he opened out his arms to emphasise his point. 'You know what young men are like... they meet a woman and they become caught up in the moment. We thought this is what had happened to Nico.'

'And why do you think differently now?' Josie tilted her head to one side as she studied them.

'No one has heard from Nico at all since he's been missing. We're starting to get worried.'

'And you've tried to contact him? I take it you've contacted his friends, other family members?'

'Yes.'

'And no one has heard from him?'

'No, this is why we are becoming worried.'

'Okay.' Ronnie stood up. 'Well, we'll be in touch as soon as we get the results back,' he told them.

They shook the men's hands, then walked outside towards Ronnie's car.

'What do you think, Gov?' Josie asked.

Ronnie glanced back towards the restaurant. 'There's a lot more to this than they're letting on. They were too rehearsed with their answers.'

Josie followed Ronnie's gaze. She had to agree. It was all too much of a coincidence that they should have a shooting take place in the restaurant, and now the owner's nephew was missing, presumed dead.

'I want you to look into the shooting. See what you can find out. There's a connection here, I can feel it.'

'I'll get on it,' Josie answered. She gave the restaurant one final glance, then climbed into the car.

George watched through the window as the officers left. He was concerned. Despite the friendly manner of the detectives, he had a feeling he had unwillingly opened up a can of worms.

11

Freddie was out of control. Matty watched warily as the older man began cutting a copious amount of cocaine on the coffee table.

'Fuck 'em all,' Freddie spat. He didn't need them. He didn't need anyone. He snorted the lines in quick succession, then looked up. 'He should have taken that cunt out when he had the chance.'

Matty had no idea what Freddie was talking about, but still, he nodded in agreement. He'd learned long ago that it was a lot easier, and not to mention safer, to just agree with him when he was in this kind of mood, which just lately happened to be all of the time.

'Get down to the estate, now. You need to sort things out for tonight.'

Matty's heart sank. He didn't want to go. He hated the situation he'd been forced into, and hated himself even more for what Freddie made him do.

'Why are you still sitting here?' Freddie roared. 'I gave you an order.'

When Matty didn't move quickly enough, Freddie leapt out of

his seat. Using a considerable amount of strength, he slapped the lad across the side of his head. 'Don't you fucking dare disobey me, boy.'

Matty curled himself into a foetal position. He brought his hands up to his head in a bid to ward off the blows.

Finally, Freddie dragged Matty to his feet and pushed him towards the front door. 'Get down to that estate, now.' He blew out his cheeks from the exertion. The look across his face was one of pure evil as he stared hard at the lad.

'I don't want to do it, Fred.'

'Unless you want to end up like Lewis, you'll do as you're fucking told.'

Tears sprang to Matty's eyes. Freddie terrified him in more ways than one, he always had. He had no other choice, he either did as he was told, or they would kill him. He'd had the same threat drummed into him for as long as he could remember, and he knew they meant every word. He'd seen them in action. They reminded him of a pack of wolves, and he knew from experience that when the kill came it would be frenzied; they had no care for their victims, life meant so little to them.

He wiped the tears away from his cheeks and opened the front door. He could feel Freddie standing close behind him, could feel his hot, putrid breath on the back of his neck.

'Unless you want to become the entertainment, you'd better start doing as you're told. Do you understand me?'

Matty nodded. He knew it was no idle threat. Freddie could make him disappear. He'd done it before.

* * *

Danny was sitting up in bed. He'd begun to feel stronger in himself. Earlier that day, the nurses had had him up and out of bed, walking around, and now he was eager to get out of the place and back to business.

The shooting was still a little bit hazy. He could remember stopping at traffic lights and that was about it. After that, he couldn't remember anything that had happened. The doctors seemed to think he was blocking it out because he'd been through a traumatic experience, they'd said. He almost laughed at that. Practically every day, in his line of work, was traumatic for someone or other.

He smiled as Moray walked towards him. He looked his friend up and down. Moray was dressed to kill, and he could see a lot more care than usual had gone into his appearance.

'Where are you off to?'

'Nowhere.'

Danny eyed his friend suspiciously. 'You've got that much aftershave on? I could smell you from twenty feet away, and I'm pretty certain it's not for my benefit.' He laughed. 'What are you up to? Where are you going?'

Moray was being coy and he averted his eyes. 'I've got a date.'

'A date?' Danny raised his eyebrows. He'd never heard Moray mention any particular women before. 'Who with?'

Moray sighed. 'If you must know, it's with one of the nurses who were looking after you.'

'Oh, I see. So while I was on my death bed, you were chatting up the nurses?' Danny had to keep the smile from his lips.

'No, it wasn't like that,' Moray answered defensively. 'I bumped into her in the cafeteria.'

'I'm sure you did.' Danny laughed. 'Well, you have a good time, mate. You deserve it.'

'Thanks, I will do.' He was clearly embarrassed and swiftly changed the subject. 'Listen, I've got something I want to talk to you about... a proposition.'

Danny raised his eyebrows. 'Go on.'

'It can wait until tomorrow. Just bear in mind, you're going to have to be open-minded about this.'

Danny threw up his arms. 'You can't leave me hanging like that.'

'I can and I am.' Moray winked. He shook Danny's hand and left the ward.

Danny lay back against the pillows. He was more than intrigued. 'Hey,' he called out to the nurse looking after him, 'when can I go home?'

The nurse shook her head. It was the fifth time he had asked the same question in the past hour.

* * *

Matty jumped off the number sixty-two bus at Gascoigne Estate. He immediately walked in the direction of the estate shops. He was bound to come across one of the junkies there. At least that was where he could usually find them, begging for some spare change so they could go out and score. If he was lucky, he might even come across someone who needed to both score and pay off a drug debt. It was one of the more desperate junkies who he was actually hoping to come across. They would sell anything for the right price, and that was exactly what he was counting on.

He stopped and casually leant against the metal shutters of one of the shops. All he had to do was wait. They would come to him. Most of the junkies around here knew what he was about, and he noticed a few turn on their heels when they spotted him. He suspected the temptation was too much for some of them, and he didn't blame them for walking away. He would do the same if he was in their shoes. In fact, he liked to think he would never

actually be in their position. He certainly would never stoop as
low as they did, if he was.

He spotted Tracey, one of the junkies. She was usually good to
use and would sell her soul for the price of some crack.

'Hey, Trace,' he called out.

Tracey Underwood swaggered purposely towards Matty. She
scratched at her greasy head as she approached him.

Watching her approach, Matty made a mental note to not
stand too close.

'You got any spare change?' she asked as she began picking at
a scab on her arm. It was a kind of game they played out each time
he came here. Eventually, she would give in. The temptation of
having money in her back pocket was too high, despite her persistent refusals to begin with.

Holding out a wedge of cash, teasing her, he watched her eyes
widen. He could see her mentally calculating how much crack she
could buy with it, and he had to hide the disgust he felt. These
junkies were all the same.

'They need to be home by twelve. Last time, you brought them
home too late,' she said, pushing a nicotine-stained finger towards
him. 'And the last thing I need is the teacher questioning me, or
social services breathing down my neck again.'

Matty shrank backwards. He didn't want her to touch him. She
repulsed him.

'They will be, I'll make sure of it.'

He followed her towards her flat. He felt physically sick. He
would never get his head around what junkies would do to get a
fix, or how his own father had done the exact same thing as
Tracey did, when he was a young boy.

* * *

Moray was nervous. He hadn't been out on a date in a long time. He stood waiting in the hospital foyer, frequently checking the time on his watch. Maybe he should have bought flowers. Did people still do that?

He felt a tap on his shoulder and turned around. Sophie was stood in front of him. With her red hair tumbling around her shoulders, and dressed in a black dress falling just above her knees, she looked stunning.

'Wow, you look beautiful with clothes on.' Immediately, he realised what he'd said. 'I meant out of your uniform.' He blushed even more, his cheeks flushing. 'I mean in normal clothes.'

Sophie laughed and slipped her hand through his arm. 'I knew what you meant. So, where are you taking me?'

Composing himself, Moray smiled. 'Somewhere up West. It's a surprise. You'll have to wait and see,' he said as they made their way across the car park.

* * *

Hayley was also getting herself dolled up for a date up West. She added the finishing touches to her makeup, then adjusted her false eyelashes, before squirting more than a generous amount of perfume over her arms and shoulders. As a finishing touch, she sprayed an ever larger amount of the sickly sweet perfume up and down the length of her short dress.

She checked the time. She had just over thirty minutes before Giorgio was due to come and collect her. Opening up a bottle of wine, she poured out a large glass. Before she knew it, she had downed half of the bottle.

'Oops,' she giggled, already feeling a little tipsy. The alcohol was making her feel braver than usual, and she decided, tonight she would tell her Giorgio that she loved him. She knew he would return the words. How could he not love her? She was stunning.

* * *

Moray pulled open the door to a little French restaurant in Notting Hill. Always the gentleman, he allowed Sophie to walk through the door first. He could see she was impressed as they were shown to a table. He knew the owner personally, and as a result, was guaranteed the very best table in the restaurant.

'Wow, this is impressive.' Sophie smiled.

Moray looked around him before answering. 'I'm glad you like it.'

They took the menus handed to them and began looking through the vast selection of dishes.

'I don't know what to choose,' Sophie stated as she studied the menu. She could see the dishes were expensive, and way out of her price range.

Leaning forward across the table, Moray's voice was gentle. 'Choose whatever you want, and don't worry about the price. Everything is on me tonight. Would you like some wine, or would you prefer something else?'

Sophie smiled. 'Wine would be perfect, thank you.'

* * *

Giorgio couldn't believe it. Talk about bad luck. Out of all the restaurants he could have chosen to take Hayley, he happened to choose the same one as Moray Garner.

He'd recognised the man as soon as he'd walked through the door. He'd spent more than enough time following him and

Danny McKay around of late to immediately know who he was. There was absolutely no mistaking him.

He looked across at Hayley. She was as pissed as a fart, and had begun slurring her words. 'We need to leave,' he said, signalling for a waiter to come over so he could pay the wine bill.

'What do you mean, we have to leave? We haven't even ordered any food yet.' Her voice was loud, causing other diners to look towards them.

'Don't make a fuss,' Giorgio hissed. 'We're leaving.'

Hayley was angry. She'd got all dressed up for nothing. 'No,' she said, sitting back in her seat with her arms folded across her chest. 'You brought me here, and we're staying here.'

Giorgio leant across the table. 'I said we're leaving, so drink up.'

Unsteadily, Hayley got to her feet. 'Fuck you, Giorgio,' she screamed. 'Don't you know who I am? Who my husband is?'

Giorgio groaned. This was all he needed. 'Sit down,' he growled.

Slumping down in her seat, Hayley pursed her lips together, sulking. 'I'm not leaving,' she stated.

* * *

Moray turned to watch the commotion. He'd noticed from the corner of his eye the young man had been watching him, yet he didn't recognise him at all. He raised his eyebrows towards Sophie.

'You can't buy class.' He grinned.

'What did you just fucking say?' Hayley turned in her seat. Her voice was loud. 'Do you know who my husband is?' she slurred, pointing her finger towards Moray.

Moray shook his head. 'No. Why, should I?'

'My husband is Terry Stevens. He works for Freddie Smith and Danny McKay, and if they were here now, and heard you disrespecting me like this, they would wipe the floor with you.'

Moray nodded. 'Excuse me for a moment,' he said to Sophie. He bumped back his chair, stood up, and walked over to Giorgio and Hayley's table. He placed his hands on the starched white tablecloth, the muscles in his forearms taking his weight.

He then brought his face close to Hayley's ear. His voice was low as he spoke. 'I think you'll find, lady, that your husband works for me now. And as for Danny McKay, if he ever heard you using his name in this manner, he would wipe the floor with you. Let me give you some advice. Do yourself a favour and keep your mouth shut and let the good people in here get back to enjoying their food, without having to listen to that big fucking trap of yours.'

Hayley's mouth fell open. Moray's words had instantly sobered her up. She swallowed deeply, as realisation set in. This man actually knew her husband. She could feel an ice cold shiver run down her spine. She was more than terrified that she'd been caught out red-handed with her lover. How would she explain this away to Terry? Gathering up her handbag, she looked across to Giorgio.

'I want to leave now.'

Giorgio immediately waved his hand in the air to gain the waiter's attention. As far as he was concerned, it was the best thing she'd said all night.

Moray returned to his seat. 'I'm so sorry about that.'

Sophie smiled. 'No need to apologise at all.'

Moray turned to watch the couple leave. Something didn't seem right about this. Who was the man with Terry Stevens's wife? He took in his dark hair and lightly tanned skin. He would put money on it that he was Greek. He fingered his scar and slumped backwards in his seat. With a sudden clarity, he realised that they had a spy in their camp. He would need to speak to Danny as soon as he possibly could.

* * *

Danny finally had the go ahead to go home. Other than the pain he could feel from his stitched wound, he felt well in himself and strong. He was waiting for Moray to bring him some clothes to change into, then he was all set to leave. Only it wasn't home he was going to, at least not the home he'd shared with Maxine for the past five years. From now on, home would be a two bedroom flat in Romford Moray had found for him. It was a depressing thought.

As Moray walked towards him, Danny smiled and clambered off the bed. He was eager to dress and get out of the hospital. He took the bag of clothes from Moray. 'How did your date go?'

Moray smiled. 'Good, but something happened which is concerning me.'

Danny burst out laughing and held up his hand, cutting Moray off. 'Whoa steady on, mate. I don't think I want to know. You might be my best mate, but what you get up to in the bedroom, isn't something I need to know about.'

Moray rolled his eyes. 'It's nothing like that. Get dressed, and on the way home, I'll explain everything.'

* * *

'Are you joking?' There was more than a hint of shock in Danny's voice.

'Straight up. She said her old man was Terry Stevens, and that he worked for you. Oh, and apparently, you're going to wipe the floor with me.' Moray laughed.

Danny's eyes were wide. He couldn't help but laugh along. 'What the actual fuck? I've never even seen this bird before.'

'Trust me, I was just as shocked, and believe me, she definitely knew who you were. What's the odds on going out for the evening and that happening?'

Danny shook his head. 'I can't believe it, mate.'

'The thing is,' Moray said, 'it was who she was with, that's bothering me.'

'Well, who was she with then?'

Moray took his eyes off the road as he quickly glanced sideways. 'I could swear it was one of the Greeks. Well, he looked Greek anyway. Same thing, as far as I'm concerned.'

'Are you fucking kidding me?' Danny's mind raced. 'One of the Greeks... are you sure?'

Moray shrugged and paused before answering. 'All I'm saying is that he looked Greek, and if he is one of them, then we have a spy in our camp, mate.'

'I can't believe this. What the fuck has she told him about all of us?'

'Your guess is as good as mine. But like I said, I'm not 100 per cent certain he was one of the Christos's, only that he looked as though he was. He had that look about him, if you know what I mean.'

Danny knew exactly what he meant. They had had more than one dealing with the Christos family over the years. 'I always wondered how they seemed to know so much. Now we know how they've been getting their information. That fucking Terry Stevens. If I find out he's involved in any of this, I'll kill him.' Danny shook his head. 'I knew I should have lamped him one, when I had the chance,' he added as an afterthought.

'Let's dig around a bit first... get our facts straight, before we dive in head long. As for Terry Stevens, well, from the look of it, he's got his own problems. His missus is definitely doing the dirty on him.'

They pulled up outside Danny's new home. Looking up at the grey apartment building, he cleared his throat. 'I never asked you if Maxine knew I'd been in the hospital, if she knew I'd been shot?'

Moray paused. He'd been dreading this question. He had a feeling, deep down, Danny already knew the answer. Why else had he taken so long to ask? 'I told her straight away, mate.'

He watched Danny swallow deeply. He could see his friend was hurting.

'Fuck her,' Danny finally replied, putting on a brave face.

Moray smiled gently. 'Come on, mate, let's get you settled into your new place. I had the lads bring all of your stuff over yesterday. You just have to unpack when you're feeling strong enough.'

* * *

'Well done.' George ruffled Giorgio's hair, then hugged his nephew towards him.

The information he'd been receiving over the past week had left him feeling puzzled. Now, everything made sense. Danny McKay and Moray Garner had obviously formed a partnership and taken over Freddie's doors.

Well, those doors would soon belong to him. He was determined to take them over, and he wasn't prepared to let anyone or anything get in his way. Taking the doors was to be his family's ultimate revenge. Only then, would George be able to rest easy.

The fact that Danny McKay was still alive niggled at him. He'd hoped the reports he'd heard about him being killed in the shooting were true. Obviously, this hadn't been the case. He wondered, briefly, if any of his nephews would be capable of finishing off what someone else had obviously started. He would speak to Alexandros, he decided, and together they would decide if the boys were up to the job.

'Can I cut all ties with Hayley now?'

George could see Giorgio was unhappy with the situation he'd put him in, yet he believed there was still more information to come. 'Just a few more weeks.'

Inwardly, Giorgio groaned. He couldn't hide his disappointment. 'You said though—'

'That was before this new information came to light,' George interrupted. 'We need to know their every move, and we can only do that if you keep seeing this woman.' His voice brooked no arguments. 'Where is your loyalty, Giorgio? Think of your father, my brother, slaughtered like a pig by those bastards. You were too young to remember your father's murder, but I remember, your uncles remember. And for your father and your cousin, Nico, we will get our justice, our revenge.'

Giorgio didn't dare answer back. For as long as he could remember, his uncle had used his father's murder as an excuse to keep him in line. The truth was, he had no recollection of the man. All he had to remember his father were a handful of tattered photographs and the stories his family told of him, and then the ultimate story of his murder by one of Freddie Smith's henchmen.

The man responsible had recently been released from prison, after serving twenty-one years inside for the murder. As of yet, his whereabouts were still unknown, but they would find him. According to the story he'd been told, his father had been gutted like a pig. The image inside his head of his father's lifeless body hanging on a meat hook, left to rot, had haunted him for months when he'd been a young boy.

'I'm sorry, uncle,' he said.

George patted his nephew's arm. 'Make your father proud, Giorgio.'

Smiling sadly, he knew he had no other choice but to do as he was told, to follow through his uncle's orders, and to keep on seeing Hayley.

* * *

Danny was bored. He couldn't settle into his new flat. He stood, looking aimlessly out of the window, just staring. He missed his boy, that was half of the problem, and it didn't help that he was used to being busy. Other than now, he couldn't remember the last time he'd had a day off from work.

It was something that used to drive Maxine up the wall. She used to say he was a workaholic. Perhaps he should have taken note of her complaining. If he had, maybe he would still have a marriage. He pushed the thought away from his mind. There was no use beating himself up over it. It was done and dusted, and there was nothing he could say or do to change the situation.

He grabbed up his jacket. Whether Moray liked it or not, he was going into work. He couldn't just sit around doing nothing. He searched around the flat for his car keys. Where the fuck were they?

'Shit,' he muttered to himself. He remembered now. He didn't even have his car; the windscreen still hadn't been fixed.

He may as well kill two birds with one stone, he decided. He would cab it to the club, then phone around to get his windscreen fixed. He would deal with Moray once he got there. Besides, he still hadn't told him what the proposition was, not to mention, they still needed to deal with his shooting. There were plenty of ample excuses for him to go to the club.

An hour later, he was given a warm welcome as he walked through the doors to Ritzy's Nightclub.

'It's good to have you back,' Callum Riley said, shaking Danny's hand. 'You had us all worried for a while there, boss.'

'Cheers, mate. It's good to be back.'

He deliberately avoided eye contact with Moray; Danny knew his friend would be more than pissed off with him.

'What are you doing here? You're meant to be resting,' Moray said as they made their way up the stairs to the office.

Once inside, Danny flopped down onto a chair. 'I was bored.' He grinned sheepishly. 'And I've still got a few things to sort out.'

Moray raised his eyebrows. 'Such as?'

'My car, for starters. Plus, you still haven't told me about this proposition of yours.'

'You're one sly dog, McKay. You'll use any excuse to get back to work, just admit it.'

Danny grinned. 'Yeah, you're right. So, come on then, what is it? You've left me hanging long enough.'

'Well,' Moray said as he spread out his arms. 'This place... I think we should buy it.'

Danny laughed hard. 'Me buy a club? Are you out of your mind? What would I know about running a club?'

Moray wasn't about to be put off. 'You've spent half your life working in clubs, and I've spent years in this place, watching how it's run. In fact, I could do it with my eyes closed, that's how confident I am that we could make a success of it.'

Danny narrowed his eyes. 'Are you being serious? You actually want us to buy this place?'

'Yes, why not?'

He thought it through. 'I wouldn't be able to afford it.'

It was Moray's turn to laugh. 'You're not short of a bob or two. You can't tell me that Freddie didn't pay you some wedge over the years? And I know for a fact you're still sitting on the dough from the gold heist. I know you, and I can guarantee you bought your house with cash, didn't you? Come on, out with it, admit it, I'm right, ain't I?'

Danny gave a shrug of his shoulders before laughing. He should have known he wouldn't be able to pull the wool over Moray's eyes. 'Well, yeah, I did actually, and yeah, I've got more than enough money to buy this place, but I wouldn't have a clue how to run a club.'

'It's a good job that I do then. Come on, Danny, this could set us up for life.' He gave a little wink. 'Plus, it has the added bonus of being legit.'

Danny glanced towards the door. In his mind's eye, he visualised the dance floor and bar area below. He had to admit, he was tempted.

'Come on, you know you want to.' Moray grinned.

Danny turned to look at Moray. He could see how much his best mate wanted this. 'Okay, I'm in. But if this does go tits up, I'll be holding you responsible.'

'As if I'd ever let you down. Honestly, mate, you won't regret it.'

Danny smiled. He could hardly believe it. He was about to become a club owner.

* * *

'Come on, Max, you'd love it, and anyway, when was the last time you had a night out?'

Maxine was indecisive. 'I can't. What about Logan? And what about...'

Jacqueline held up her hand to cut Maxine off. 'You know your mum would babysit, and as for Danny, what are you worrying about him for? You're not even together any more.'

'It's not as easy as that, though, is it? He works the doors, so he's bound to find out, and the last thing I need is him causing a scene, which you know full well he will.'

Jacqueline grinned, and there was a twinkle in her blue eyes. 'Ahh, but he doesn't work in Romford, does he? And that is exactly where we will be going.'

'I don't know, Jac.' Maxine pushed a lock of dark hair behind her ear. She wasn't so sure about this. As much as she would love to go out, she really didn't want to bump into her husband, now that he was out of hospital. He wasn't the type of man to sit around doing nothing; he would have dived straight back into work.

'Trust me, Max. He will never find out, not that it would even matter if he did. Let's face it, you're getting divorced, so who cares what he thinks?'

Mentally, Maxine was sorting through her wardrobe. What would she even wear? It had been so long since she'd had a night out. As if she was reading her mind, Jacqueline spoke.

'You've got that lovely black dress, the one you wore for Danny's birthday. Put that on with a pair of nice heels, and you'll look stunning.'

Maxine was tempted. She could do with a night out, and to be able to dance off the stress the last few weeks had caused her, sounded like heaven. 'Go on then, you've twisted my arm.' She grinned. 'But only if we definitely stay in Romford. I mean it, Jac,' she warned.

'I promise you, we will stay in Romford.' Jacqueline grinned. 'Let me quickly run home and grab my clothes and a bottle of wine, while you sort out Logan, and then we can blast out some music while we get ready, just like we used to do years ago.'

Maxine smiled as she recalled the laughs they used to have when they were getting ready to go out clubbing together. She missed those days. 'Go on then, you go and get your stuff, while I sort out this little boy,' she said, kissing the top of her son's head.

* * *

Danny walked around the club. It was nearing 9 p.m., and the first few customers would soon start streaming in. The early birds – as they called the first arrivals – were the punters who liked to take advantage of the club's happy hour of half-price beers and spirits. It was a well-known ruse to tempt customers inside, and was also effective. Those customers were usually the first to end up getting pissed. So long as they were behaving themselves, and handing over their hard-earned cash, they were more than welcome to stay. If not, his and Moray's men would quickly and efficiently escort them out of the venue.

Once he was satisfied that the men were all ready for the night's work ahead of them, he wandered back to Moray's office. He'd promised his friend not only that he would stay at the club, but that he would also stay out of trouble. Moray was like an over-protective parent, and he couldn't help but smile as he recalled the look on his face as he'd made him promise to stay in the office with his feet up. They both knew that was never going to happen.

Danny checked that the CCTV cameras were working, before taking a seat behind the desk. He still couldn't believe he was actually going to own this place.

He only wished he could tell Maxine about it. He knew she would have been proud of him. Not only was he about to become a businessman, but everything was legit – no more skulking around the Old Bill or having the threat of prison looming over him. He would finally become what she'd always wanted, only it was too late. She wasn't here any more for him to be able to share his news.

He had to stop thinking about her, only it wasn't as easy as that. She was the only woman he'd ever loved. How was he supposed to just forget about everything they'd shared? He couldn't just erase all of the years they'd spent together. The bottom line was, he couldn't switch his feelings off as easily as she obviously could.

He would need to speak to her at some point, though. He was still Logan's dad, and he wanted his boy in his life. He wasn't about to become one of those dead-beat fathers, who only remembered or saw their kids at Christmas or on birthdays. Whether Maxine liked it or not, he was here to stay.

* * *

Maxine was sipping on a glass of white wine. It felt good to actually be out for the night. She was pleased that Jacqueline had talked her into coming out. They were in The Bull public house in Romford, and despite the hour, it was already heaving with customers. They were sharing a bottle of wine, their second in the past hour, and Maxine was beginning to feel a little tipsy.

'Don't look now, but that fella over there hasn't stopped staring at you.'

Maxine blushed. 'Stop it, Jac. You know I'm not interested in anyone. It's too soon after Danny.'

'Well, it isn't my fault, is it? I can't help it if someone is giving you the eye. Go on, take a sneaky peek at him.'

Maxine casually looked over her shoulder, before turning back towards her friend. She wrinkled up her nose and giggled.

'I don't know, he isn't that bad. I would.' Jacqueline pouted her lips and gave the man in question a seductive wink.

'Jac,' Maxine cried. She could hardly believe her friend's

brazenness. 'Stop, don't encourage him,' she pleaded, as Jacqueline went on to wave at him.

'Too late, he's already coming over. Remember to smile.'

Maxine groaned. She could feel her face begin to blush once again. 'I can't believe you just did that.'

'Hi,' Jacqueline said to the approaching man. 'I'm Jac, and this is my friend, Maxine. And before you even ask, she's newly single.'

Maxine shot a look towards Jacqueline, her eyebrows arched. She really didn't feel comfortable with this.

'Is that right?' he answered, looking towards Maxine and giving her a wink. 'I'm Steve. Can I get you ladies a drink?'

Jacqueline raised her glass. 'White wine for us both, please.'

'See, I told you he's a bit of all right,' Jacqueline whispered into Maxine's ear, as Steve went to the bar to get the drinks.

'I don't want to be stuck with him all night though, Jac.'

Jacqueline sighed with irritation. Her friend was easily the most stunning woman in the pub, and she had a body to die for. In fact, she was surprised there wasn't a queue of blokes waiting to chat her up. 'Don't be such a bore, Max. You're young, beautiful and single. Enjoy yourself.'

Looking towards the bar, Maxine sighed. Maybe Jac was right. She should learn to enjoy herself more. She wasn't used to getting attention from men, and she couldn't help but feel a little bit self-conscious. That was half the problem.

'So, where are you ladies off to next?' Steve asked, as he handed over their glasses of wine.

Maxine took a sip, before answering. 'We were thinking of staying here. How about you?'

Steve looked to Maxine as he answered. He couldn't take his eyes off her. She was just his type. 'I'm just waiting for my mates to arrive, then we're heading off to Ritzy's Nightclub. Why don't you join us?'

The two women glanced towards each other. 'We'd love to,' Jacqueline quickly answered. She wasn't about to give her friend the chance of declining the offer.

'Good. I'm looking forward to getting to know you a lot better.' Steve grinned.

Maxine could feel Jacqueline give her a nudge and she gave a small smile. She may have felt out of her comfort zone, but she was determined to enjoy her night out, and if that meant spending the evening with Steve and his mates, then so be it.

* * *

Danny sat forward in his seat. He was watching the long line of customers on the CCTV monitors as they stood queueing up outside the club waiting patiently to be admitted inside. Tonight was going to be a busy night, if the queue outside was anything to go by.

Moving closer to the monitor, he stared intently at the screen. 'What the fuck?' he muttered under his breath. That was his Maxine, queueing up outside the club. What was she doing here, and who the hell was looking after his son? He could see her mate, Jacqueline, stood beside her. He'd never liked the woman and knew without a doubt the feeling was mutual. He still had a feeling she'd been the one putting ideas into Maxine's head about him having an affair.

He stood up from his seat. He could feel his heart begin to pound inside his chest, and he balled his fists at his sides. Who were the men with them? They were a little too close for comfort, for his liking. A wave of jealousy swept through him. When one of the men snaked his arm across Maxine's shoulders, he'd seen just about enough, and tore out of the office. He would kill the bastard stone dead. Who the fuck did he think he was, touching his wife?

12

Weaving through the club, Danny felt as though he was about to explode. Where the fuck was she? He pushed his way outside the club doors, and stood out on the pavement, before walking up and down the long line of punters waiting to be admitted inside. In the time it had taken him to race down the stairs from the office, she'd obviously snuck inside.

'Everything okay, boss?' Callum asked.

Danny looked around before answering. 'Where did she go? The woman with long dark hair. She was with a blonde tart.'

Callum nodded towards the doors. 'They just went inside. You must have passed them.'

Danny raced back inside the club.

'What's going on, boss?' Callum called out to Danny's retreating back. Shrugging, he turned his attention back to the waiting line of customers. It couldn't be that important, he thought to himself.

Danny was oblivious to everything else around him as he searched frantically for his wife. He would fucking kill her for this. Who the fuck did she think she was? They'd only just separated, and already she was allowing another man to drape himself all over her.

He pushed through the crowd of customers and made his way towards the bar area. It was the most obvious place they would have headed to. His fists were clenched into tight balls. This was not the time for pleasantries. As soon as he found her, he was going to go absolutely fucking apeshit.

* * *

Maxine was swaying in time to the music. She loved all of the old skool classics from the nineties and couldn't wait to get on the dance floor. She leaned in closer to Steve as he tried to make himself understood above the heavy beat.

'I can't hear you!' She smiled, pointing to her ear.

Steve pulled her closer. 'I said, I think you're beautiful.'

Maxine's cheeks blushed pink. 'Thank you,' she mouthed back. She glanced across to Jacqueline and took a sip of her wine. Despite her earlier reservations, she was beginning to enjoy herself. Turning back towards Steve, she felt an ice cold chill run through her body, and the smile froze across her face. Striding towards her was Danny. What was he doing here? Before she even had the chance to open her mouth to speak, he was upon them.

'What the fuck are you doing here? And where the fuck is my son?'

Maxine's eyes were as wide as saucers. 'Please, don't start, Danny,' she begged, pushing him away from her.

Watching the interaction, Steve moved closer. 'Is this bloke bothering you?' he shouted above the music. He placed his arm protectively around her shoulders. 'She's with me, mate, so go and bother someone else. Go on, fuck off, jog on.'

Danny stared hard at the man before taking a step forward. He could feel his temper rising. His firm body was taut, a vein pulsated at the side of his neck and his fists remained firmly clenched at his sides. Jog on? Was this prick taking the piss? He battled not to lose his rag in front of Maxine. He didn't want her to see him for the animal he really was. 'She's with you? Are you for fucking real? I'm her husband, you no good fucking cunt, so get your hands off my wife, now, before I end up doing you some serious damage.'

Immediately, Steve dropped his arm. The man in front of him looked insane. It was just his luck to pull a bird with a crazy ex. He took a step to the side, creating a respectable distance between them. 'Come on, mate, there's no need for that.'

'You call me mate once more, and I'm gonna bounce you across this fucking club. Now, fuck off away from me and my wife.'

'Yeah that's about right, resort to violence. That's your answer to everything, isn't it? Go on, piss off, Danny. No one wants you here, especially Maxine.'

Turning to face Jacqueline, Danny sneered. He couldn't stand the stuck up bitch. She'd always had a bit too much to say for herself. 'Keep your nose out of my business,' he shouted, stabbing his finger towards her face.

'Danny, please, just leave us alone. Don't spoil our night, and don't talk to Jac like that.'

Grabbing hold of his wife's wrist, Danny began pulling her away. His grip was tight and she tried desperately to claw his hand away. 'I don't want to go with you. Stop it, you're hurting me.'

'Leave her alone, she said. She doesn't want to go with you,' Jacqueline screamed, pulling at the back of his shirt. She turned to Steve. 'Stop him, will you?' she pleaded. 'Do something.'

Danny shrugged Jacqueline away from him. 'I told you to fuck off. This is between me and my wife.'

As much as he hadn't wanted to intervene, Steve yanked hard

on Danny's arm, trying to release the grip he had on Maxine. 'Get your hands off her. I'm warning you,' he yelled. He'd played rugby for years, and knew he could take the man down if he needed to. He was physically strong, and if it came to it, he would simply rugby tackle him to the floor. He would have no other choice.

In a white hot temper, Danny pulled back his fist, knocking Steve to the ground. It happened so fast, Steve didn't stand a chance. As he lay on the floor, with blood streaming from his nose, he was too dazed to even speak. He was seeing stars.

'I told you to fuck off.' Danny looked up at Steve's friends. 'Which one of you cunts wants it next?'

The revellers around them screamed as they ran for cover. Glasses smashed to the floor in their panic to get away from the fight. Within seconds, the door men were on the scene. They were stunned to see it was Danny who'd caused the commotion.

'I want this bastard thrown out,' Danny demanded, his breath coming fast.

Maxine crouched down beside Steve; tears welled up in her eyes. 'You animal,' she cried. 'Why did you have to do this?'

'Max, get up and get away from him. He's fuck all to do with you.'

'No,' she sobbed, as she cradled Steve's head on her lap. 'Stay away from me, and from now on, I want you to stay away from my son. He doesn't need someone like you in his life,' she cried, hysterical.

Danny swallowed deeply. She didn't mean that. No way would she stop him from seeing their son, would she? He wiped his hand across his face and looked around him. He could see contempt for himself in the faces staring back at him. Fuck them all. The only one who meant anything to him was his wife, and despite everything, she was still his wife.

'Max, come away from him,' he beckoned. 'Come up to the

office. We can talk in private there. We can sort this out. Things just got a little bit out of hand here, that's all.'

'You're unbelievable, do you know that? She isn't going anywhere near you,' Jacqueline spat, looking down her nose at him. 'Haven't you done enough damage? Look at her. Look at what you've caused, with your big "I am" attitude. The worse thing she ever did was to get involved with you. Right from the start I warned her about you, that this is what you are.'

Ignoring Jacqueline, Danny looked to his wife. 'Please, Max,' he implored. He took a step towards her and watched as Maxine cowered away from him. In that instant, his heart sank. He would never actually hurt her, despite how angry she made him feel at times.

'Just go, Danny. I never want to see you again.'

Callum held out his arms. He was more than hesitant. After all, this was Danny McKay he was dealing with. 'Boss, I think it'd be a good idea if you went back to the office. Let us deal with this, okay?'

Danny stared hard at Callum, before looking back to Maxine. He couldn't believe what he was seeing and hearing. Why the fuck was she so bothered about some random bloke? He held up his hands as Callum tried to usher him away from the scene. 'All right,' he spat. 'I'm going, and you'd better get this wanker out of here, before I end up going to town on him. Do you hear me?'

'We're on to it now.' Callum had absolutely no idea of what had just gone down. He was as baffled as the rest of the men on Danny's payroll.

Danny sneered at the man on the floor. He contemplated giving him one last dig. Instead, he shook his head and began to walk away. As he walked across the dance floor towards the staircase that led to Moray's office, Jacqueline called out after him. 'You're a fucking animal, McKay.'

Danny stopped and turned; the look on Maxine's face broke his heart. A tiny voice at the back of his mind told him that he'd gone too far, that he'd shown his wife his true colours, a side of himself that he'd always been so careful to conceal from her in the past. They couldn't come back from this; he couldn't erase what he'd done. Shame filled every ounce of his being. He'd always known his temper would be his downfall, he just hadn't thought it would be Maxine who would have to witness it. 'Make sure that bitch is thrown out and barred for life,' he said stabbing his finger in Jaqueline's direction. It was a small victory, but it gave him some satisfaction, nonetheless.

* * *

Moray was on the warpath. He ran up the stairs towards the office, taking the steps two at a time. After receiving a telephone call from Callum, explaining the situation, he'd charged back to the club in double quick time.

He pushed open the door to the office. Danny was sitting in darkness, the monitor screens giving out the only light in the room. He blinked his eyes rapidly, as they tried to adjust to the dark surroundings. He could see Danny had been drinking, and if the near empty brandy bottle was anything to go by, he was fast on his way to getting smashed.

'Are you out of your fucking mind?'

'He deserved it.' Danny shrugged. He couldn't even be bothered to look up.

Moray threw up his arms. 'He deserved it? Is that all you can fucking say about the situation?'

Danny turned to face Moray. He could see the anger across his mate's face. 'What else do you want me to say? He was touching my wife. Was I supposed to just swallow that? Or maybe I should have shook his hand and told him to crack on. Would that have been more to your liking?' he asked sarcastically.

'Don't try to be funny with me, Danny. This is serious.'

'I know it's fucking serious. This is Maxine we're talking about. Any other man would have done the exact same thing, and you fucking know it.'

'You do know you could be sitting in the nick right now, don't you?' Moray asked, changing tact.

Danny gave a shrug of his shoulders. At this precise moment in time, he couldn't give a shit about what happened to him. 'She's my wife, Moray. Come on, man, what did you expect me to do?'

Moray blew out his cheeks. He slammed the office door closed, and then leant against the glass panel. On the one hand, he could see Danny's point, yet, at the same time, he needed to make his friend see the consequences of what could have happened. If the bloke, whoever he was, had decided to press charges, the end result could have been Danny being sent down at Her Majesty's pleasure for a number of years. 'I take it they've left the premises?'

Danny gulped at his brandy and nodded towards the monitor screens. 'I watched them leave.'

Moray sighed. At least that was something to be thankful for. 'Listen, mate, I understand you're hurting, but steaming in like that isn't going to help the situation, is it? Think about it rationally, mate.'

Danny momentarily closed his eyes. He looked back at the monitor screens. 'I've lost her, mate.'

Walking across the office, Moray placed his palms down onto the desk. 'You have to move on, Dan. Getting yourself into situations which could end up putting you away for years isn't going to help anyone, is it? You need to think of your son now. He's the one you need to focus on.'

'What's the point?' He let out a bitter laugh. 'She isn't going to let me see him again anyway, especially not now. That's what she said. Those were her exact words.'

Moray could hear the bitterness in Danny's voice. He watched him gulp at the brandy. 'That was said in anger. She won't stop you from seeing your boy. Think about it logically. It's the only thing she could say that would hurt you.'

Danny turned his face away. He was embarrassed, and he rubbed at his eyes in a bid to hide the emotion he was feeling. 'Well, she sounded convincing enough to me,' he said, his voice cracking.

Now that he'd calmed down a bit, he could see the bigger picture, and he knew, without a doubt, his wife would never forgive him for his actions. In his mind's eye, he could still see her cowering from him. His behaviour had scared her, and for that alone, he felt ashamed.

'Let her calm down a bit first. You'll see. Everything will turn out okay.'

Danny could only hope that was true. He remained silent. All the while, a thousand thoughts raced through his mind. His Maxine had always been too good for him, too nice. That was half the problem.

After taking a fresh glass from the drinks cabinet, Moray picked up the brandy bottle from the desk and poured himself out a generous measure. He then gulped it down and wiped the back of his hand across his lips. 'You'll be the fucking death of me, McKay.'

Danny looked up. He could only hope his friend didn't mean that literally.

* * *

Ronnie Dellow was about to break some bad news. This part of his job was always tough, yet, at the same time, he felt it was something he needed to do himself, rather than send uniformed officers to do the job for him, like some of his colleagues did.

He'd telephoned George Christos earlier that evening. Apologising for the lateness of his call, he had something to tell them, which couldn't wait until the following day. He suspected George already knew the reason for the meeting by the urgency in his voice, and the speediness in which he had arranged for him to come and see them.

He pulled up outside a house in Manor Park, East London, and looked over to the front door. Wearily, he climbed out of his car. He opened the small wooden gate and walked down the path. He knew his arrival had already been noted when the door was flung open before he'd even had the chance to lift the brass knocker.

'Detective Inspector.' There was a note of concern in George's voice. 'Is it Nico? Are the results back?'

Ronnie gave a sad smile. 'Can I come in, please? I'd like to speak to you all together.'

'Yes, yes, come in.' George pulled open the front door, allowing Ronnie to step inside. 'Please, go through,' he said, indicating for Ronnie to walk through to the lounge.

Ronnie introduced himself as he walked through to the small room. He took note of the gold crosses hanging on the wall, and averted his eyes. He then shook hands with the few family members who had gathered to hear his news.

'Please, would you sit?' Alexandros gestured. He nodded towards the high-backed, over-stuffed couch. 'This is our sister, Elini, Nico's mother.'

Ronnie took a seat and looked directly towards Elini. She was a small, thin woman with greying hair pulled into a bun at the nape of her neck. He could see the despair in her brown eyes, and he didn't want to prolong her agony.

'I'm afraid it is bad news.'

A high shrieked wail came from the woman. She rocked backwards and forwards, whilst clutching rosary beads in her clasped hands. Her obvious distress was heart-breaking to witness.

Ronnie glanced away. He wanted to at least give her some privacy, and he felt nothing but a sense of relief when a younger woman ran across the room to sit beside her, offering comfort.

'Are you certain it is Nico?' George asked. His skin was clammy, and once again, he could feel the tightening inside his chest.

Ronnie nodded sadly. 'I'm afraid it is. The dental records are a match.'

'How?' Alexandros asked. 'How did he...' He left the sentence unspoken.

Words were not needed for Ronnie to understand the question. He glanced across to Elini before speaking. 'Is there anywhere else we could speak, somewhere private?'

Ronnie followed the two men into a small dining room, then took a deep breath. 'I'm afraid this isn't going to be easy for you to hear. Nico sustained several injuries. The post mortem showed tissue and organ damage, caused by fire, which was the cause of death. I'm afraid the fire would have caused Nico to suffer substantial loss of blood and body fluids, causing his body and organs to go into major shock.'

George grabbed onto the back of a dining chair. His head began to swim. He could barely breathe, and the pain in his chest intensified.

'No,' he cried. 'Not our poor Nico, no.'

Concerned, Ronnie moved across to the older man. He guided him towards a chair. The drastic change of colour in

George's face was more than enough to tell him that medical help was needed.

'I think you need to call an ambulance,' he stated to Alexandros. He watched the man dash out of the room, and he loosened George's tie for him. He was no medical expert, but unless he was very much mistaken, for all intent and purposes, George Christos looked as though he was having a heart attack.

* * *

George was sitting on the edge of a hospital trolley in the Accident and Emergency Department of Newham Hospital. He was bare chested, and had numerous electrodes connected to an ECG machine, stuck to his chest. An oxygen mask helping him to breathe was strapped across his face. He looked away as a nurse took a vial of blood from his arm. He could feel his heart beating wildly inside his chest, and he willed it to return to its normal rhythm. The pain inside him had subsided, and for that he was thankful.

He felt as though his heart had been torn in two. Poor Nico, he hadn't deserved to die the way he had. He'd always been such a good boy.

'You must make sure that Elini is okay,' George said to Alexandros. He couldn't help but believe the doctors would give him bad news regarding his heart.

Alexandros was concerned. The way George was speaking, it sounded as though he already knew the outcome. 'You're going to be okay, George.'

George shook his head. 'No,' he said. 'Something isn't right with my heart. I can feel it.'

'When will we find out if he's going to be okay?' Alexandros asked the nurse.

'It shouldn't be too long,' the nurse replied as she began wrapping a blood pressure cuff around George's arm.

As if on cue, the doctor opened up the cubicle curtain. 'Everything seems okay.' He gave George a reassuring smile. 'There are no signs of a heart attack.'

George was amazed. He could feel the relief seep out of him. 'Then what is wrong with me?'

The doctor flicked through the notes. 'Have you ever suffered from anxiety or panic attacks in the past?'

George was shocked. 'No, never.'

'I think this could be an anxiety attack. Have you been under any stress lately?'

Alexandros answered for his brother. 'Yes, our nephew has recently passed away.'

The doctor nodded. 'I'm going to give you a letter to take to your General Practitioner. They will give you some medication, which should help if you feel an attack coming on.'

George was astounded. He was a strong man, and he'd never suffered from panic attacks before. He tried to think back to when the problem had first started. It was the day Nico's severed fingers had arrived at the restaurant. Anger coursed through his veins; in his mind there was only one person to blame for his ill heath, and that was Freddie Smith.

* * *

Taking a tissue, Jacqueline wiped the mascara away from underneath Maxine's red-rimmed eyes. She had finally stopped crying, leaving her face red and blotchy. As Maxine's breath came out in little shudders, Jacqueline placed her arm protectively around her shoulders and pulled her close so she could lean her head against her.

They were sitting in the waiting room of the Accident and Emergency department at Oldchurch Hospital in Romford, just a short walk from Ritzy's Nightclub.

Jaqueline stroked Maxine's hair in a bid to comfort her. 'He's an animal, Max. He's evil. What kind of man does something like that?'

Maxine turned her head to the side. 'I'm so sorry,' she said again to Steve.

Steve gingerly touched his nose and grimaced. It was obviously broken. He could barely breathe through it, and he could hear a cracking noise each time he touched it. 'You don't need to apologise. It wasn't your fault.'

Maxine couldn't help but feel like it was all her fault. She should have stayed at home, then none of this would have happened.

'He's an animal, always has been,' Jacqueline stated as she leant forward to look at Steve. 'The quicker you get that divorce, the better, Max, and stick to your guns. Don't let him see Logan. He can't be trusted around him.'

'He wouldn't hurt the baby, Jac, he loves him.'

Jacqueline pursed her lips. 'Maybe he wouldn't hurt him, but if you're not careful, he'll mould him into a younger version of himself.'

Maxine shuddered. She couldn't allow that to happen. Danny had always been a good father to their son, he'd been a good husband too once. Oh, she knew he had a temper on him, but this wasn't like him to be so violent. This wasn't the man she'd married; he'd changed beyond recognition. The Danny she knew had been decent, he had a caring side to him. Look how he was with Logan: from the moment she'd found out she was pregnant he'd wrapped her up in cotton wool, he'd taken care of her. Maybe she'd never known him at all, perhaps it had all been a charade. He'd cheated on her easily enough after all. As for their baby, Logan was innocent, and she was determined he wouldn't grow up anything like his father. Her son may look like Danny, and bear his name, but that was where the similarities would end.

When Steve's name was called out, Maxine sat up straight in her seat. 'Would you like me to come in with you?' she volunteered. It was the very least she could do, after all of the damage she'd caused.

Steve paused. Every instinct inside of him told him to run away from this woman, as far and as fast as he possibly could. He'd recognised her husband's name, and would have never got involved if he'd known it was Danny McKay he was dealing with. He wanted to say no to her, yet her eyes looked so sad he didn't have the heart to turn her away.

'Okay.'

Maxine stood up and followed Steve through to the cubicle. In all her life, she had never felt so ashamed, or sorry, before. She eased her body down onto a plastic chair beside the hospital trolley and listened in amazement as Steve told the doctor he'd fallen over, after having one too many drinks. Did her husband really scare people that much that they felt the need to lie? It was definitely an eye-opening moment.

13

'So, you've got no idea who could've been behind the shooting?'

Danny shrugged. He'd been thinking about it nonstop, and in his mind, there was only one person it could have been. 'It has to be Freddie. I can't think of anyone else.'

'Big Tone mentioned the Greeks had been causing a lot of problems lately.' Moray steepled his fingers in front of his chest as he looked across to Danny.

'Well, yeah, they have been, as you well know. But seeing as I'm not working for Freddie any more, I can't see them bothering with me now. And if we're going with the train of thought that Terry Stevens's missus is giving out information to them, then they would definitely know I'm working with you now.'

Moray swivelled on his chair as he thought it through. What Danny had said was true. 'So, you think it's definitely Freddie who's responsible then?'

'Don't you? It's got to be him. I can't see who else it would be. Who else could have that much of a problem with me that they would want to see me dead?'

Raising his eyebrows, Moray looked across to Danny. His expression said it all.

Sheepishly, Danny grinned. 'Okay, so maybe there's more than just Freddie out there who would want to kill me, but what I actually meant was, all of that's in the past. Why bring it all back up now?'

'Could be someone just out of the nick, or someone who's let everything die down, before exacting their revenge.'

'Nah, I just can't see that happening, mate.'

'Well, stranger things have happened, and let's face it, what we do know, is someone out there was definitely sending you a message. I'll dig around and see if anyone's recently been released, who could have had an issue with you.'

Danny leant back in his seat. Moray had him thinking now. The problem was, after twenty years of working for Freddie, it could be absolutely anyone coming out of the woodwork. He didn't have a clue. Let's face it, he hadn't exactly kept track of everyone he'd had a problem with over the years.

Moray cleared his throat. He had to get this off his chest. The shooting had been playing on his mind, something didn't seem quite right about it. Whoever was responsible hadn't intended to kill Danny, he was pretty certain of that. If it had been a serious hit, then they would have made sure he was dead, not just wounded.

'I'm just surprised no one's owned up to it yet, that's all I'm saying. Whoever it is, they're keeping it close to their chests, which makes you wonder why, doesn't it? Maybe it was a warning shot, or even a "hello, remember me?" kind of thing.'

Danny could feel Moray's eyes boring into him, and he kept his head down low. He knew exactly what it was his friend was getting at: Adam Christos, and the circumstances surrounding his murder.

It was something they hadn't spoken about since they were seventeen years old, yet it had always been there in the background, hanging over their heads, remaining unspoken between them.

'I don't think it's anything to do with him.' Even now, Danny couldn't bear to say Adam's name out loud.

'You can't know that for sure, mate.' Moray rubbed at his temple. 'I don't know, maybe it's me being paranoid. It's just the fact that the Greeks have started all of this up again, causing problems with Freddie, after all those years of them doing zilch, nothing. It's more than a little bit odd, don't you think? Maybe they know something that we don't?'

Danny shook his head. 'I really don't want to talk about this.' After all these years, he still felt ashamed of what he and Moray had been through, for what they had done. It had always been their dirty little secret, one they'd sworn to take to their graves.

Moray paused. That was the problem – Danny had never wanted to talk about it; even when Christos had done what he'd done, Danny hadn't wanted to discuss it. It had been him who'd found the courage to finally bring the subject up, and the look of horror coupled with shame in Danny's eyes had told Moray it hadn't only been him who Adam Christos had abused, it had been Danny too. 'It's not something I want to talk about either, but it happened to us, and' – he took a deep breath – 'we did what we had to do to survive. We can't turn the clock back, can we? We both know that.'

Danny stood up and walked across to the window, turning his back on his friend. 'We were kids. We didn't know what we were doing.'

'Yes, we did, Danny.' Moray's voice was low. 'We did it to save our own arses' – he stabbed his finger forward – 'and you fucking know it. We fitted Lee Hart up with Christos's murder, and one day he'll be released from the nick, and then what, eh? What happens next? Who is he going to tell our secret to?'

Danny's face paled. 'Enough,' he growled. 'I can't think about any of that now. It's in the past. We buried it a long time ago, and that's exactly where it should stay, in the past.'

'The thing is, though, it's not going to stay in the past, is it? He's going to come back and haunt us one day; he'll open that big trap of his and then everyone will know.' His voice was barely louder than a whisper. 'And I'm not just talking about the murder, I'm talking about what happened to us, what Christos did to us.'

Danny remained silent. He knew, deep down in his heart that Moray was right, he just didn't want to admit it to himself.

* * *

Maxine was perched on the edge of the bath. She glanced quickly at her watch, then looked around the bathroom, her eyes darting everywhere other than the home pregnancy testing kit resting beside her on the sink. She couldn't believe she was actually having to do this. Why now? she thought bitterly.

Surely, she couldn't be pregnant. The truth was, she just couldn't bear the thought of bringing another child into the world, not the way her life was at the moment. She had only just escaped from Danny, and she didn't want a further reason for him to be in her life any longer, or more than he needed to be.

She looked down at her watch for a second time. Please, be negative, she prayed. She held her breath, then glanced across to the pregnancy test. Already, she could see the outcome, and her heart lurched. Two strong pink lines stared back at her, taunting her. The test was positive.

Tears welled up in her eyes and her heart broke all over again. The pregnancy should have been something to celebrate, and she knew without a doubt that Danny would have been over the moon. He'd often talked about Logan having a sibling; he hadn't wanted their son to grow up as an only child like himself. Danny had loathed his childhood, and he'd been determined that their children wouldn't be dragged up in the same way that he had, that their children would have two parents who loved them, no matter what. For as long as she'd known him, Danny's relationship with his parents had always been strained, he hadn't seen them in years, he wasn't even so sure that they were still alive.

She hastily wiped away her tears. She could always get rid of it, no one even needed to know the baby existed. Only she would know, wouldn't she? But how would she be able live with herself afterwards, knowing that she'd denied Danny another child, and Logan a brother or sister?

Standing up, she slipped the test back into its box, and as she made to walk out of the bathroom, she paused in front of the large mirror on the wall and studied her reflection. It was such a stark contrast to how she had felt when she'd fallen pregnant with Logan. She could still recall how happy and excited she'd been. She looked down at her still flat stomach, and her heart went out to her unborn child. The fact she was even considering terminating the pregnancy, tore her apart.

In that instant, she knew she couldn't get rid of the baby. All she could hope and pray was that the pregnancy didn't give Danny false hope, that he didn't assume everything would be okay between them, because it wasn't and never would be. She didn't want her children to grow up between two parents who despised each other, because that's what would happen. Her mistrust of Danny would finally drive a wedge between them, they would end up resenting one another and would become that couple who were only together for the sake of their children.

What kind of a role model was that? She didn't want her children to grow up believing that was how a marriage worked.

By the time she'd walked down the stairs Maxine had made up her mind; she would keep the baby and as for Danny, well he would have to see their children when and as often as she deemed fit, no more and no less.

* * *

Moray held up his hands. 'Okay, we'll dig around first and get our facts straight, before we jump to conclusions.' He could see he had unnerved Danny by dragging up the past.

'I still think Freddie's the one responsible for this.'

'Time will tell, mate, and until someone talks, we're not going to find out, are we?'

'Yeah, I suppose so.'

Moray couldn't believe how calm Danny was being about the shooting. It was actually quite refreshing to see him thinking things through, rather than wanting to go out and head straight for Freddie's jugular vein. Especially when he was convinced Danny was putting the blame onto the wrong man. Maybe the talk he'd had with him after the incident with his wife had sunk in.

'Any news on Maxine? Have you heard from her?' he asked, changing the subject.

Danny sighed. 'She's letting me see Logan for an hour today. I've given her three weeks to calm down, so hopefully there won't be any more dramas.'

Moray flashed a smile. 'See, what did I tell you? Give her some space and she'll come around.'

'Yeah.' As much as Danny wanted to see his son, he was actually dreading seeing Maxine. He couldn't bear to see the contempt she felt for him in her eyes. The problem was, he still loved her, and he had a nasty feeling he always would. 'Right then, mate. I'm gonna shoot off and go and see my boy.'

Moray stood up, shook Danny's hand and watched him walk out of the office. 'Good luck,' he shouted out after him. He watched Danny raise his hand in acknowledgment, then closed the office door and took his phone out of his trouser pocket.

He had a contact who worked for the prison service. He needed to find out, one way or another, if the hunch he had was right. He knew if he left it to Danny, they would never find out. He had a feeling his mate was still blocking it all out, and a part of him didn't blame the man. He only wished he could do the same.

* * *

Even though, deep down, it was what he'd been expecting, Moray was still shocked. He switched off his phone and dropped it onto his desk. Two fucking months Lee Hart had been out of prison? How the fuck had they not found out before now?

He sat down heavily and rubbed at his scar. The six-inch slash across his cheek had been the start of the whole sorry saga; it had been Adam Christos who'd found him on the street bleeding out and after taking him and Danny to hospital he'd kept in touch. They had only been fifteen at the time, impressionable. To begin with they'd thought Adam was a nice bloke, they'd had a laugh with him, only it didn't take long for the abuse to start, less than a month in his case, Danny he wasn't so sure about, but he guessed the timeframe would have been similar – how else would Christos have kept them quiet for so long? It had been around that time that Danny had gone off the rails, that he'd become uncontrollable; he'd seemingly changed overnight from a carefree kid to someone who lashed out at every available opportunity. In hindsight, Moray should have guessed his best mate was going through the same horror that he was, but being a kid he hadn't linked the two, why would he. The only difference was, unlike Danny, each and every time he looked in the mirror, he was forced to not only remember what had happened to them, but also remember what they had done in the aftermath.

Lee Hart. The name echoed around inside his mind. It had been almost twenty-one years since they'd last seen him, since they had fitted him up for murder. That meant that Lee had had half a lifetime to sit brooding on what they had done to him. Moray knew if the roles were reversed, he or Danny would have plotted out their revenge. So what made Lee any different?

Moray knew, without a doubt, if Danny had been targeted, then surely he would be next. Why would Lee stop at Danny, when they had both been involved? After all, it had been the two of them, together, who'd wronged him. They were equally to blame.

Only Danny's pig-headedness would stop him from seeing what was going on right underneath their noses. He didn't want Lee to be responsible for the shooting, that was the problem. After all these years, Danny still couldn't face up to what they'd done. It was one of the only things Moray had ever known his mate to have a conscience over.

Moray was more than just concerned. He picked his phone back up. He needed an address for Lee. The three of them would have to sit down and talk the situation through, bash it out between them, if that's what it took – maybe even let Lee throw a few punches around to get it out of his system.

At the end of the day, they would need to suss out his intentions, and find out what his plans were. If they sat around doing nothing, then the problem wouldn't go away by itself, and could very well end up escalating. Setting up a meeting with the man was the only viable solution to the problem. Whether they wanted to or not, they would have to front Lee out.

He needed answers from them, an explanation for their actions, and after spending twenty-one years inside for a crime he didn't even commit, it was the very least he deserved.

The only other alternative was too much for Moray to even think about. Even though he knew, if needed, they would carry it through. They would have to. They both had too much to lose, not to mention, they had their own children to think about. No, if it came down to it, they would have no other choice but to keep Lee quiet, by whichever means they could. After all, a dead man couldn't talk, could he?

In fact, killing Lee had been a part of their original plan, all those years ago. He'd known too much about what had happened that night. Lee had a big mouth, and they didn't trust him to keep quiet, so together, they'd decided he had to go. They would need to dispose of him.

Only at the last minute, before they'd had the chance see it through, Moray had grown a conscience. Somehow, and it had taken a lot of persuading, he'd managed to convince Danny to set Lee up instead. In their naivety, they'd believed, if they planted the evidence on Lee, then he would be sent down for five years, instead of the life sentence he was actually handed out.

Now, Lee was back to haunt them. If they couldn't keep him quiet now, then they would have no other choice but to see the original plan through. Moray knew he definitely wouldn't be able to convince Danny a second time around not to kill the man, and if he was being totally honest, deep down in his heart, he knew he wouldn't even try.

Looking back on it now, Danny had been right all along. They should have killed Lee from the off. As callous as it sounded, it would have been the best option. They wouldn't have had to spend the best part of twenty-one years feeling guilty for having Lee sent down for a murder they, themselves, had committed. The whole sorry situation would have been done and dusted years ago.

* * *

Danny was excited to see his boy. He pulled up outside his old house and climbed out of the car. He had to admit, though, he felt more than a little bit nervous. If he was being even more truthful, he had to admit, he was terrified at the prospect of seeing Maxine.

His wife held all the cards where his son was concerned, and she could easily stop him from seeing their boy. At this moment in time, Maxine was probably the only person in the world who actually scared him, as daft as that may sound.

He walked down the path and tapped lightly on the front door. After a few moments, Maxine pulled the door open. Logan was nestled on her hip, and Danny held out his arms as his boy gave a gummy grin and kicked his legs out excitedly.

Taking Logan from his wife, Danny kissed the top of his son's head. 'How's he been?'

'Fine.'

He followed Maxine through to the kitchen. She was being frosty with him, and in a way, to a certain degree, he supposed he deserved it.

'I was thinking I could take him to the park. Would you like that, eh?' he smiled down at Logan.

Maxine shook her head. She didn't trust her husband to be left alone with their son. 'No, Danny, you're not leaving the house with him.'

Danny sighed. He could see this was how things were going to be from now on. 'Why not? I won't be long.'

'I said no.'

'Okay, calm down. Keep your hair on, it was only a suggestion.'

'Don't ever tell me to calm down.' Maxine bristled at his words. 'You've got an hour with him, and then I want you to leave.'

Closing his eyes, Danny's heart sank. Even though he could understand her frostiness, there was no need for her to be like this. He'd apologised over and over for what had happened at the club.

'I know I've got an hour with him, Max. It's what we agreed on.'

Leaning against the breakfast bar, Maxine watched as he hugged their son to his chest. He was a good father to Logan, she couldn't deny that, and it was obvious that he loved their little boy, in fact his eyes shone with love for him. Guilt swept through her veins. How had it even come to this? Just months earlier they had been happy; she would never have even contemplated not having Danny by her side, let alone thinking about divorce.

'He needs his lunch. He's probably hungry. Here, take this,' she said, handing over a small Tupperware tub of pureed food she'd prepared earlier that morning. 'You can feed him, if you'd like.'

Danny took the bowl and sat Logan in his highchair. 'When can I see him again?' he asked as he spooned the food into his boy's open mouth.

Maxine passed over a wet wipe to mop around Logan's lips. 'I don't know. I'll have to think about it, and then let you know.' It was the only answer she could give him. She hadn't thought through what would happen after today.

He walked across the kitchen. 'Well, we need a routine, don't we?' he asked, trying to be as civil as he possibly could. He was about to drop the wet wipe into the pedal bin, when he paused.

Something had caught his eye. 'What's this?' he asked, scooping down to pick up the pregnancy test box.

Rushing across the kitchen, Maxine's cheeks were flushed pink. How could she have been so careless? 'Give it to me,' she demanded.

Danny held her off. 'What the fuck, Max? Are you pregnant?'

'Give me it, Danny.'

Glancing across to his wife, Danny tipped out the contents of the box. He picked up the testing wand and turned it over in his hand. Immediately, he could see the test result, and his heart leapt. He was going to become a father for the second time. A wide smile spread across his face. 'When were you going to tell me about this?'

'I don't know.' In a panic, the words tumbled out of Maxine's mouth.

The smile froze across his face, and he stared at her. 'But you were going to tell me?'

Maxine could hear the hurt in his voice, and before she could stop herself she shrugged. Of course she would have had to tell him at some point; she wouldn't have been able to hide it in the long run, would she? He was bound to have guessed when her clothes became tighter.

'Well this changes everything.' He picked Logan up and kissed the top of his head. 'We're having another baby; you can't expect me to walk away from them.'

Snatching the pregnancy test out of his hand, Maxine walked across the kitchen and tossed it back into the bin. 'It changes nothing,' she said, turning to look at him. 'I don't trust you, Danny. Whatever we had is gone.'

Danny rubbed his hand across the nape of his neck. He felt as though she'd taken his heart out of his chest and stamped all over it. He could feel a hard lump form inside his throat, and he quickly swallowed it down. She'd hurt him in more ways than she could ever imagine. He was devastated. 'I see,' was all he could manage to utter. He kissed Logan goodbye, then made his way to the door.

Without even looking at his wife, he spoke. 'I have to go,' he said, pausing beside the open doorway. He didn't wait around to hear her response. He didn't trust himself to stay around her for a minute longer.

* * *

Lee Hart had aged considerably over the years. Prison hadn't been kind to him. He bent over the snooker table to take a shot, the cue stick resting between his thumb and forefinger. His dirty blond hair was now receding and beginning to thin. He looked much older than his thirty-eight years. He potted the ball, then straightened up and nodded at the man walking towards him.

'Freddie,' he said in a greeting.

Freddie shook Lee's hand. Seeing Lee now, with a cue stick in his hand, reminded him instantly of Lewis. They were like two peas in a pod. Lee definitely wouldn't have been able to get away with saying Lewis wasn't his son. The similarities were plain for everyone to see. It was just a shame Lee hadn't had the chance to get to know his boy. Maybe if he had, if he'd taken Lewis under his wing, the boy would still be alive.

Like Lewis, Lee had been one of Freddie's boys. Talk about like father like son. The only difference being, Lee had a vicious streak inside of him. He supposed prison did that to a man, and after spending twenty-one years banged up at Her Majesty's pleasure, he was bound to have a lot of pent up anger inside of him.

Lee downed his lager. 'I'll have the same again, Freddie,' he said, tipping his glass towards the older man.

Freddie swallowed down the irritation. He was no lackey. 'Get Lee a lager and get me a double scotch,' he ordered Matty, passing across a twenty-pound note.

'You've got him well trained, haven't you?' Lee asked, throwing Freddie a sly look. 'Was my Lewis as good as him?'

Freddie didn't bother to answer. Lee was pissed. It was the only time he ever mentioned his son. Either that, or he was after something from him.

Taking his lager from Matty, Lee drank deeply, his beady eyes watching Freddie over the rim of his glass. 'So, when are we having another one of your parties?'

Freddie quickly swallowed down his scotch before he choked on it. 'Keep your fucking voice down.'

Lee was the picture of innocence. 'What?' he asked, shrugging.

Having Lee around was beginning to take its toll on Freddie. He was becoming a liability. That big mouth of his never shut up, and it was going to end up getting the both of them into trouble, sooner or later.

'We don't talk about that in public,' he said, looking around, checking that no one else was within earshot. He kept his voice neutral, low. More than anything, he was treading carefully. The last thing he needed was for Lee to start blabbing out his business.

Lee gave a cocky grin. 'I didn't realise it was such a big secret.'

Freddie had heard just about enough. He grabbed Lee by the scruff of the neck and dragged him outside the snooker hall. 'Let's get something straight, you little cunt,' he hissed as he pushed him up against the outside wall. 'Despite what you might think, you still work for me. That means you keep that trap of yours shut. One more sly remark from you, and I'll cut that bastard tongue out of your fucking head myself, do you understand me?'

Shaken up, Lee nodded. 'All right, Fred, fucking hell I was only joking.'

'Do I look like I'm fucking laughing? I need your idea of a joke like I need a hole in the head. I mean it, Lee. One more fucking word, and I'm seriously going to lose my rag with you.'

Straightening out his T-shirt, Lee was contrite. 'I'm sorry. I don't want any aggro with you, Fred. It was a joke, that's all. I didn't think you'd be so touchy.'

'You didn't think I'd be so touchy? You do realise what we do is not considered fucking normal, don't you? That's without mentioning that it's highly fucking illegal. If anyone gets wind of it, there'll be hell to pay. Do you even have any comprehension of what happens to people like you and me in the nick?'

Lee understood exactly what happened to people like them. When he'd been inside, he'd seen first-hand the violence dished out to nonces. It had happened right in front of his very own two eyes. It hadn't been pretty, and even to this day, he could still hear the poor bloke's screams.

He shuddered. He didn't plan on going back to prison any time soon. He hadn't had the best of times in there as it was. Belmarsh had been the worst. He couldn't wait to get out of that shithole. He wasn't well liked, that was the problem. He had a big mouth and couldn't be trusted to keep it shut. If they weren't pushing him around, they were giving him a wide berth – Billy No Mates, they called him, and that was just the screws.

'I said I'm sorry. What more can I say?'

'What you can do, is learn to keep that mouth of yours shut, before you end up getting us both nicked.'

'I will do. I swear.'

Freddie narrowed his eyes. 'Okay,' he said, giving Lee the benefit of the doubt. 'Tell me the latest news on McKay.'

Relieved to be back on neutral ground, Lee gave Freddie a

quick rundown. 'The bastard is back out of the hospital now, living the life of Riley with Moray Garner, by all accounts.'

Freddie scowled. 'I ordered you to kill him, not piss around.'

Lee lifted his shoulders in a shrug. 'How was I to know he'd survive the shooting? I aimed for the bastard's heart; my hand must have slipped.'

'Time to step up the game then, and this time I want no mistakes.'

Grinning, Lee nodded. 'McKay and that didicoy pikey bastard, Garner, are gonna wish they'd never messed with me.' It was said with a confident air, and Lee thoroughly believed what he was saying to be true.

14

Moray was starting to become worried. Danny had been on the missing list for more than forty-eight hours. No one had seen hide nor hair of him. He wasn't even answering his phone. Knowing just how much of a workaholic Danny was, the fact that he hadn't shown his face was highly unusual. In normal circumstances, he couldn't stay away from the club, and would check in at least two or three times, every day.

Standing outside the grey apartment building, Moray tapped in a three-digit number on the intercom system, then pressed call. When there was no answer, he pressed the trades button. Much to his surprise, the door unlocked. He walked across the foyer, then took the lift to the third floor.

He knocked on the front door, silently willing Danny to answer. Where the fuck was he? He thumped on the wooden door once again, only harder this time. He was hoping this was simply just a case of his mate shacking up with some random bird for the weekend, even though he knew that wasn't Danny's usual style. But seeing as it was Danny, let's face it, anything was possible.

'Can I help you, dear?'

Moray turned to his side. With all the banging he'd been doing, he hadn't heard Danny's neighbour open her front door. In fact, he was surprised he hadn't knocked the door off its hinges, he'd hammered on it that hard.

'I'm looking for my mate. Have you seen him at all?'

'He's definitely inside. I've heard him moving around.'

Glancing at the front door, Moray turned back to the neighbour. 'Are you sure?'

'Oh yes, I'm quite certain.'

Moray thanked the woman and knocked again. Lifting up the letterbox, he called through the tiny gap. 'Danny, open up. I know you're in there. If you haven't opened this door within thirty seconds, I'm sending the boys around to smash it open.'

He straightened up as the door was flung open. 'Jesus Christ,' he said, wrinkling his nose. The stench of stale booze wafted out of the door. It smelt worse than the club on a Sunday morning, and that was saying something.

'What do you want?'

'Well, to be invited inside would be nice, unless you're going to make me stand out here all day.'

Danny moved aside, giving Moray enough space to squeeze through the tiny gap.

Looking around him, Moray took in the empty brandy bottles. 'What the fuck is going on in here?'

Barefoot and dressed in just a pair of grey jogging bottoms and a T-shirt, he shrugged. 'What does it look like?'

'I don't know. That's why I'm asking.'

'Unless I sit in here doing fuck all, I'm gonna end up doing some serious bird,' Danny answered as he flopped down heavily onto the sofa. He took a swig from the brandy bottle, and continued. 'You should be proud, I'm finally taking your advice,' he said, stabbing the bottle forward. 'I'm keeping schtum, instead of going off my fucking head.'

'What the fuck are you going on about?'

Danny looked across to Moray, his eyes flashing dangerously. 'I blame you for this. You were the one who stopped me from seeing her earlier, we could have talked it out. But oh fucking no, let her calm down first, you said. You, with your high and mighty fucking morals. Well, you weren't so high and fucking mighty, once upon a time though, were you? Or have you conveniently forgotten all about that? I know you, remember,' Danny spat. He stabbed the bottle towards Moray again, oblivious to the alcohol that slopped over the sides, staining his jogging bottoms. 'I know all of your dirty little secrets. I know, because I was there with you, and trust me, you ain't no saint. And you've got the audacity to stand there and question what I do, treating me like I'm some naughty little kid? You're always on at me in my fucking earhole, that's your problem. Don't do this, don't do fucking that. Well, bollocks to you and all. You're as bad as she is, looking down your nose at me, like your own shit don't stink. Well, trust me, it fucking does,' he said, giving a bitter laugh.

Moray was taken aback. For the first time in a long time, he was actually speechless. He eyed his mate cautiously. He had absolutely no idea of what he was even talking about. He was making no sense at all, and was obviously in a world of his own.

He watched Danny through narrowed eyes, unable to tell if he was pissed, or if he'd actually taken some kind of narcotic. Noting the amount of brandy bottles lined up on the coffee table, he took a wild guess at him being pissed, or maybe even both. Who fucking knew? The only thing he knew for sure, was that Danny McKay had finally, completely and utterly, lost the fucking plot.

Walking across to the window, Moray pulled back the heavy curtain. Immediately, Danny squinted and covered his eyes as sunlight streamed in. 'Close the curtain,' he growled.

'Not until you've told me what's going on, and how all of this, whatever the fuck it is, is my fault?'

'Just get out, I need to be by myself. I need to think all of this shit through.'

Moray frowned. This was so unlike Danny. In the twenty-odd years he'd known him, he'd never seen him behave like this before, and to be perfectly honest, it wasn't just unnerving, it was downright scary. What the hell was going on inside that head of his?

Now the curtain was open, he could see his mate much better, and just one glance in his direction was enough to tell him that he clearly hadn't showered or shaved in days – if the dark stubble across his jaw line was anything to go by. 'You need to sober up, shower and have a shave. Come on,' he said, yanking Danny to his feet.

Pushing Moray away from him, Danny hurled out abuse. 'Just fuck off, Moray. I told you to get out of here and leave me the fuck alone. What are you still doing here, eh? Go on, fuck off.'

Moray wasn't concerned by Danny's words. The first advantage, when working on the doors, was that they were pissed and you were sober. He treated Danny as though he was one of their customers, and half dragged him into the bathroom.

'Get in that fucking shower now, otherwise, I'll throw you in there and hose you down myself, fully clothed or not,' he growled as he twisted on the shower tap. 'I mean it, mate. Don't tempt me not to follow this through, because you know full well, I will.'

Danny was about to open his mouth to speak, when Moray took a step towards him, his large frame dominating the bathroom. 'Seriously, Danny, I'm not in the mood for all of this shit from you today, and if you want it to come to blows, then trust me, I'll give back twice as good as anything you attempt to throw my way. Now, get in that fucking shower.'

Moray waited outside the bathroom door until he could hear Danny step into the shower cubicle, before walking through to the kitchen. He'd known, without a doubt, that Danny wouldn't physically lash out at him. In all the years they'd known each other, not once had it ever come to blows between them. At the end of the day, they had too much respect for one another, for it to ever come to that.

Thirty minutes later, Danny emerged from the bathroom. Moray could see he was freshly shaved and that he looked relatively like his old self – other than his eyes, which were still red and bloodshot. Flicking the switch on the kettle, Moray heaped in two generous spoonfuls of coffee granules into a mug. Once the kettle had boiled, he poured in the water. Moray passed over the steaming mug of black coffee, just how Danny liked it, and watched as his mate sipped at the scalding liquid.

'Feeling better?' he asked. He waited for Danny to nod his head, then asked the burning question that was at the forefront of his mind. 'So, what the fuck is going on? C'mon, spit it out.'

Danny paused before speaking. He leaned back against the kitchen counter and folded his arms across his chest. It hurt him to even say the words out loud. 'She's pregnant.'

Moray raised his eyebrows. Surely that was something to celebrate?

Taking note of Moray's expression, Danny explained himself further. 'She said it doesn't change anything, she still wants a divorce. That's two kids I'm walking away from.'

To say Moray was stunned was an understatement. He didn't

know what to say in return. No wonder his mate was in such a state. 'You're not walking away from them,' he finally managed to utter.

'No? Then why does it feel like I am? I'm gonna be a weekend dad, that's not what I ever wanted for them or myself.'

'I'm so sorry, mate. I don't know what to say to you.'

'There's nothing you can say, is there? It's already happened, she doesn't want me around.'

Danny could feel the hard lump form in his throat once again, and he swallowed it down. He wouldn't cry. He was determined of that. He might smash the place up, or drink himself into a stupor, maybe even do both, but he wouldn't cry. He was a man, and in their world, men didn't blubber like babies.

Taking a seat at the kitchen table, Moray rested his forearms on his knees. 'As a mate, I'm gonna give you some advice. You can't sit cooped up in here for days on end, drinking yourself into oblivion. It isn't healthy. You need to get back to work, mate, focus on something else. Moping around in this flat isn't going to change the situation, is it? The only person you're hurting is yourself.'

Danny could see the truth in Moray's words. It was just so bloody difficult for him to even think straight at the moment. 'I'll be back tomorrow, probably. I just need to sort myself out.'

'No probably about it. I want you back to work, tonight.'

Danny sighed and nodded. There was no point in arguing. Moray was like a dog with a bone once he'd set his mind to something.

'You'll feel better for it, trust me. It'll take your mind off all of the other shit you've got going on.'

More than anything, he needed Danny back in his right frame of mind. What with the news of Lee's release, they had things to discuss. Now was not the right time, though. It could wait. After all, the man had already been out of prison for about two months, so waiting another day or two wouldn't hurt.

'Come on, get dressed. I'll take you down to the café. You need to eat something to sober you up and mop up all of that booze you've consumed.'

* * *

Dressed in dark blue jeans and a white shirt, Danny felt a lot more human than he had that morning, and after splashing a generous amount of aftershave over himself, he smelt a lot better, too. He walked purposefully across the empty dance floor towards the stairs leading up to the office.

Moray was right. He needed to be back at work. He needed something to take his mind off Maxine. Eight missed calls he'd had from her. He knew nothing was wrong with Logan. He'd listened to her voicemails, telling him she was sorry he'd found out about the pregnancy the way he had. Well, bollocks to her. From this moment on, she meant nothing to him. As long as his son and unborn child were okay, then he was happy. Logan and the baby were the only ones who mattered to him.

'Danny, have you got a minute?'

Danny stopped and turned around, as Big Tone walked towards him. 'Yeah.'

'I was talking to Mick Johnson. He was wondering if you had any work going for him?'

Weighing it up, Danny chewed on the inside of his cheek. How many more of Freddie's men were going to end up jumping ship. He looked up to where the offices were situated. Really, he should run it through with Moray first. They were meant to be making decisions together. 'Tell him to come and see me tomorrow. I can't promise anything, mind.'

'Cheers, Danny. I'll do that.'

Danny watched as the big man walked away, then carried on his way up to the office. As he was nearing, Moray waved out to him.

'I'm glad I caught you. These need signing,' he said, pushing paperwork across the desk.

'What are they?'

'It's the forms from the solicitors for this place. All I need is your autograph, and it should be ours, as soon as the brief has pushed your divorce through.'

'I'm surprised you still want me as your partner.' Danny grinned sheepishly. 'I've not exactly been easy to be around of late. I'm sorry, mate, truly, I am. I shouldn't have taken my shit out on you this morning. I was bang out of order.'

Laughing, Moray, shook his head. 'I've known you since we were fifteen, you tosser. I think I know what I'm getting myself involved with. And yeah, you are a loose cannon, and some days, I don't think you're quite right up here,' he said, pointing to his temple. 'But I'm pretty certain I can handle you, so sign the bloody paperwork.'

Danny burst out laughing. Moray certainly had a way with words. He quickly signed the forms, then handed them back.

'That's it now. You've signed your life away.' Moray grinned. 'And trust me, you won't regret it.'

Danny smiled. He knew he wouldn't regret it. This was exactly what he needed, to take his mind off everything else that was going on in his life.

* * *

Big Tone had been in the game a long time. Not much got past him, without him noticing first. He was standing outside the doors of the Earl of Essex public house on Romford Road in Manor Park, East London. He looked handy, his cropped hair giving him a thuggish appearance. Most of the punters steered clear, not wanting to mess with him, and that suited Big Tone down to the ground. His heavy frame was intimidating, and on more than one occasion, he'd heard people whisper, 'Look at the size of him. You wouldn't want to meet him down a dark alley,' or, 'I wouldn't want to get on the wrong side of him.'

Of course, he could look after himself, if need be. He wouldn't have lasted all these years if he couldn't. Right now, he had his eye on a man who he'd let into the pub over an hour ago. Every instinct had told him to watch the bloke. He couldn't exactly put his finger on the reason why. Maybe he just had one of those faces.

Speaking into his earpiece, he told Lloydy to change positions with him. He had a feeling the geezer was dealing. He had to be. From his position at the door, Big Tone had seen so many people approach him that it was blatantly obvious he was up to no good.

Quickly switching places with Lloydy, he came to stand just ten feet away from the man, so he could keep a closer eye on what he was up to. Freddie had allowed dealing when he ran the doors, taking a cut from the profit. More often than not, they were instructed to turn a blind eye; as long as the dealer passed over the cash at the end of the night, then everyone was happy.

Under Moray Garner, dealing was forbidden. He wanted to run a legit business, and it was more than Big Tone's job was worth to turn a blind eye now. Not to mention, he didn't want Danny or Moray coming down on him like a ton of bricks.

He continued watching the man. He couldn't believe how bait he was. Every instinct he had told him something wasn't right about the situation. Unless they'd had prior permission, he'd never known a dealer to be so open about what they were doing before.

Grabbing the man by the collar, Big Tone hurled him towards the door. 'That's it, you're fucking out.'

The man protested as he was being dragged outside. 'What have I done wrong?' he shouted. His irate screams caused customers to turn and look.

Big Tone ignored him. Seeing the commotion, Lloydy ran inside to help drag the man outside. 'Get back,' Big Tone shouted out. He had a bad feeling this was an attempted takeover. He'd seen it once before – distract the doormen, and then bang them out, while they were preoccupied.

Once out on the street, the man ran as if his life depended on it. As Big Tone had predicted, four men walked towards the pub. He and Lloydy may have been outnumbered, but they were prepared. The takeover had been foiled. It was a poor attempt, thanks to Big Tone's eager eyes.

Seeing the men off, Big Tone blew out his cheeks, the exertion causing him to breathe heavily. He really needed to go on a diet and lose some weight.

'Keep an eye out,' he instructed Lloydy once he'd got his breath back. 'I'll get on the blower to Danny.'

* * *

Speeding down Romford Road, Danny brought the car to a screeching halt outside the pub. He jumped out of the motor and strode purposefully towards Big Tone, his fists balled at his sides.

'Who the fuck was it?' he demanded.

'The fucking Greeks, mate.'

Danny was momentarily taken aback. He was certain the big

man was going to say Freddie. He narrowed his eyes. 'Are you sure it was the Greeks, not one of Freddie's lot?'

'I'm positive. If it was one of Freddie's lot, I would have recognised them from the off. These were definitely Greek.'

Immediately, Danny recalled his previous conversation with Moray. He just couldn't understand why the Greeks would want to cause trouble now. He'd been convinced the issue had been about Freddie, and not the actual doors themselves. It was a startling revelation. He couldn't help but think of Lee Hart – the two went hand in hand, after all.

'Keep your eyes peeled,' he said as he made his way back towards his car. 'And call me, immediately, if anything else happens.'

'Will do, Danny.'

Starting the ignition, Danny decided to drive around to the remaining clubs and pubs before going back to Moray and telling him the score. Something seemed off about all of this. Why would they half-heartedly attempt to take over the doors? Why not just go all out and take them, like he and Moray had done? No, something just didn't sit right about any of this. It made no sense to him, and that was the problem.

* * *

George chuckled to himself. Alexandros may not have been the sharpest knife in the drawer, but at times, he came up with some good plans. He had to agree that his brother's plan for taking the doors was good this time around. In fact, it was pretty much foolproof.

They were planning to have a few half-hearted attempts at taking the doors over, just enough to make their presence known to the men working them. They would rattle a few cages, put them on edge, so to speak, before they went out, all guns blazing, in attack mode.

Unlike the previous attempts, this time, they really would take over, and just like all the other times, McKay and Garner would believe, wrongly, that they could maintain their stronghold. In other words, they were luring them into a false sense of security. The plan was genius, and was exactly what they all needed to pick them up after Nico's funeral.

Poor Nico. He still hadn't come to terms with what had happened to his favourite nephew. As he watched Nico's coffin being carried into the church, he'd had to bury his anger deep inside. They couldn't even have his body on display, as was their custom, because his death had been that horrific.

He still believed Freddie was responsible for the murder, even though he had no proof. Nonetheless, he blamed him for the deaths of two of his family members. The first had been his brother Adam, by that murdering scumbag, Hart, who'd worked for Freddie Smith.

They would find the bastard, eventually. He'd promised his brother's widow and son of that, and when they did, they would leave his gutted body swinging on a meat hook to rot, just like Adam's body had been left, rotting away, for days on end. He'd had so many maggots crawling all over him, eating away at his flesh, that the police couldn't even tell if he was a human being or an animal carcass at first.

George swallowed down the hatred he felt for Smith and his firm. He knew the day for revenge was fast approaching. He could feel it in his bones.

* * *

'Do fucking what? Why the fuck didn't you tell me he was out?'

Moray raised his eyebrows. Was Danny seriously asking him that question, after his escapades just that morning? 'It wasn't the right time, mate, and I know you don't like dragging up the past, where Lee is concerned. But all of this that's going on with the Greeks, there's got to be a connection. There has to be. None of it makes sense. My main concern is the truth coming out. That's why we have to speak to Lee. We've got to keep him quiet.'

'Well, where the fuck is he? Have you seen him?'

'Of course I haven't seen him. What do you take me for? But we do need to speak to him at some point in the very near future, and let's face it, the sooner the better.'

'Well, first thing's first. We need to locate him.'

Locating Lee was turning out to be a lot harder than Moray had anticipated. 'I spoke to Jonny Carter. He's gonna keep an eye out for him.'

'Jonny Carter, as in Tommy Carter's younger brother? What the fuck did you go to that ponce for? I've had nothing but agg from that little prick, and believe me, he's lucky I haven't caught up with him yet.'

Moray held up his hand. 'The reason I went to him is, between the Carter brothers, they know most of what goes on around here, and I'm guessing someone would have mentioned Lee Hart was out and about to them.'

'Well, does he know where he is then?'

'Not as yet. I'm still waiting to hear.'

Danny began to laugh. 'If Carter finds out we're working together, you're gonna have a long wait hearing back from him. Trust me.'

Moray didn't doubt that for a second. In fact, Danny's name had been one of the first things Jonny had mentioned, when he'd called him up. 'Thing is, I sort of told Jonny I'd smooth things over between the two of yous.'

'You did fucking what? No way. That bastard tried tucking me up, not once, but twice. I'm not letting him get away with it.'

He'd had a feeling Danny would say this, and Moray was prepared. 'If Carter tells us where Lee Hart is shacked up, then in the grand scheme of things, we've had a result, mate.'

Danny tilted his head to the side as he thought it through. In a way, Moray was right, and Tommy Carter had tried to make amends for his brother's wrong doings on more than one occasion. Twice Jonny had come to him asking to borrow a considerable amount of cash and twice like an idiot he'd fallen for his sob story. What was he supposed to do, Tommy was a good mate, and Jonny was his youngest brother, he'd not only trusted him, but he'd also believed he would repay his debts. He should have known something wasn't right the minute Jonny had even come to him, it wasn't as though the Carters were short of a bob or two – not only were they hugely successful bank robbers but they were also sitting on the profits of the gold heist. He supposed he only had himself to blame; the fact Jonny hadn't wanted his elder brother to know about the loans should have been enough to set alarm bells ringing in his head. 'All right, I'll do you a deal: as long as I don't have to be nice to the little bastard, then you can use him to get what you need. But you tell him from me, I'm still gunning for him.'

Moray smiled. They both knew that he would say no such thing, at least not until he'd learnt of Lee's whereabouts. 'It's a deal.'

* * *

Jonny Carter had a finger in a lot of pies. You name it, he was involved in it, or knew someone who was, much to his elder brother's chagrin. A gifted boxer, by the time he was nineteen he'd hung up his gloves and begged his eldest brother, Tommy, to let him join the family business. His poor dad had been left heartbroken, with six sons he'd hoped that at least one of them would lift a title belt, and as the baby of the family, Jonny had been the only one left interested in the sport. He would have carried on boxing if it hadn't been for the fact he'd seen how well his elder brothers were doing. Not only were they all driving flashy motors but they were also loaded, and he wanted a slice of the action. He'd taken to debt collecting and bank robberies like a duck to water, it was in his blood.

After a hard day's graft, he was standing in the snooker hall, enjoying a well-deserved pint.

He'd spotted Lee Hart as soon as he'd walked in through the doors. He didn't know him well, admittedly, being that much younger than the man, but he knew who he was, all right. Everyone in the club did, and as a result, they gave him a wide berth.

After spending twenty-one years inside for murder, naturally, most people were wary of Lee, and would whisper about the atrocious crime he'd committed. The severity of the murder went down in folklore, giving Lee a huge amount of kudos. The truth was, people were just scared of Lee dishing out the same treatment to them. After all, he'd done it once. What was stopping him from doing it a second time?

Downing his pint, Jonny placed the empty glass down onto the bar, then walked outside. He took his mobile phone out of his pocket and dialled Moray Garner's phone number. He just hoped Moray had had a chance to speak to Danny first. He didn't fancy him breathing down his neck and all. He was already getting it in the neck from his brothers over not paying Danny what he owed.

'You never fucking learn, do you?' Tommy had bellowed at him after his latest escapades. Tommy was right. In all fairness, though, he didn't have to learn. He'd always had his big bothers to bail him out.

* * *

Grinning from ear to ear, Moray switched off his phone. 'See, what did I tell you? Jonny Carter came through with the goods.'

'Where is he?'

Moray stood up, grabbing his jacket as he did so. 'In the snooker hall down the road. The cunt's been under our noses this whole fucking time.'

The two men bolted out of the office. 'Just remember to go easy on him,' Moray reminded Danny. 'This was all our fault to begin with.'

'What do you fucking take me for?' Danny answered, his voice low. 'We're just gonna have a nice, quiet, friendly chat with him, that's all.'

'Well, make sure it is friendly.' He knew what Danny was like. It didn't take much to push his buttons, and what with the mood he'd been in lately, he didn't fancy Lee's chances, should he start getting lairy.

* * *

Pulling up outside the snooker hall, Danny and Moray jumped out of the car. Spotting them, Jonny Carter took a step backwards. He was wary of being anywhere near Danny McKay, without having his elder brothers around to back him up.

'Is he still inside?'

'Yeah, he's still in there.' Jonny nodded.

'Don't think I've forgotten about you, either. Pay up what you owe me, otherwise, my fist will end up sending you for a kip,' Danny growled.

He stabbed his finger towards Jonny and meant every word. Being a Carter wasn't going to save him this time. It was only the fact that he had bigger fish to fry, that he was giving the younger man a swerve, for the time being.

'Right,' Moray said, as he peered through the doors leading to the club. 'Let's get this over and done with.'

* * *

Lee Hart felt the colour drain from his face. Despite his big 'I am' attitude in front of Freddie, he was nothing but a coward, and seeing the two men striding towards him, he felt his insides instantly turn to mush. They were a lot bigger than the last time he'd seen them. Back then, they'd only been kids. Now, they were men.

'Lee, long time,' Danny said. 'We wanna have a quick word with you. Come out to the motor.'

Lee shook his head. 'Nah, you're all right. I'll stay in here, thanks.'

'Wrong answer. Move your fucking arse out to the car, now, before I end up dragging you out.'

'We just want a quiet word, that's all,' Moray interrupted, changing tact. Danny had never had much patience, and he could see this going wrong if they weren't careful.

Looking around him, Lee had no choice but to go outside with them. He didn't want to lose face, especially not now, seeing as he had a reputation to uphold.

* * *

'See, that wasn't so difficult, was it?' Danny asked as he climbed onto the back seat beside Lee.

'I suppose not. What do yous want from me?'

'The thing is, Lee, and I'm sure you're going to understand where we're coming from on this,' Moray stated as he turned in his seat. 'You know a bit too much about what happened that night for our liking, and other than Danny and me, you're the only other person who really knows who killed that Greek.'

'I'm not going to say anything about it. Honestly, I'm not.'

'But, we only have your word for that, don't we? Which leaves us in an awkward position, doesn't it?'

Lee shook his head furiously. 'I swear to you, I'm not going to say anything.'

'What do you think, Danny? Do you believe him?' Moray asked. There was a hint of humour in his voice.

Danny shook his head. 'Nah, I don't, mate. Maybe we need to cut him up a bit, to make sure he understands to keep that big trap of his shut.'

Lee was almost crying. 'I swear to you both, I'm not going to say anything to anyone. I swear I won't, not even to Freddie.'

Immediately, Danny raised his eyebrows towards Moray. 'Why the fuck are you bringing Freddie's name up in all of this?'

'I don't know. Just please, don't hurt me,' Lee babbled. He could barely string his sentences together he was that terrified.

'He's told fucking Freddie,' Danny snapped. He knew it. He knew they should have killed this big-mouthed cunt at the same time as they'd killed the Greek, all those years ago.

Moray held up his hand in a bid to calm Danny down. For all intents and purposes, it was looking that way. The problem was: what did they do about the situation now?

'It's my boy. He was shot and killed, see, and Freddie's been helping me out like. That's the only reason I mentioned his name.'

Danny was stunned. He hadn't even known Lee had a kid. 'So what's Freddie got to do with your kid?'

'He was there when my boy was shot. He cradled him while he died,' Lee answered, talking fast.

The truth was, he had no feelings for the kid, whatsoever. He hadn't even known him, but still he turned on the waterworks. Lewis had to come in handy for something, and if the sob story of his boy being shot and killed was going get him out of trouble with these two thugs, then he would raise his glass to the kid in a toast later on.

Astounded, Danny took in Lee's mop of blond hair. Surely not! Surely the kid he'd shot wasn't Lee's son. And as for Freddie cradling the dying boy, well, that was complete and utter bollocks. Freddie had run out of the restaurant as fast as he himself had.

'I'm sorry for your loss, mate, but at the end of the day, that doesn't make any difference to the predicament we're in now, does it?'

Lee swiped at his crocodile tears. 'Please, Danny. I'm not going to say anything. You know me, and you know I wouldn't be that stupid. As if I'd ever tell anyone about what yous both did. I still have nightmares over it.'

Moray raised his eyebrows before shaking his head. 'It's up to you. What do you want to do with him?'

'If we let you go, can we trust you not to say anything?' Danny asked.

'I promise I won't say a word. If I could, I would get down on my hands and knees, and beg, just to prove it to you.'

Danny looked across to Moray, before reluctantly climbing out of the car. 'Don't make us regret letting you go, because next time, we won't be so friendly. Do you understand me?' he asked, opening the rear passenger door.

Lee nodded. 'Thank you, thank you,' he grovelled.

'Well, go on, piss off.' Danny watched as Lee ran back inside the snooker hall, then climbed into the front seat beside Moray. 'Twenty-one fucking years I spent feeling guilty over that useless, poxy, sly, big-mouthed wanker. We should have just killed him from the off, and left him hanging from a hook, next to that Greek bastard.'

'Yeah, we should have done,' Moray agreed as he started the ignition. He had a feeling they hadn't heard the last from Lee.

15

Danny had completely forgotten all about Mick Johnson paying him a visit. He hastily shook his hand, recalling the last time they'd seen each other. It was when the Greek lad had been killed, and he could still recall telling Mick, Big Tone and Freddie that he would kill them all for their parts in the murder.

'I told Freddie straight he was bang out of order, and I still stand by that.'

'So, what can I do for you, Mick?' Danny interrupted. He was keen to get down to business, and not only did he not have the time for small talk, but he also didn't want to hear his excuses for not helping him give the boy a more dignified death.

'I was hoping you might have some work for me. Nothing too heavy. I'm getting on in years. So, I was hoping you might have a small venue, somewhere relatively quiet, that you feel like you're wasting your manpower on.'

Danny's thoughts went immediately to The Golden Goose in Stratford. The boozer was a typical East End family run pub. The majority of the regulars were getting on in years themselves, and he'd always thought of the place as a waste of time in using their heavies on. In all the years he'd known Freddie to run the doors, there had never been any trouble there.

At the same time, they were reluctant to sever the contract. You never knew what might happen in the future. It could have a new run of owners and become one of the hippest venues for youngsters to go to.

'Let me speak to Moray. I've got a place in mind for you.'

In fact, he was pretty certain Moray would agree to taking Mick on solely to work there. Most of the lads complained if they were sent to do a stint at the sleepy boozer. They'd even nick-named it the graveyard shift.

'Cheers, Danny. I'd really appreciate it.'

'I'll give you a bell when I know for sure, okay?'

Mick shook Danny's hand and thanked him once again. He was glad he'd come and cleared the air with Danny. It would be good to get back to work, and he whistled happily as he walked across the dance floor. In his own way, Danny wasn't so bad, and as Big Tone had pointed out, working for Danny McKay had to be a lot safer than working for Freddie. Yes, he'd definitely done the right thing in coming here.

* * *

Matty was eavesdropping. Freddie usually discussed all types of business in front of him, but today, he and Lee Hart had cossetted themselves away, out of ear shot.

Standing with his ear against the lounge door, he tried to listen to what was being said. He didn't like Lee. When he'd first been introduced to him, he'd been pleased to have Lewis's dad around. He thought it would be good to have someone else to talk to about his best mate. He'd thought Lee would like that. But he was wrong. Lee had shown no interest in Lewis whatsoever.

Pushing his ear closer to the door, he listened intently as the two men talked. He could pick up strangled pieces of the conversation, just enough to put two and two together, to understand what was going on.

'I'm telling you, Fred, they know I've told you. I could see it in their eyes.'

'If they thought that, then you wouldn't be alive to tell the tale.'

'It still sickens me seeing the bloke's corpse swinging on that hook. Gutted him like a fish, they did. And now, they're going to do the same to me.'

'I think you're panicking over nothing. McKay isn't stupid. He'd have gutted you there and then, if he'd thought you'd told someone.'

Astounded, Matty walked away from the door. So it was Danny McKay all along, who'd carried out the murder, not Lee. He gave a little shudder. Lewis hadn't been his first victim, after all. No wonder the man slept so easily at night. He was used to killing anyone who got in his way.

He wondered briefly if Danny would kill Freddie and Lee. He would like that to happen. He began to daydream about it, before pushing the thought from his mind. He had been doing a lot of daydreaming lately. He enjoyed thinking up new ways for the two men to disappear.

So far, they'd been eaten by a pack of wild dogs, or Freddie's car had blown up with the two of them in it. His absolute favourite was for them and the rest of the men to be lined up against a wall, just before one of Freddie's infamous parties got underway. And then for him to personally gun them down, with a machine gun, no less, spraying bullets everywhere, laughing while he did it. He only wished he had the bottle to really follow it through.

There wasn't much he could do with his new-found information, other than secretly smile at Lee's obvious distress. It briefly crossed his mind to let it slip to Danny that Lee had told Freddie about the murder. It was something he would definitely do, if he thought he could get away with it. But he didn't want to put himself into a precarious position, and he didn't want to become the next person to swing on a hook, after being gutted like a fish.

* * *

'So, are you planning on taking that bird out again?'

'What bird?' Preoccupied with a mountain of paperwork on his desk, Moray didn't even look up.

'The nurse. What's her name?'

'You mean Sophie, and yeah I am. I like her, a lot.'

'Love must be in the air, eh? Don't forget to consider me when it comes to the best man duties.'

Moray looked up now. 'You're being a bit premature, mate, and what's with all the questions?'

'I'm trying to take my mind off that scumbag Lee Hart, before I get back in the motor and drag him out of the snooker hall.'

'For your information, we've only had a couple of dates, so it's hardly love yet, is it? And as for getting married, nah, mate, I've been there, done it, and got the bloody T-shirt. I won't be going down that road again.'

'I dunno, these things can quickly escalate.' As Moray gave him a cold stare, Danny held up his hands and laughed. 'Sorry, like you said, it's a bit too soon.'

Turning back to his paperwork, Moray tried his hardest to ignore the sighs and fidgeting coming from his mate. Slamming his fist down on the desk, he'd had enough. 'For fuck's sake, Danny, I'm trying to concentrate here. When the lads end up with no wages, are you going to be the one who deals with them, eh? Haven't you got something better you can go and do?'

Hoping Moray would say that, Danny leapt to his feet. 'Yeah, I do actually. I'll be back later.'

Watching as his mate walked out of the office, Moray stared after him. What the fuck was that all about? Shrugging, he turned back to his paperwork. As he looked over the figures on the sheet of paper in front of him, Danny was already gone from his mind.

* * *

Tommy Carter had known Danny McKay for years. There was a fair amount of respect between them, and as long as they didn't step on one another's toes, then they were more than happy to maintain their friendship.

'What can I say, Danny? Jonny has always been a bit head strong. You know what he's like, and it's all our fault. We fully take the blame for how he's turned out. He's the baby of the family, see, and clearly, we've given him too much of a free rein, and let him do as he pleases for far too long, and this,' he said, throwing up his arms, 'is the fucking outcome. But from the bottom of my heart, I apologise for all the grief he's caused you of late.'

Tommy was a good looking man. In fact, all of the Carter boys were good looking, each of them a clone of one another.

Danny sipped at his brandy. 'I get what you're saying, Tommy, and I hate to have to come to you like this, but as you can imagine, I'm not happy, and I've given him plenty of swerves over the years, because of our friendship, but he's taking the piss out of me now, and I can't let that slide.'

'We'll sort him out, Danny, don't you worry about that. Our Mitchel and Sonny have gone out searching for him, as we speak.'

Turning to look across at Jimmy, the second eldest of the

Carter brothers, Danny nodded in gratitude. 'Thanks, mate. I'm sure, as you can appreciate, this isn't something I can swallow. He's making me look like a mug, and if I let him get away with it, then others will think they can follow suit. If you were in my position, you'd do the same.'

'I would have fucking battered him long ago if I were you, so I get where you're coming from.'

'Jonny's always been the same. He's a lairy little bastard who thinks we're gonna bail him out all the time,' Gary Carter, the third eldest Carter brother, stated. 'I've told them,' he said, jerking his head towards his elder brothers, 'that they're too soft on him. As soon as everything goes up in the air they fight his battles for him. He needs a fucking slap; I've been saying that for years.'

Tommy and Jimmy nodded at their younger brother's words. They'd been expecting this day to come, and in recent months had warned Jonny on more than one occasion, to wind his neck in and start behaving himself. The fact Jonny was the baby of the family didn't wash with Tommy; he'd had enough of making excuses for his brother's reckless behaviour. He himself had only been nineteen when he'd first started working for his former boss Davey Abbott, a damn sight younger than what Jonny was now. They had their own reputations to uphold, and their youngest brother was beginning to make them look like fools. 'It'll end today, Danny, I can guarantee you that.'

'I ain't done nothing wrong, so let me fucking go.'

Tommy sighed. 'Speak of the devil himself. Here he is.'

Man-handled by his two brothers, who at that precise moment were flanking him on either side, Jonny Carter took one look at Danny McKay, and tried to bolt out of the door.

'Jonny, stop where you fucking are.' The authority in Tommy's voice stopped Jonny dead in his tracks.

'Why have you let him in here? You know he's after me. You've fucking set me up. My own brothers! Why would you do that?'

'They've let me in, Jonny, because your brothers are sensible men. They don't want your stupidity to cause a feud. Shit's about to hit the fan, Jonny boy. You keep trying to fuck me over, and I'm not having it any more. I've already warned you, time and time again, I want my money back,' Danny said. He stood up and drove his fist hard into Jonny's stomach.

Doubled over, Jonny groaned in pain. Winded by the blow, he tried to catch his breath. 'You dirty bastards,' he croaked.

'So, Danny, now that the pleasantries are over with,' Tommy said with a grin, 'what's this job you want us to do for you? Oh, and Jonny, get up. Even I can see he didn't hit you that hard, at least not as hard as I would have done, in his shoes,' Tommy stated, dismissing his youngest brother's obvious distress.

Danny sat back down in his seat and kicked his legs out in front of him. 'The job I've got in mind is going to take all of you to carry out, even soppy bollocks over there,' he said, nodding his head towards Jonny. 'Once it's done, you can consider the debt owed to me by Jonny boy, to be paid off.'

Tommy nodded. It was a fair request. 'So, what do you want us to do?'

'I want someone disposed of. Actually, that should be plural. I want persons disposed of.'

Tommy raised his eyebrows. He hadn't expected Danny's request to result in them committing murders. They were bank robbers, not hitmen.

'You still fucking owe me, Carter. You might have forgotten, but I haven't.' Danny stabbed his finger in the air, a half-smile spread across his face to take the edge off his words. 'I haven't forgotten how you tried to tuck me up over the gold, all those years ago.'

Tommy sighed. There was more than a hint of truth to what Danny had said – he had tried to tuck him, not in a malicious way of course, more to make sure Danny stayed on side and worked with them rather than against them. He looked across at his brothers, before reluctantly agreeing. 'Okay, when do you want it done?' Tommy had been in the game a long time, and knew the score. They wouldn't ask questions, and he knew Danny was counting on that.

'Soon. I'll get back to you with the specific details... the whys and the whens, and so forth.'

'Good, good. Well, we'll be here, ready and waiting, so just say the word. Another drink, Danny?' Tommy asked, raising his own glass towards the big man. He was relieved that the air had been cleared between them.

'Go on, you've twisted my arm. I'll have one more for the road.' Danny grinned.

* * *

Armed with Terry's credit card in her hand, Hayley decided to treat herself to a few new outfits. She had to maintain her image, and more than anything, she wanted to continue to impress Giorgio.

She strolled into a boutique on Brentwood High Street with a confident air. She had money, and in her eyes, she had class. She treated the sales assistants abysmally. Her attitude stank, and they couldn't wait to see the back of her.

Laden down with bags, she made her way back to her car. Slamming down the boot, she glanced across to a wine bar situated just feet away from where she'd parked. What she saw made her stop dead in her tracks. That was her Giorgio, draping himself over some dark-haired tart.

Fuming, Hayley stormed into the bar. She stood with her hands on her hips.

'What the fuck is going on here?' she yelled, her Dagenham roots pushed to the fore. Gone was the classy image she worked so hard to maintain.

Startled, Giorgio inwardly groaned. This was all he needed. 'She's no one. She's crazy,' he said to the petite brunette sitting beside him.

Puffing out her chest, Hayley's eyes flashed dangerously and that was when all hell broke loose.

* * *

George Christos was furious. He'd spent the past thirty minutes screaming and shouting at his nephew.

'How could you be so stupid?' he roared. When Giorgio remained silent, George stabbed his finger towards him. 'Do you even realise, or care for that matter, that we have now lost the only person who can give us information, and for what? Some stupid whore you've taken a fancy to?'

'She's not a stupid whore. I love her, and I'm going to marry her.'

'Love! Love? You don't even know the meaning of the word,' George screamed as he lashed out at his nephew.

Giorgio bristled with resentment. He knew what love was. He'd secretly been dating Rosita for over two years. It was only his family's attitude that had stopped him from introducing them to her.

'You will get on the phone now, to this Hayley woman, and apologise for your stupidity. If we are lucky, we can salvage this.' It was the only hope George had.

'No.'

'I gave you an order.' George was visibly shocked. How dare Giorgio disobey him like this. He was the head of the Christos family, and as such, he deserved his nephew's respect.

'I said no, I'm not doing it. I love Rosita.'

'You've no loyalty, Giorgio. Your father would have been ashamed of you.'

Giorgio shrugged. 'My father never even knew me, and I didn't know him,' he said, beginning to walk away.

'If you walk away, then we will never accept that woman into our family,' George roared.

Shrugging again, Giorgio carried on regardless.

* * *

Freddie had been getting it in the neck to arrange another one of his parties. They were starting to become a bit too frequent for his liking. In the past, he'd been more than happy to put them on. He'd needed to keep his friends in high places happy. Only it wasn't them taking the majority of the risk. It was him who had to deal with everything. They even used his house.

Over the years, his friends had come in useful for some things, though. The fact that he'd never had his collar felt was proof of that. In fact, he was surprised no one had ever questioned why he'd had such a lack of police interest in him before. He had a feeling McKay had guessed, though. He had a nose like a copper. The constant questioning of his use of Matty was proof of that. Yes, McKay definitely suspected something wasn't right.

The truth was, the swerve he was given came from the very top, and obviously, that was something he didn't want to give up. Hosting his parties meant more than one blind eye had been turned over the years, and he wanted to keep it that way.

'Matty, I've got a job for you,' he growled into the phone. He could hear the boy's reluctance and screamed into the mouth-piece, 'Get your lazy fucking arse over to that estate, now.'

This boy and his attitude were starting to take its toll on him. Maybe it wouldn't be such a bad idea to get rid of him after all. He pondered it over. It wasn't as though anyone would miss him, other than his old gran, and she was a senile old bat as it was.

No, Matty's days were numbered. He'd had enough, what with him and Lee wearing him down, he needed to take action, and fast, before he ended up losing the plot.

16

Moray had never seen Danny laugh so hard. At one point, he'd been doubled over in stitches.

Callum was a funny fucker and you could always count on him to cheer everyone up. More often than not, he had a funny tale or two to tell. Whether they were real or a figment of his imagination, was anyone's guess.

'And so this fella is refusing to pay for the upkeep of the greyhound I was training for him. And I thought to myself, "Well, bollocks, I've had enough now." So, I drive up to the south of Dublin, a proper posh area like, and on the drive there, I'm feeding this dog as much as it can eat. Now, this dog is getting through cans of dog food like you wouldn't believe. I pull up outside the house, get the dog out of the car, and knock on the fella's door. This posh woman opens the door. "Can I help you?" she says, looking down her nose at me. You know the type... proper hoity toity. Anyways, there they are, having this fancy dinner party, and so I let the dog off the lead. The dog's jumping all over her, and she's screaming. Her husband comes running out to see what's going on. Well, he starts coughing and spluttering. "I'll pay the money, just take it away, take it away," he says. And I say to her, his wife, "It's all fecking yours, darlin', and by the way, the dog needs to take a shit." And as if on fecking cue, the dog squats and shits in their hallway on the Axminister rug, of all places, and what with the amount of food it's eaten, this dog is shitting for Ireland. Was proper funny, I can tell yer. I lost money, but it was worth it, just to see the look on their faces.'

Doubled up with laughter once again, the men were cracking up.

'You're a funny fucker,' Danny said, laughing.

'All true, Danny. On my life.'

Once they had all calmed down, Moray clapped his hands together. 'Come on, lads, let's get back to work.' He watched them leave, then grinned at Danny. 'He's a character, eh?'

'He's definitely funny. I needed that. I don't think I've laughed that hard in ages.'

Moray smiled. 'Right, I'm gonna shoot off. Make sure you ring me if anything happens on the doors.'

'I will do. Now, go on, piss off and enjoy your date, and don't do anything I wouldn't do.'

Raising his eyebrows, Moray grinned. 'That's not going to leave me much I can't do then, is it?'

'Oi, sod off.' Danny laughed. 'I'm not that bad,' he shouted out to Moray's retreating back.

'If you say so, Danny, if you say so,' Moray shouted back.

With a smile across his face, Danny shook his head. He was hoping tonight was going to be a quiet one. There had been more than enough drama over the past few months.

* * *

'Dad's gonna kill us.' Moray Garner's youngest son, Colm, said to his elder brother, Aaron.

'What Dad doesn't know won't hurt him, and if we keep this schtum and between us, then he's not even gonna find out, is he?'

Peering down into a plastic carrier bag full of white pills, Colm was hesitant. 'You know what he's like with drugs. He's gonna go fucking mental. Where did you even get them from?'

'Some geezer down The Spotted Dog. Lee something or other, and these little pills, Colm, are gonna make us a fortune. We can pop 'em out for two quid a pill. You do the math. That's a lot of fucking cash in this bag, bruv.'

Colm narrowed his eyes. 'Where did you get the money from to buy this lot? You didn't pinch it from Dad, did you?'

'Course I fucking didn't. I haven't paid for them yet. They're on tic. Once we've sold them, then we give the geezer the money.'

'Sounds dodgy to me. Why would some random bloke in a pub give you a bag of pills?'

'You worry too much, little brother,' Aaron said, slinging his arm across his brother's shoulders. 'Trust me, we're gonna be raking it in.'

Colm Garner couldn't help but worry. Their dad was going to kill them stone dead, if he ever found out they were dishing out pills in the clubs.

* * *

Sophie Nolan was fast on her way to falling in love. She slipped her hand into Moray's as they made their way inside the little French restaurant where they'd had their first date. The restaurant was fast becoming one of their favourite places to eat out. Sophie smiled up at Moray as they were shown to a table.

Once seated, she reached over and clasped his hand, her thumb softly caressing his palm.

'I was thinking... maybe you could come down to the club one night. I want you to meet my boys. They're going to love you.'

'I would love that.' Thrilled, Sophie smiled widely. She couldn't wait to meet Moray's sons. He spoke so highly of them, and she knew he was proud of his two boys. She could tell by the way his eyes twinkled whenever they came up in conversation.

'Not forgetting, you can meet Danny properly. Him laid out on a hospital bed doesn't really count, does it?'

'No, not really,' Sophie laughed. 'Just don't mention I had to give him a bed bath. I wouldn't want to see him blushing.'

'Ah no, that's the best bit. I have to tell him that.'

Playfully, Sophie slapped Moray's hand. 'No, don't you dare. Save me from blushing instead, then, and keep quiet about it.'

'Ah, go on then. You've convinced me. I don't want to see my girl blush.'

'Your girl?' Sophie arched her eyebrows. There was a twinkle in her blue eyes.

'Well, that's what you are, aren't you?' he asked, giving her hand a squeeze.

Sophie nodded. A wide smile was spread across her face. 'Of course I am,' she said gently. She could feel her stomach do a little somersault. It was too late... she'd already fallen in love.

* * *

Tracey Underwood snatched the money out of Matty's hand. There was enough there to feed her kids for a month, not that they would see a penny of it. The whole lot would be gone within days. The majority of it spent on crack cocaine, the rest, on cheap cider, cannabis and cigarettes.

'This is the third time this month you've took 'em. Looks like you've taken a shine to my kids.'

'I don't touch them. I'm not like that.' Matty could feel the disgust rise up inside of him, and he quickly swallowed the accusation down. He was telling the truth; he would never do anything to harm them.

Narrowing her eyes, Tracey squinted at the lad in front of her. 'So, what do you take them for?'

'It doesn't matter why I take them, and if you had any sense, you wouldn't ask that question.'

'Okay, keep your bleedin' hair on. I was only asking, making conversation, like.' Tracey tilted her head to the side and pointed her finger towards him. 'You're Barry's boy, aren't you? I thought I recognised you from the off.'

Matty's cheeks blushed at the mere mention of his father's name. He hated his old man, almost as much as he hated Freddie. 'No, I'm not. Are the kids ready yet? I need to get going.'

'Hmm, I could have sworn you were. I knew you when you were a little nipper. Don't you remember me? I used to come up to your dad's flat and have a smoke with him.'

'I've already told you, I'm not Barry's kid, and I really need to go now.' If he was late, Freddie would have his guts for garters, and that was the last thing he needed.

Tracey shrugged. 'Ah well, you look like Barry's boy, my mistake.' She gave a high-pitched cackle, her open mouth showing what was left of her decaying, nicotine-stained teeth. 'I bet a lot of people around here say that to you, don't they?'

'No, not really.' Matty was getting fed up. 'Look, either get the kids now, or I want the money back.'

The thought of the money being taken from her spurred Tracey into action, and she ran into the bathroom to hurry the boys along.

Pushing his hands into his jeans pockets, Matty leant against the wall whilst he waited. She'd unnerved him by mentioning his dad. He hadn't seen the man in years, but he could still feel his hands on him.

He bit down hard on his lip. He used to do the same thing when he was a little boy, to stop himself from crying out loud, whenever his dad took his belt to him. He'd learnt from an early age to focus on biting his lip, rather than make any noise. He hadn't wanted to give his dad a reason to become even more angry with him, or to give him any more of an excuse to hurt him. Matty could taste the blood inside his mouth, and he wiped the back of his hand across his lips.

'All ready.' Tracey smiled, dragging two solemn little boys behind her. 'Don't forget to have them back by twelve, otherwise the little bastards won't get up for school.'

Matty looked down at their sad little faces. They reminded him of himself, when he was the same age. He'd had the same solemn expression. He took their tiny hands in his, and gave them a little squeeze. He always did that. He'd told them that he did it because he understood how they were feeling, and he really did. He was them once.

'You make sure you behave yourselves, otherwise, I'll bloody well slap the skin off your arses,' Tracey called out after them, before slamming the front door shut. Instantly, her two little boys were gone from her mind. Her only thoughts were on where she could score. The money was already burning a hole in her pocket.

Walking across the landing towards the lift, Matty's heart was breaking. He didn't want to take them to Freddie's party. Every single ounce of his being wanted to scream out at how wrong it was. They should have been tucked up in bed, not traipsing across London where unimaginable horror awaited them.

He adjusted their little coats. The thin material would offer no protection from the bitter cold wind and rain. He stopped and looked back towards Tracey's front door. He was in half a mind to knock there and see if they had hats, gloves and scarves they could put on. Instinctively, he knew they wouldn't. Tracey wasn't the type of parent who would have seen buying her kids thick coats for protection against the winter elements as a necessity. How could people like Tracey and his dad even call themselves parents?

He swiped away the tears that had begun to glisten his eyes, before they slipped down his cheeks. The unfairness of their lives made him want to cry. More than anything, he didn't want the boys to see him upset. He didn't want to scare them.

'Don't cry, Matty,' Sam, the eldest of the two boys, said, his brown eyes wide with innocence. 'We'll be okay. We've got you to look after us, haven't we, Jack?' Jack nodded. They liked Matty. He was always nice to them. Much nicer than their mum was.

Matty sobbed harder. Sam's words broke his heart into a million little pieces. When he felt their arms go around him, he pulled them closer. He only wished he had enough money, so they could run away. He would give anything to be able to jump on a train with the two boys, to get as far away as they possibly could, from the horrors of a parent who didn't care about what happened to them.

All three of them were victims. They'd been let down by the one system that should have been protecting them. If they did run away, then wherever they ended up, Matty would make sure the boys were looked after. No one would ever hurt them, not with him around to protect them. One day, they would really do it, he vowed. They had to. He'd already promised the boys they would.

* * *

Lee Hart couldn't resist sneaking into the club to watch Moray Garner's two sons as they worked. He'd supplied the pills to one of them earlier that day, when he'd been in The Spotted Dog in Barking. He'd told the lad he was a supplier with connections in Amsterdam, and that there was plenty more where they came from. Aaron, he'd said his name was, cocky little bastard he was and all, just like his father had been at the same age.

He drank deeply from his pint of lager, watching both boys over the rim of his glass. From his position, he could see everything that went on, and his beady little eyes missed nothing.

In actual fact, he couldn't believe how easily the boy had fallen for it. They say money talks, and he'd grabbed the boy's attention by telling him how much profit there was to be made from the little white pills. Of course, the boy didn't have that kind of cash to hand, so Lee kindly let him have them on tic. For anyone with a bit of savvy, that would have rung alarm bells, but not this little prick. All he was thinking about was the easy cash.

Lee kicked his legs out in front of him, making himself comfortable. Moray Garner's cozy little world was about to shatter into pieces, right in front of his very eyes. He put his head down as he sniggered. He didn't want to draw attention to himself. It was just a shame he wouldn't be there to see Garner's face when it happened. That really would have been the icing on the cake.

* * *

Sipping on a mug of coffee, Ronnie Dellow stifled a yawn. This case had him working flat out. He couldn't make head nor tale of it. Not one iota of it made sense. Why would a respectable law student end up murdered and half buried on a scrap of wasteland?

There was no forensic evidence at all, not even a damn finger-print, no eye witnesses, and no leads. Whoever was responsible obviously knew what they were doing.

Ronnie rubbed at his tired eyes. It was time to call it a night. Glancing across to Josie, he spoke. 'How are you getting on with the shooting? Have you dug anything up? Any connection to our victim?'

'Not that I can tell, Gov,' she said and gave him a quick rundown. 'Lewis Hart, brought up in care, shunted from one foster home to another, was released from the local authority at age sixteen. That's where the trail goes cold.'

'What was he in care for?'

'Neglect, physical abuse, the list goes on. Mother was a crack addict, now deceased, OD'd.'

'Father?'

'I'm still trying to track him down. There's no mention of him in the social services reports.'

Ronnie sighed. 'Poor kid didn't stand a chance, did he? Come on, time to head home. Enough for tonight.'

'Nope, he really didn't stand a chance.' Josie felt sorry for the boy. Kids like Lewis were the hardest cases for her to deal with. She would never say it out loud, what with all of the political correctness and human rights activists out there, but if it was left to her, anyone who harmed a child would be lined up against the wall and shot. She grabbed her coat. 'See you in the morning, Gov. Night.'

'Night.' Ronnie took one last glance at his computer screen before switching it off. He couldn't shrug off the feeling that there was so much more to this case than met the eye. As of tomorrow, he would start again, and go right back to the beginning and piece everything together. There was more to come. He could feel it in his bones, and his hunches had never let him down before.

* * *

'See, what did I tell you? We're fucking raking it in.' Aaron was grinning like a Cheshire cat. They'd made almost five hundred quid in one night. If they carried on at this rate, then by the end of the week they would have made thousands.

They were sitting in Aaron's car, and Colm watched as his brother counted out the cash. 'What if it's all on camera, though? You do realise there's CCTV in there, don't you?'

'And you know Dad's not going to sift through hours of CCTV, is he? He'd have no reason to. When have you ever known him to do that, eh? C'mon, stop putting a downer on it. We're fast on our way to becoming rich, bruv.'

'I think you should give the bloke the money from what we've already sold, and then give him back the rest of the pills. I'm telling you, Aaron, there's something fishy about all of this.' Colm couldn't shake off the feeling that all of this was dodgy, and he didn't mean the illegal side of selling drugs. The fact that his brother had got the pills off some random geezer in a pub didn't sit right with him. What was that saying their dad had always said to them when they were young? Oh yeah, that was it. 'Trust no one. Even the devil himself was an angel once.'

Blinded by the cash he was looking to earn, Aaron ignored his brother. Colm had always been cautious. It was in his nature. He took after their mum in that respect. She always found a negative in everything, too. Even if he won the lottery, she would find something bad to say about it. He could hear her voice now: 'It's too much money, Aaron. It'll turn your head.' He wanted his head turned, though. That was the problem. He wanted respect, and he wanted people to come to him to buy their drugs. He wanted a reputation of his own, rather than just being Moray Garner's son.

'Aaron, are you even listening to me? We should give the pills back.'

Aaron punched his brother on the arm. 'I'm keeping them. You're either with me or against me, Colm, but when I get rich and you're still working the doors for Dad, earning peanuts, don't come running to me. It'll be too late.'

Colm sighed. 'I'm with you, bruv. I just don't like it, that's all.'

'You don't have to like it. You just have to like all of that lovely dough we're gonna make.' Aaron grinned.

* * *

'They're taking the fucking piss now.' Moray was furious. 'That's the third attempted takeover this week. How many more are we going to let slide, before we take action?'

'We can't take action. We're stretched as it is. Where are we meant to get the muscle from? If we take them from the doors, then we're leaving the venues wide open. It's a vicious circle, Moray. We either just keep fighting them off, or we recruit more men, and that actually is something I was meant to talk to you about. One of Freddie's men came to me looking for work. He's getting on in years, but still handy. So he was hoping we might have something a bit quieter for him. I was thinking of The Golden Goose in Stratford. You know the lads always complain if we send them there.'

'Can you trust him?' Danny was right, every man on their payroll was accounted for. Maybe it was time they recruited a few more heavies, and have them floating around the venues, in case of trouble.

'Yeah, I trust him.'

'Okay, well send him to The Golden Goose then. That'll save a few arguments when we allocate the doors.'

'I'll give him a call tomorrow and let him know when to start.'

'You know this George Christos, don't you?' Moray asked, changing the subject.

'I've dealt with him, yeah,' Danny said, sitting forward in his seat. 'I arranged the meeting between him and Freddie. Why, what are you thinking?'

'I'm wondering if it's worth us arranging a meeting with him.' Now that they were pretty certain Lee wasn't going to talk, Moray could see no risk in them meeting with George Christos.

Danny blew out his cheeks and flopped backwards in his seat. 'It took a lot of negotiating to get him to agree to that meeting. He's hard to get close to. You have to go through his brother first.'

'But it's a possibility. He might agree to meet us.'

'Maybe. I couldn't really say, mate. At the end of the day, there's a lot of history between him and Freddie. I think that's what swayed him in the end,' Danny answered as he rubbed his hand across his jaw.

Moray thought through Danny's words. 'In Christos's eyes, he might think of it as having a lot of history with you, too, then. You stayed with Freddie's firm for a lot of years after I left. He would see you as being one of Freddie's lot still, wouldn't he? More so than he would me?'

'Maybe.'

'What we need, is something we can barter with.' Moray chewed on the inside of his cheek as he tried to think of something, anything, they could use to get George Christos to meet with them.

'I think I might actually have something we can use as a bargaining tool. There's some information I know of that would be of interest to them.' Danny was pretty certain the information he had regarding Nico would get their attention. The problem he had, was if he would be able disclose it without bringing risk to himself. If he knew the Greeks as well as he thought he did, then he had a feeling Christos would snap up the chance to hear what he had to say. He knew if he were in their shoes, then he would. 'We need to get that meeting first. That's gonna be the tricky part. As I said, he's hard to get close to.'

'Can I leave it with you then, to arrange a meeting with just you, me and Christos present?'

'I'll do my best, mate.' Danny wasn't particularly hopeful. Christos rarely travelled anywhere alone.

* * *

'We have them worried.' George Christos grinned widely. 'Your plan has obviously unnerved them, Alexandros. Well done for thinking it up.'

Alexandros took the compliment. It was rare for George to hand out any form of praise. 'So, what shall I tell him?'

'Tell him no, there will be no meeting. The doors are not negotiable. For Adam and Nico, we will take them over.'

'Maybe we should hear them out and listen to what they have to say. McKay said he has information that would be of particular interest to us,' Alexandros answered wearily.

He was tired and growing older. All he wanted was a quiet life. He and his wife had even talked about returning home to Greece to retire. He wanted to grow lemons and to feel the sun on his back once again. In fact, he'd already decided, once they had their revenge for his brother's and nephew's deaths, then he would sell up and leave England.

'This was your plan. Are you having doubts that we can't pull it off?' George eyed his brother suspiciously.

Alexandros shook his head. 'I'm going home, George. I want all of this tied up, so I'm free to leave. Enough blood has been spilt... Adam, Nico, both of them dead. They would still be here, if we hadn't wanted to make our family the most feared in London.'

'We have waited over twenty years for this day to come, and now you want to leave?' George was astounded.

'Twenty years ago, we were younger, stronger and full of hate for Freddie Smith and his firm. Now, we are old, George. Look how your own health has suffered. Let us put it to rest. Arrange the meeting, and negotiate for our family to live in peace. We've already lost Giorgio by forcing him to do things he didn't want to do. And he lost a father and cousin, because of this war. Our sister lost a son. Don't allow them to lose anyone else because of us and our need for power.'

'But...'

'Do the right thing,' Alexandros urged. 'Swallow your pride, brother, and let me go home, knowing we did the right thing for our family.'

George reluctantly nodded. He knew if he didn't agree, then he would lose his last remaining brother, and Alexandros was right. His own health was suffering. Still, the panic attacks plagued him. He had a feeling they always would. 'Arrange the meeting then, and we will put our affairs to bed.'

* * *

Matty was in a lot of trouble. Freddie was definitely going to kill him over this. Instead of taking the boys to Freddie's house, Matty had hid with them in McDonald's. Sitting in a corner booth, out of sight from the main doors, he'd fed the boys cheeseburgers, fries and strawberry milkshakes. To see their little faces light up at their first trip to the fast food restaurant had made the trouble he was in now, worthwhile.

He'd taken the boys home, just before midnight, satisfied that their little bellies were full for once. They'd even made him laugh by referring to the restaurant as Donald's, instead of its full name, and had told him it was the best night they'd ever had. He recalled smiling sadly when they had said that. The fact that hiding out with him, eating burgers, was one of their happiest memories, said a lot about their home life with Tracey.

He'd then crept around to his gran's house and let himself in through the dodgy bathroom window. He'd been on at his gran for months to get onto the council to get the latch fixed. Luckily for him, she must have forgotten. He'd needed somewhere to kip, and he knew without a doubt, he couldn't go to his own home. That was the first place Freddie would have gone to search for him.

He'd resigned himself to the fact that he was going to die. In fact, he'd known this day had been coming for a long time. That afternoon, he'd said goodbye to his gran. He'd hugged her tight, knowing this was the last time he would ever see her. His gran had been the only woman who'd ever been kind to him, and for that alone, he loved her.

He stood outside The Hope public house, just waiting. He knew it wouldn't take Freddie long to find him. And he wouldn't run away, not this time. He was going to stop being a coward. He was going to do what he should have done a long time ago. He was going to break away from Freddie and his firm. In fact, death would be a welcome release for him – a release from all of the pain and torment he'd suffered in his short life.

He had just one last thing to say to the man he despised, and that was, if he chose to kill him, then he would never find out who it really was, who'd tried to shoot and kill him, that fateful day in Christos's restaurant. No matter what Freddie did to him – and he knew, instinctively, it would be harsh and painful – he would take the secret to his grave.

He was going to leave the ball in Freddie's court. If he let him live and get away, then he would tell him who was responsible for the shooting. Or he could choose to kill him, and then he would never know.

17

Sophie Nolan was excited. She'd taken extra care with her outfit for this evening. She needed to make a good impression with Moray's sons, not to mention his best mate, Danny.

They were going to Ritzy's Nightclub for the evening, and Moray had told her that the VIP section was exclusively theirs for the night. His boys would be working, though, so she would only see them at fleeting intervals, but Danny had the night off. She couldn't help but feel a little nervous, too. What if they didn't like her? Even though Moray had told her they would all love her, she couldn't help but feel worried. Tonight was a big night for them as a couple. It could make or break their relationship.

She sprayed a light mist of perfume over her. It was an expensive fragrance and Moray had bought it for her as a gift. She knew he loved the scent as much as she did. She had butterflies in her tummy. Just be you, she told herself, as she studied her reflection in the mirror. Other than that, there really wasn't much else she could do.

* * *

Moray had warned Danny, over and over, to be on his best behaviour. In the end, Danny had felt like a little kid about to go and meet the queen.

'I'm gonna behave. Stop worrying.' Danny laughed. 'I'll even bow down to her, and keep schtum the whole night, if that'll stop you from worrying.'

'See, you're already starting.'

'What have I done now?' Danny couldn't help but grin. This woman had obviously got underneath Moray's skin.

'Just be yourself, but a nice, calm, friendly and polite version of yourself.'

'Give over, Moray, fucking hell. What do you take me for? And before you even say it, I'll mind my language in front of her, too.' There was a hint of humour in his voice, and Moray couldn't help but laugh along.

'Sorry, mate. I just want this to be perfect for her, that's all.'

'It will be, so stop your worrying. Go and pick her up, and I'll meet you back here about ten.'

'Yeah, you're right,' Moray answered as he searched around his desk for his car keys.

Danny lifted up a stack of paperwork and scooped up the keys. 'Here, go on, go,' he said, handing them over to Moray.

As he watched Moray walk out of the office, Danny couldn't help but smile. It looked as though his mate was in love, after all.

* * *

Danny wasn't the only one to have had a warning to be on their best behaviour. Aaron and Colm had been told the exact same thing. This was the first time their dad had introduced a woman to them, so they knew it must be serious.

'I wonder what she's like?' Colm pondered as he adjusted his black tie in preparation for the night's work ahead of them.

Aaron shrugged. 'Gawd knows.' If he was being honest, he couldn't give a toss what she was or wasn't like. 'It won't last,' he stated. 'Come on, let's face it. This is Dad we're talking about. All he's interested in is the clubs, and always has been. Why'd you think Mum left him?'

Colm ignored his brother. Unlike Aaron, he was close to their dad, always had been. 'Well, I'm happy for him. He deserves to have someone in his life.'

'Here, take these.' Aaron handed over a fistful of white pills. 'Stick 'em in your pockets, and remember, they're two quid each.'

'Are you mad? We can't deal 'em out right underneath Dad's nose.'

'Dad's gonna be too busy with his tart. He won't even notice what we're getting up to.'

'And what about Danny? You know he doesn't miss a trick. He's got eyes like a bleedin' hawk.'

'Just bloody do it, Colm. Jeez it's like having a fucking baby tied around my neck. When no one's looking, just dish 'em out. It's not rocket science.' He was losing patience with his brother. He knew he should have kept quiet about the pills, instead of bringing Colm on board.

Colm pushed the pills deep into his pockets. He wasn't happy about it, but at the same time, he didn't want to fall out with his brother. 'Okay, keep your bloody hair on. I'll do it.'

* * *

Moray picked Sophie up just after nine. On the short drive to the club, he kept squeezing her hand. Sophie wasn't sure if the reassurance was for her benefit, or his own. She could tell he was just as nervous as she was. He hardly said two words to her in the car, and when he did speak, he became tongue-tied, making her laugh.

'Anyone would think we were fifteen and I'm about to meet your parents for the first time.' Moray laughed as they climbed out of the car outside the club. 'I'm that nervous.'

'So this is how you're going to be when you actually do meet my mum and dad, is it?' Sophie answered, laughing.

'Don't.' Moray broke out in a cold sweat just thinking about it. He pulled Sophie into his arms and kissed her on the lips. 'Are you ready?'

Taking a deep breath, Sophie looked across to the club and nodded. 'As I'll ever be.' She slipped her hand into his and held on tight as they walked across the car park towards the club.

'That's one of my boys there. Aaron, my eldest,' Moray said, pointing out a dark-haired young man stood at the doors. The likeness between father and son was uncanny, except the boy's skin tone, which was a lighter shade than Moray's brown skin.

'He's a handsome boy.'

'Of course he is. He takes after me.'

Playfully, Sophie nudged him. 'That head of yours is going to get bigger and bigger.' She laughed. She could tell Moray was trying to ease her nerves, and it was working. She felt more relaxed.

After the introductions, Moray guided Sophie into the club. He placed his hand gently on the small of her back as they walked towards the VIP section, pointing out who the members of staff were.

'And this here, for my sins, is my best mate, Danny. He probably looks a bit different to when you last saw him.'

Danny pulled Sophie into a bear hug and kissed her cheek. 'Nice to finally meet you. Moray's talked a lot about you.'

'All good, I hope,' she answered, laughing.

'Of course all good.' Moray winked, placing his arm around her waist and pulling her towards him.

'I've ordered champagne, so let's celebrate and have a good night.' Danny grinned as he popped the cork.

Sipping her champagne, Sophie looked around her, before smiling across to Moray. She felt as though a whole new world had opened up to her, and she couldn't believe how lucky she was to have this man in her life.

* * *

Aaron spotted them before they'd even climbed out of their cars. They weren't exactly inconspicuous, for a start, the flashing blue lights were a dead giveaway. 'Shit,' he muttered. Immediately, his thoughts went to the little white pills he'd stuffed into his pockets earlier that night.

He could feel the colour drain from his face and the hairs on the back of his neck stand up on end. He didn't know what to do for the best. He couldn't exactly tip the pills out of his pockets. He was bound to be caught trying to get rid of the evidence. In a blind panic, he ran inside the club. He had to warn Colm. They would need to get rid of their stash, chuck the bloody lot down the toilet and flush them away, if need be.

Weaving in and out of the revellers on the dance floor, he looked around him. Where the fuck was his brother?

'Aaron, come over here.'

Aaron turned towards his dad as he called out to him from the VIP section.

'Come and have a glass of bubbly with your old man,' he grinned, raising his glass in the air.

'I will later on.' He had to find his brother first. He could feel his heart in his mouth as a cold sweat broke out across his fore-head. He and Colm were both in deep shit.

Hearing a commotion coming from behind him, Aaron turned to look. He already knew what he was going to see, and he felt sick to his stomach. Police officers swarmed inside the club. They were being raided. He slipped his hand inside his trousers pocket. He could feel the pills. He was in half a mind to tip them out all over the dance floor. It had to be better than being caught red-handed with them. This was all his fault. He shouldn't have been so fucking greedy.

* * *

Moray was stunned. He looked across to Danny and saw the same surprise etched across his face. He knew they had nothing to worry about. The club's anti-drugs policy ensured him of that. Anyone found dealing or using, was thrown out immediately. It simply wasn't tolerated.

The club was in chaos as the Old Bill rounded up the customers to begin their searches.

'I'll deal with this,' Moray said confidently. Other than one or two stragglers who may have made it through the doors carrying, he knew the police would find nothing. 'Won't be long, darling.' He smiled to Sophie. 'Danny will look after you. The Old Bill will be in and out within minutes.'

He gulped down the remainder of his champagne, then began to make his way down the short few steps from the VIP section. He reached the bottom in time to watch Aaron being slammed to the floor. 'What the fuck is going on? That's my son you're manhandling. I'm in charge of the doors here, and I can assure you, no dealing goes on inside any of my clubs.'

'We've had a tip off your own security is dealing in here,' the officer replied as he began a thorough search of Aaron.

'No, we have a strict anti-drugs policy in here. There's been a mistake.' If the situation hadn't been so serious, Moray would have laughed out loud. No fucking way. His boy had nothing to do with drugs, he was certain of that. He'd drummed it into both of his sons, from an early age, to stay away from them.

'We're also going to need your CCTV footage. So if you don't mind, can you show an officer where it's kept?' the officer asked.

Moray watched in disbelief as Colm was then brought out. His hands were behind his back in handcuffs. He searched his boy's face, hoping against all hope, to see his innocence there.

'I'm sorry, Dad.'

As his boy looked down at the floor, averting his eyes, all Moray could see was his guilt. Immediately, his eyes darted to the polythene bag held in the hand of the police officer escorting his son. The bag was full of pills. In denial, he shook his head. No way, he would never believe it. The dirty bastards must have planted them on his boy. His Colm would never do something like this.

He was about to open his mouth, to hurl out a torrent of abuse, when Aaron's pockets were emptied out. In despair, he watched as hundreds of pills spilled out. If he hadn't of seen it with his own two eyes, he would never have believed his sons were capable of such a thing.

Bringing his hands up to his head, Moray felt as though his world had shattered into pieces. He wasn't gullible. He knew both of his sons would go down for this. They were looking at serious bird. How could they have been so fucking stupid, to think they could get away with dealing in the clubs? He had to fight the urge to not barge the Old Bill out of the way and batter his sons to within an inch of their sorry lives, for their stupidity.

He felt Danny's hand grip hold of his shoulder. 'Get yourself down to the nick, mate. I'll get on the phone to our brief, and tell him to meet you down there. We'll get this sorted out. Don't worry.'

Moray turned to look behind him. He could see in his mate's eyes, he already knew the outcome, just as he himself did. His sons had been caught bang to rights. No matter how good their brief was, the boys were not going to get off with this. In fact, they were going to go down for a very long time.

* * *

'The stupid fucking bastards, they've ruined their whole fucking lives, and for what? Fucking greed?'

Danny remained silent, letting Moray get it out of his system. They were in Moray's house, and he'd already destroyed the lounge. Coffee tables and sofas were overturned, and the television set had been thrown against the wall, in a fit of rage.

'They're my boys. What am I meant to do? They must have been dealing, right underneath my fucking nose. How did I not know what they were doing? I should have watched them more closely. I should have kept them separated.'

'You can't blame yourself, mate. And you can't do anything to change what they've already done. Not only were they caught in possession of supplying, the whole fucking thing is on camera.' Danny blew out his cheeks. He was still in shock himself. He was close to Moray's sons, and was gutted for them. They were only young, nineteen and eighteen. Now, it looked as though they would spend the best part of their lives locked up.

'I need to speak to them. I need to know where they got the pills from.'

'They're not going to let you in to see them, you know that. The brief will have to get it out of them on the quiet.'

Overwhelmed, Moray sank into a chair. He placed his head in his hands and sobbed.

Danny hadn't seen his mate cry since the night he'd disclosed the abuse Adam Christos was subjecting him to. There and then his heart went out to him, and moving closer, he sat on the arm of the chair. 'I'll get the brief to find out the score, and then when we find out who it is, we'll make them pay the fucking price.'

Wiping away his tears, Moray nodded. Now that he'd cried, he wouldn't shed another tear. He was gunning for blood, and he wouldn't stop until enough blood had been spilt to satisfy his anger. 'Find out who it was who supplied those fucking pills, and then I'm going to tear the bastard apart with my own bare fucking hands.'

Danny didn't disbelieve Moray for a second. He had a feeling his mate could very well end up sitting in the cell next to his boys, if he wasn't careful.

* * *

Aaron Garner had spent the best part of twenty minutes crying. How could he have been so stupid? The coppers had taken everything from him, even his shoelaces. He sat gingerly on the edge of what was meant to be a bed. The thin layer of foam acting as a mattress, offered no comfort. He and Colm were going to go to prison. He knew they were, and it was all his fault.

He wished he could talk to Colm. He was bound to be terrified. He hated confined spaces, always had done, ever since they were kids. He could still recall the good hiding he'd got off his dad, when he was young, all because he'd locked Colm in the wardrobe, causing his brother to hyperventilate and pass out.

His brother hadn't even wanted to sell the pills. He'd only gone along with it to keep him happy. Colm had always followed his lead. Ever since they were little kids, he'd followed him around like a puppy, copying everything he did.

He would take full responsibility. When they came to question him, he would tell the coppers that Colm had wanted nothing to do with it. He doubted it would help his little brother out, but he had to try, he decided.

He wanted to speak to his dad. Maybe his dad's brief would be able to get Colm off, if he explained everything. Aaron stood up and walked towards the cell door. He banged his fist on the metal grill. 'Oi, I'm entitled to a phone call.'

He received no reply. In all honesty, he hadn't even expected one.

18

As he'd predicted, Matty didn't have to wait long for Freddie to find him. He didn't run away. He stood leaning against the wall of the pub, waiting for the big man to hurl him inside the car.

'You little bastard, you're gonna pay for this. Think you can fucking show me up, do you? Think you can disobey my orders?' So tangible was Freddie's anger that spittle formed at the corners of his snarled lips. Matty had embarrassed him by not turning up with the boys. He'd had to apologise profusely to his friends for ruining their night, and causing disappointment.

Matty didn't resist as he was thrown onto the back seat of the car. He dragged himself into a sitting position and stared out of the window.

'We'll gut you like a fish for this and leave you to hang on a fucking hook. I've done it before, and I'll do it again.'

Matty ignored Lee's words. He knew for a fact that he'd never killed anyone before. He'd heard him tell Freddie exactly who it was who'd carried out the murder, and it definitely wasn't Lee.

The short drive to Hainault seemed to go on forever, and still, Matty didn't speak, not even when Freddie punched him in the side of his head. He bit down on his lip, blocking everything out, and continued staring out of the window at the passing blur of oncoming traffic.

They didn't even need to drag him into Freddie's house. He walked in freely, wanting to get the inevitable over with as quickly as possible.

The beating that followed was immediate. He let his body go limp, knowing it wouldn't hurt as much as it would have, if he'd tensed his muscles. Within minutes, he could barely see out of his left eye. It was swollen and bruised. The heavy ring on Freddie's pinkie finger had ripped open the skin below his eyebrow. Still, he didn't make a sound.

'You should cut him up, Fred. He's embarrassed you in front of your friends. You can't let him get away with that.'

Matty could hear the excitement in Lee's voice. He was a vicious, spiteful bastard, and he was glad Lewis had never got the chance to meet him. His mind wandered to his friend now. He hoped when they finally did end his life, he would get to see Lewis. That was if heaven was even real and not some make-believe story. He hoped it was real. He wanted to see his mate.

After punching the lad one last time, Freddie walked through to the kitchen. He grabbed a knife from the utensils drawer. 'I should have finished you off months ago, boy. You've been nothing but an albatross hanging from around my neck since the day I fucking met you,' he wheezed, pointing the blade towards Matty.

'I know who tried to kill you.' Finally, Matty spoke, stopping Freddie dead in his tracks.

'He's lying. He knows fuck all, Fred.'

Freddie held up his hand, cutting Lee off.

'If you kill me, then you'll never know who it was.'

Matty could see Freddie thinking it over. He was eyeing him suspiciously, his mind weighing up if he was telling the truth or not. 'Who tried to kill me?' His voice was low, menacing. 'Who was it?'

Matty pulled himself into a sitting position. His whole body hurt and his stomach muscles felt like they were on fire.

'I asked you a fucking question. Who tried to kill me?'

Easing himself to his feet, Matty grabbed onto the back of a chair for support as he steadied himself. He needed to be able to put one foot in front of the other, before he spoke, before he uttered the words out loud... before he told Freddie who it was who'd tried to kill him.

'Don't play fucking games with me. Who was it?'

'Just kill him, Fred. Get it over with. He's not going to tell you.'

Matty blocked out the pain. He was an expert at doing that. He'd been doing it all his life. From the corner of his eye, he could see the front door. He would have just a split second to make a run for it. He bent his knees, testing his legs were strong enough, capable.

He watched as Freddie took a step towards him. He didn't take his eyes off the man. The knife was in his fist. The glint of steel danced across the wall behind him, as Freddie prepared to thrust the blade forward. Matty had to time this just right, to catch Freddie off guard with the words he was about to speak. More than anything, he needed to shock him enough to make him hesitate, just long enough for him to have the chance to dart away.

'Kill him, Fred.'

He looked Freddie in the eye. He wasn't scared of him any more. There was nothing left that Freddie could do to hurt him that he'd not already done. He welcomed death, only not today, not yet. There was something he needed to do first. 'It was Danny McKay.' He then bolted towards the front door. He fumbled with the door handle, before flinging it open, then ran as fast as his legs could carry him. He could hear Freddie screaming behind him, but he didn't stop, he didn't look back. He kept on running.

* * *

Josie Morgan held a sheet of paper aloft in her hand. 'Gov, I've got something.'

Ronnie got up from his seat and walked over to where Josie was sitting at her desk.

'Look, I've found a social services report, dating back to when Lewis Hart was born. He'd been placed under child protection from birth.'

Ronnie peered at the sheet of paper.

'Look at the father's name, a Lee Hart. I've checked him out and he was released from Belmarsh prison a couple of months ago.'

Josie now had his full attention. 'What was he in for?'

'You're not going to believe this. He served life for the murder of Adam Christos, the uncle of our victim.'

Ronnie could feel his heart begin to beat wildly inside his chest. 'So, this Lee Hart murdered Adam Christos, then Lewis Hart, the son of said Lee, was shot and killed in the restaurant owned by the Christos family? And now Nico Kallas, nephew of Adam Christos, is found murdered. Am I getting this right?'

Josie nodded. 'It's a revenge killing, Gov. You kill one of mine, I'll kill one of yours, type of thing. It's got to be.'

Ronnie punched his fist in the air. 'I knew it! I knew there was more to this case than met the eye. Right, everyone,' he shouted out. 'Lee Hart has just become our number one suspect. He needs to be found, and I need to have a serious word with him. In fact, the first person to find out his whereabouts, gets a drink, on me.'

* * *

Danny slammed down the phone. He'd just ended a call to their brief, and as a result, he was fuming. 'Lee fucking Hart. It was him who gave the pills to Aaron.'

Moray's eyes were wide. 'So the bastard sold my boy the pills, then tipped off the Old Bill?'

'Yep, that cunt is a fucking snake in the grass, mate. I told you we should have left him hanging from a hook.'

Moray could taste his anger, so palpable was his fury. 'The dirty, no good bastard.' He grabbed up his car keys. 'I don't care if I go down for this. That wanker is finished.'

Danny didn't need telling twice. He already knew Moray would kill him. He quickly punched a number into his phone, then brought it up to his ear. If anyone could find the bastard, it would be the Carter brothers. He and Moray were going to need all the help they could get in locating him. Lee Hart's days were numbered.

* * *

All of the Carter boys had gathered at Tommy's home in Epping, Essex. Tommy shook Danny's and Moray's hands, as he ushered them inside. 'Jonny, pour out the drinks,' he ordered as he led the two men into the lounge.

He had a nice house, and was proud of it. His wife, Stacey, had excellent taste, and had decorated the place to a high standard. It was like a show home.

'Give me the low down.'

'That cunt Lee Hart, has set my two boys up. They're looking at doing a lump, and I want the bastard found and brought to me.'

The father of a daughter and two sons himself, Tommy could

feel Moray's pain. 'Finish up your drinks, and then get out and find this bastard. Make sure you're tooled up,' he told his brothers. He'd known Lee vaguely, when they'd been kids, and even then, he hadn't liked him. Everyone knew Lee couldn't be trusted, and that he had loose lips. 'We'll find him, Moray, don't you worry about that.'

'I want him alive.'

'Of course. You heard him, lads, make sure the bastard is alive. You can give him a couple of digs, but that's it, nothing more.'

* * *

'That fucking McKay. I knew it. I knew it was him, all along.' Freddie was furious. He stabbed the knife in the air as he spoke. 'I told you, you should have killed that fucker stone dead, instead of pissing around and leaving him still alive. Well, now you can get out there, find the bastard, and bring him to me.'

'Can't you get one of the other lads to find him?' Lee wiped at his clammy forehead. He didn't want to go out looking for Danny McKay. A coward through and through, he was scared of the man. He only liked intimidating the youngsters, such as Matty, and then, only because he knew they would be terrified by his reputation, all thanks to the murder he'd supposedly committed.

'No, I fucking can't.' He wasn't prepared to have his business interests known publicly. His firm was hanging by a fine thread as it was, and more than anything, he didn't want to lose face.

'What about Matty? What are you going to do with him? You can't let him get away with what he's done. He knows too much.'

'Don't you think I already know that? I'll find him. I've always found him before, and besides, he can't run forever.'

* * *

Moray was pumped up as they drove from Epping, towards Romford. Every muscle was straining. In his hand, he held a house brick. It was a makeshift tool, and the beauty of it was that no fingerprints could be taken from it.

For the past ten minutes, they'd been sitting in silence, each of them trying to think of where Lee Hart could be holed up.

'He has to be living local, if he uses the snooker club in Romford.'

'It's still a big area to cover though, mate. He could have travelled there from Barking, Dagenham, or any of the surrounding areas. He could even be living in Romford itself.' Danny flicked the switch on the indicator as they approached Hainault. They were in Freddie's neck of the woods. 'He could even be living with that bastard, Freddie. Do you want to swing by his place, and check he's not there?'

'Nah, I can't see him being there. He knows you know where Freddie lives. He'll be hiding out elsewhere.'

'Maybe.' Danny continued driving. He glanced towards Freddie's turn off anyway, just in case. 'I reckon it was him, who had me shot. I still think Freddie was involved in it somehow. But after what he's done to the boys, he's not gonna let me get off scot-free, is he?'

'I've been thinking the same thing. Well, I can tell you now, he's not gonna get away with this.' Moray gripped the brick tighter. He couldn't wait to smash it into Lee's face. In fact, the thought of what he was going to do to the slimy bastard was the only thing stopping him from going insane.

'Oi.' Danny pushed his foot down hard on the brake, causing Moray to throw his hand down on the dashboard to save himself from crashing head-first through the windscreen.

'Is it him?' Moray turned back in his seat, craning his neck to see why Danny had pulled the car over.

'No, but someone who'll know where he is.' Danny threw the seatbelt away from him and jumped out of the motor.

Matty was fast, but not as fast as Danny. He grabbed hold of Matty's jacket and dragged him back towards the car.

Climbing out of the motor, Moray looked the young lad over. He looked to be about the same age as his Colm. He could see from the blood and bruising on the lad's face, that someone had recently done him over. He looked towards Danny expectantly.

'One of Freddie's boys,' he stated to Moray. 'I want a fucking word with you, you little bastard, and I want you to tell me everything,' he growled, throwing Matty into the front passenger seat.

* * *

Matty was scared. His stomach lurched and he could feel his heart begin to pound inside his chest. He may not be scared of Freddie any more, but Danny McKay was a completely different kettle of fish. The story about the murder and the hook were still fresh in his mind, and as a result, he was terrified.

He'd always had a feeling it would be Danny who sussed out his secret about Freddie and the other men abusing him and countless other boys. That had to be the reason he'd grabbed hold of him. Maybe Freddie had even told Danny it was him who went out and collected the boys, knowing full well the man would kill him stone dead, saving Freddie the trouble of getting his own hands dirty.

He began to cry. Within seconds his cheeks were wet. Snot hung down from his nose in tendrils, and he swiped at it with the cuff of his sleeve as he tried to catch his breath between each sob. 'I'm sorry. I didn't want to do it! They made me. I never touch them, I'm not like that. Honest, I only go and pick the boys up. Please don't kill me. It's Freddie and the others who do it, not me.'

* * *

Danny stared hard at the boy. He had no idea what he was talking about. He watched through narrowed eyes as his small frame cowered beside him. He turned to look at Moray in the back seat, and saw the same confusion spread across his face.

'I promise, I don't touch them, on my life. It's Freddie who does it, not me.'

'What the fuck is this?' Moray glanced towards Danny before staring back at Matty.

Danny shrugged. Matty's words were echoing inside his head. He couldn't make head nor tail of it. What did Freddie have to do with boys?

'Fucking hell, Danny.'

Danny turned back to look at Moray. He gave a tiny shake of his head, his forehead furrowed. He still didn't understand.

Sitting forward, Moray's fingertips turned white as he gripped onto the leather headrest. 'Boys, Danny? Think about it. Boys.' He pressed his hand towards his mouth, and he swallowed down the repulsion he felt. Of all the things he thought Freddie was, a nonce wasn't one of them.

Danny's eyes widened. He wiped his hand across his ashen face and turned to look across at Matty. He felt physically sick, the trauma he'd been through himself at the forefront of his mind. How could he have been so stupid not to have seen the signs? They were all there in plain sight. Freddie was another Adam Christos. No wonder Freddie had surrounded himself with kids in the firm. He lunged towards the boy and roared. 'You dirty, no good cunt.'

It took all of Moray's strength to pull Danny off the lad. 'Not here. It's too open. We'll be fucking seen. We need to find out what's going on first.'

Feeling sickness rise up inside of him, Danny opened the car door and hung his head out. He took deep breaths to quash the sickening wave of nausea that rippled through him. How had he never guessed what Freddie was? He thought back to when he was seventeen and had joined Freddie's firm. Had the man intended to use him, too, just like Christos had?

He tried to think back to when he was young and had been in the man's company. So many times, it had been just the two of them alone. There had been so many opportunities for Freddie to make a move.

His mind instantly went to Logan. Freddie had always taken an interest in his son. The innocent remarks he'd made about his boy being a handsome little lad, now appeared sinister. He began to heave. He couldn't stop the wave of nausea, and tipping his head forward even farther, he vomited until his stomach was empty.

Wiping his hand across his mouth, Danny sat up. He took a swig from a bottle of water, and then promptly spat it out onto the roadside, before closing the car door. His face was pale, drained of all colour.

He looked across at Matty and felt him flinch as he leant across him. He opened up the glove box, searching for a piece of paper. Anything would do, as long as it could be written on. He pulled out a tattered envelope and a pen, and then thrust them into Matty's hands. 'Write down the names of everyone involved. I want the kids' names, I want the nonces names, everyone.'

Matty stared down at the envelope in his hand. 'I can't.'

'Write it all fucking down,' Danny roared.

Shaking his head, Matty looked Danny in the eyes. 'I can't. This is not big enough.'

'Fucking hell.' Slumping backwards, Moray gasped from the back seat. What the fuck had they stumbled across?

* * *

After a quick trip to a supermarket, Danny walked out with a pad of paper. He climbed back into his car and handed the pad over to Matty.

'What are we going to do now?' Moray asked. 'We can't just sit in the car park all day, waiting for this piece of shit to write everything down. We'll have to take him to your place, then I can get back out searching for that cunt, Lee. If we're lucky, he and Freddie might even be together... kill two birds with one stone.'

Matty was alarmed. While he was out in the open, he felt relatively safe that they wouldn't hurt him. But if they took him to Danny's flat, he knew for sure he wouldn't come out of there alive. They would kill him stone dead, maybe Danny even kept his hook there. He began to cry once again. The enormity of the situation was hitting him full on. 'Please, don't kill me.'

'Is this bastard getting on your nerves, or is it just me?' Danny asked.

'Just take him back to your place. I can't be doing with all of this snivelling bollocks.'

After starting the ignition, Danny eased out of the car park. Other than the sobs which came from Matty, the men remained silent, each of them lost in their own thoughts as they were transported back to when they, themselves, were fifteen and at the mercy of Adam Christos.

* * *

'Sit there and write down two lists, one for who the perpetrators are, and a second one for the kids,' Danny ordered as he pushed Matty down onto the sofa. 'And make sure you put down everyone involved, do you understand me?'

Matty nodded. He didn't dare speak. Sitting as still as a statue, he began writing.

'I need to get out looking for Lee, mate. I can't sit in here all day doing nothing. I need to keep active.' Moray clenched and unclenched his fists. The thought of what he was going to do to Lee was the only thing stopping him from thinking too much about the fate of his boys.

Danny paused as he thought through their next move. 'Get on the blower to the Carters. Find out where they've already searched. You don't want to be going back on yourself. I'll stay here with this little bastard.'

Moray shot a glance in Matty direction. The hatred he felt for nonces was enough to make him want to commit murder. 'Yeah, I'll do that.' He walked through to the kitchen to make his phone calls and closed the door behind him as he did so.

Hovering behind Matty, Danny watched as the boy jotted down the names. Already he could see a few he recognised, and he felt a sense of anger begin to bubble inside of him. No wonder Freddie had never had his collar felt. He had enough Old Bill in his pocket to ensure him of that. He closed his eyes. He still couldn't get his head around it all. How had Freddie kept this hidden for so long, and right underneath their noses, too?

'Right, the Carters have had no joy as of yet. I was thinking of trying The Tavern.'

'I doubt he'd show his face in there. People don't forget easily, and everyone knows what a tosser he is. You'd be better off trying all the snooker halls. If I remember rightly, he used to play a fair bit, before he went inside.'

'Yeah, you're right, he did. I'll start there, instead.'

'Let me know when you find the bastard and just keep a hold of him. Wait for me to get there, before you do anything.'

Reluctantly, Moray nodded. 'I'll try, but I can't promise I won't tear him limb from limb.'

'He's with Freddie at his house.'

The two men turned to look at Matty. What with everything coming out about Freddie, they'd completely forgotten to ask the boy if he knew of Lee's whereabouts.

'What did I fucking tell you? I knew he'd be with that cunt. Get back on the blower to Tommy Carter. You're going to need them. Oh, and take these, the keys for Freddie's lock up. You'll have to take them somewhere.' Danny handed over a set of keys that Freddie had given to him, before all of the trouble had started up. No doubt the man had forgotten he still had them.

'Is it secure and out of the way?'

'It's perfect, mate. I picked the place out myself.' Scribbling down the address, Danny passed across a scrap of paper.

'I'll give you a bell when we've got them then. What are we going to do with him?' Moray glared towards Matty.

'Once you've got Freddie and Lee at the lock up, I'll bring him over.'

Satisfied, Moray nodded. He couldn't stay in the room a moment longer. He didn't trust himself to not grab Matty around the throat and throttle the life out of him.

Danny waited until Moray had left the flat, then sat down heavily. Resisting the urge to kick the boy in the head, he didn't take his eyes off him while he sat quietly brooding over his fate. He'd always felt a hatred for the kid, he'd just not been able to put a finger on the reason why. Now, everything made sense to him. He now knew why the boy had got underneath his skin so much. He must have had some kind of sixth sense as to what he was.

* * *

Matty continued writing down the list of names. He was almost finished, and had just two more to add, yet he could barely bring himself to write them down. He'd promised the two little boys so many times that he would take them away from their mum, and now, he knew that wouldn't be possible. It was out of his hands. Danny McKay was going to kill him.

He began to cry. What would the boys do now? He wrote down the names, Sam and Jack, then passed the sheets of paper across to Danny. He felt so ashamed as Danny studied the lists. He couldn't even look at the man. He looked down at his lap, and allowed hot salty tears to slip down his cheeks. He didn't wipe them away, he let them fall freely. His heart was breaking all over again.

* * *

Moray and the Carter brothers regrouped a few hundred yards from Freddie's house. They couldn't risk themselves being spotted by the two men. More than anything, they didn't want to give them a heads up to try and escape.

'How do you wanna play this out?' Tommy asked.

Glancing towards Freddie's house, Moray took in the neighbouring houses. There would be a lot of witnesses if they kicked down the front door and dragged them out in broad daylight. Fuck it, he decided. Taking them by force could well be the only means of getting them out the house. 'We smash the fucking door down, if need be. I want them out.'

'Fair enough. You heard him,' Tommy addressed his brothers. 'Just try not to bring too much attention to yourselves, and Jonny, have the car ready and waiting for our signal.'

Jonny nodded and took the car keys from his brother. The fact that he was an excellent getaway driver was his only saving grace, where his brothers were concerned.

'Right, are we ready?' Tommy gave the signal for his brothers to move forward. Silently, they walked towards Freddie's house.

'Remember, I want them both,' Moray added as an afterthought.

Putting up his hand, Tommy indicated for the men to stop. Confident that his brothers and Moray were hidden out of sight, behind privet hedges of a neighbouring house, Tommy walked a few paces ahead to suss out Freddie's gaff. Walking back towards them, he kept his voice low. 'There's a back gate about six feet or so high. Gary and Mitchel, I want the two of yous to jump over, just in case they try to escape out the back, and then the rest of us, stay at the front. Moray, are you happy with that?'

Moray hastily agreed. All he wanted to do was to get his hands on Lee Hart.

They moved forward and watched as Gary and Mitchel expertly scaled the back gate. They then waited a few seconds for them to get into position, before kicking down the front door. They were inside the house within seconds. The splintered door brought further proof that despite Freddie's paranoia, he'd thought of himself as untouchable.

* * *

Studying the sheets of paper, Danny read each name the boy had written down. He wasn't surprised to see Lee Hart's name there. How the fuck did these people even find each other? It was a question he didn't want to know the answer to, he decided. He moved on to the second sheet of paper, containing the list of boys' names. He felt physically sick. So many kids, so many innocent victims.

Danny paused before glancing across to Matty. His and Lewis Hart's names were amongst the list of victims. He didn't speak. He was actually at a loss for words. He didn't know what he was meant to say. Was Matty even telling the truth?

He watched as the boy cried his heart out, and in that instant, he felt his mood soften towards him. Matty had been a victim just as he and Moray had been. Massaging his closed eyes, he rubbed his hand across his face.

Somehow the boy had managed to pull at his heart strings – an emotion he would never, in a million years, have believed he was capable of when it came to Matty Payne. For his son, yes, or Maxine, even Moray's two boys, but not for this young lad in front of him, whom he'd despised for so long.

'When did it start?' Even though he'd asked the question, Danny wasn't so sure he wanted to know the answer.

'When I was fourteen. They target kids like me, because no one cares about us. It's easy to make us disappear, see.'

Danny knew all too well what Matty meant. Look at himself; his own parents hadn't given a shit about him. He'd tried to tell his mum once about the abuse he'd suffered at Adam Christos's hand and in return, she'd slapped him around the face and thrown him out on to the street. That had been the last time he'd seen her or his dad.

Matty cleared his throat, the lump there choking him, so gut wrenching was the emotion he was feeling. He'd never been forced to relive the horrors of what had happened to him out loud before, and every emotion he'd kept hidden away for so long, had now been dragged out from the box inside his mind, where he'd kept the abuse locked away.

Danny closed his eyes. He didn't understand any of this. How had Freddie managed to keep the fact he was a nonce hidden for all of these years? Why hadn't he seen the signs? In hindsight he knew they had been glaringly obvious. Perhaps he hadn't wanted to see them, perhaps he'd been scared that if he'd had to acknowledge what Freddie was then he would have to admit he'd once been a victim too. He stood up and walked towards the window. He could barely bring himself to look at the boy, and he didn't want to listen to any more of what he had to say, he knew that much. He continued staring out of the window. He placed his palms on the window sill, his strong arms taking his weight. Finally, he forced himself to turn back around.

As Matty sobbed, his heart actually broke for the lad. Gingerly, he took a step closer, unsure if he was doing the right thing.

He couldn't understand the turnaround inside of him. How could he go from wanting to kill the boy one minute, to wanting to offer comfort the next? He must be going soft, he decided. Whatever it was, it was certainly a revelation.

* * *

Lee was so scared, he'd actually wet himself. 'I didn't do anything,' he'd protested as the men dragged Freddie and himself out of the house. 'Tell 'em, Fred. Tell 'em how it was all your idea.'

As they were thrown into the car, Freddie knew when to keep schtum. With no firm around to protect him, he knew his days would be numbered if he started getting lairy. He was only grateful it wasn't actually Danny McKay who'd grabbed a hold of them. After being on the receiving end of that famous temper of his, he didn't relish the thought of round two.

'Shut your fucking mouth,' he hissed, giving Lee a swift kick in his shin. If they wanted to get out of this alive, they would need to keep their wits about them, and if they weren't careful, Lee's loose lips were going to make the situation ten times worse.

'It wasn't me,' Lee continued to protest. 'It was you, Fred. You told me to give the kid the pills.' Despite his terror, Lee smirked. If he could get them to believe it was all Freddie's doing, then they might let him walk away.

The brick that smashed into Lee's face came out of nowhere. Such force was used that he actually watched his teeth fly out of his mouth. As blood gushed from his split gums, he began to cry. With a sudden terrifying clarity, he knew for certain that this was one situation he wouldn't be able to talk his way out of. Moray Garner and the Carter brothers obviously meant business.

* * *

Hesitating, Danny sat down on the edge of the sofa. He moved his arm towards Matty, and then just as quickly, he pulled it back. He continued watching as the boy cried, and knew, instinctively, he was telling the truth. Blowing out his cheeks, he took the plunge and pulled the lad into his arms.

'It's okay,' he whispered, as he pulled him close. 'It's okay.' Only it wasn't okay, and he knew that. Kids like Matty, even himself, never got over something like this; it stayed with you and was always there in the background.

Matty clung onto Danny for dear life. His fingertips clasped hold of him tightly as he let out heart wrenching sobs. He'd never had anyone hold him before, and his grief for the childhood that had been ripped away from him, tumbled out. He was unable to stop the tears from flowing. The horror of what he'd been through throughout his young life, was too raw.

Over the course of the next hour, the horrifying tale of the beatings from Matty's dad, Freddie's parties, the other men, and the kids who no one cared about, came flooding out. At times, Danny had to hide the disgust he felt. None of this was the lad's fault, of course he understood that, and he could feel the rage build inside of him, when Matty had stated that if Freddie had indeed killed him that morning, then there would have been another boy to take his place within hours.

Watching Danny as he got up from the sofa and walk through to the bedroom, Matty sniffed back his tears. He dragged his hand across his face, drying his sodden cheeks.

'Take this and get as far away as you can. No one will come looking for you, I can promise you that.' Against his better judgement, Danny handed over five thousand pounds in cash.

Matty held the money in his hand. With a solemn expression spread across his face, he passed it back. 'I can't.'

'Yes, you can. Take the fucking money and run. If you stay here, I can't guarantee that they won't kill you when all of this comes out. They will be gunning for blood, you should already know that. I'll tell them you made a run for it while I was taking a piss or something.'

'I can't. The two boys... I promised I would take them away.'

'What two fucking boys?' Danny narrowed his eyes. Immediately, he was suspicious.

Matty gulped before speaking, his voice hoarse from crying. 'Sam and Jack. They're only little, and their mum doesn't care about them. All she'll do, is find another Freddie and use the money to buy crack. It's easy money for her, see.' Matty looked up at Danny, his eyes were wide, imploring him to help the two brothers. 'I have to help them. I promised I would.'

Danny chewed on the inside of his cheek as he thought the situation over. Finally, he took out his phone and punched in a number. 'Moray,' he said into the mouthpiece. 'I need a huge favour.'

19

After warning Matty not to leave his flat, or open the door to anyone under any circumstances, Danny drove to Freddie's lock up. He just hoped and prayed he wasn't too late. He had a proposition of his own for Moray, and he had a feeling this could be exactly what they needed to get the Greeks off their backs. Convincing Moray, however, was going to be the hard part.

He walked through the doors and took in the scene before him. It was exactly what he'd been expecting to find. Sitting back to back, in the middle of the vast concrete floor, were Freddie and Lee. Their hands and feet had been bound tightly together, making it impossible for them to move.

'I see you didn't waste any time,' Danny stated as he took in Lee's obvious facial injuries.

Moray didn't answer. He was too busy unravelling a length of rubber tubing.

'We need to talk,' Danny said. Coming to stand beside Moray, he kept his voice low as he watched his friend place the rubber tubing, a plastic funnel, staple gun, pliers, and a litre bottle of bleach onto a table.

'Go on.'

'We could use these two wankers in exchange for the doors. Barter with the Greeks and get them off our backs for good.' Glancing towards Freddie and Lee, Danny then placed his arm across the table, forcing Moray to stop what he was doing and to look at him.

'No.'

'Listen, if we hand them over—'

'I said no,' Moray interrupted. His voice was loud and brooked no arguments.

'Fair enough. I understand you want to kill him, but you're making a huge mistake by doing it yourself.' Danny hadn't seen this side of Moray for many years. The steely glint in his mate's eyes warned him to back off and not argue the case.

'I want that bastard to die for what he's done to the boys.'

'And he will do. Let the Greeks have him, in exchange for the doors.' Danny understood where Moray was coming from, but at times, you had to look at the bigger picture. He'd lost count of how many times he'd told Freddie the exact same thing over the years.

There had always been a method to his madness, and at the end of the day, it didn't matter if it was Moray or the Greeks responsible. Lee Hart was going to die. Everyone, other than Lee, was a winner. 'C'mon, mate, business is business, and besides, you should have bought a bigger funnel. You'll be there all day with this poxy little thing.' Flicking the small plastic funnel across the table, Danny smiled, trying to lighten Moray's mood.

'Yeah, well, it's been quite a few years since I've had to torture anyone, unlike you, by the sound of it.' There was a note of sarcasm in Moray's voice.

'Trust me, mate, you don't want to go down this road, not when you've worked so hard to get out of the life. If you do this now, and get blood on your hands, then I can guarantee you won't stop there. You'll do it again and again, just like I have.'

'All I want is to see the fucker dead. Don't try and talk me out of it.'

'Moray, you'll end up as fucked up as me. Think of what you're doing.' Despite what his mate said, Danny could see he was beginning to waver. It was all well and good, him carrying out such a heinous act in the heat of the moment, but in the cold light of day, he knew that if Moray carried it through, then it would haunt him for the rest of his days.

'How do you even know the Greeks will kill him?' It was the closest Moray would ever get to hearing Danny show any kind of remorse for the brutal acts he'd committed over the years, and his words were beginning to make him think through what he was doing.

'They think he killed one of their own. They're gonna want revenge. Can you honestly see them letting him live?'

'And what if he talks and tells them the truth?' Moray glanced across to the two men tied up on the floor. He kept his voice low. 'You know what he's like with that big fucking trap of his. The quicker one of us kill him, the better.'

'Easy solution to that,' Danny stated. He snatched up a knife from the table, and lightly touched the point of the blade, testing its sharpness. 'The bastard can't talk without a tongue, can he?'

Striding towards Lee with the steel knife in his fist, Danny indicated for one of the Carter brothers to hold Lee's head still for him. Quickly and efficiently, he forced apart the terrified and protesting man's jaws, and as though it were a hot knife gliding through butter, he sliced off the top half of Lee's tongue. Throwing the bloody matter to the floor, Danny turned back towards Moray and wiped the blood from his hands as he did so. 'There you go, problem solved.'

Jonny Carter's eyes were like golf balls as he watched Lee Hart choking on the blood that filled his mouth. For future reference, he was given a stark reminder not to upset Danny McKay in any way, shape or form. He could see now that he'd had a lucky escape, all thanks to his elder brothers, and the surname he'd been lucky enough to be born with.

* * *

Freddie had almost felt his heart stop as he'd watched Danny McKay walk through the doors. He'd been convinced the man would immediately begin a thorough beating of both Lee and himself. Instead, through hooded eyes, he had watched McKay, as he'd stood talking to Moray Garner for over ten minutes. He couldn't hear what was being said, but took a wild guess from the glances they threw in their direction, that Lee and himself were the topic of conversation.

As Danny purposefully strode towards them with the knife in his fist, Freddie had closed his eyes tightly. Dishing out violence was one thing, but receiving it was a totally different matter, and he didn't want to see the blade plunging towards him.

He'd felt his body sag with relief, when it was Lee who'd begun screaming. He was only thankful it wasn't his tongue the man had cut out. McKay had always been a mad bastard. He'd known that from the moment he had first clapped eyes on him. Even when he'd been just a kid, it was clear for everyone to see that the boy was a loose cannon, hence why he'd never laid a finger on him or the gypsy. Seeing how close the two boys were, Freddie had given them both a wide berth, not to mention, he didn't fancy a backlash from the rest of Moray's pikey clan, if they were to ever find out that he'd interfered with him.

As he took deep breaths, Freddie's racing heart began to slow back down to its normal rhythm once again. He could feel Lee squirming against his back. He was obviously in distress and a great deal of pain. 'Shut the fuck up,' he hissed. The more attention Lee brought on them, the worse the outcome would be, he was certain of that.

For the first time since he'd arrived, Danny looked Freddie in the eyes. He snarled as he came to crouch down beside him.

Pulling back his head, Freddie spat into the younger man's face. It was the only thing he could physically do. They had him trussed up like a chicken, and he could no longer feel his hands or feet. The sensation had begun as pins and needles, until numbness had taken over several hours earlier. He could tell by the mottled purple colour his hands had turned, that the plastic cable ties tightly binding them together, had cut off all blood supply.

Danny wiped the spittle from his cheek. He remained composed and chillingly calm, and brought his face closer to Freddie's ear. 'I know what you are, and I know what you did to those boys.'

In that instant, Freddie knew he was a dead man. He felt an ice cold chill run down his spine, and beads of cold sweat began to break out across his forehead. Warily, he looked Danny in the eyes, unsure of what the man was going to do with the new-found knowledge he had. He could see repulsion spread across his face, and in that instant, he knew. He didn't speak, he didn't need to. The fact that Danny now knew exactly what he was, was more than enough to tell him he wouldn't be walking out of the lock up alive.

* * *

Hastily, Danny had arranged a meeting with George Christos. The ongoing situation with Freddie and Lee had forced them to move fast. Both Moray and himself were in the office above Ritzy's Night-club, and he poured them both out a tumbler of brandy. 'Look, I'll do you a deal, okay? If the Greeks don't kill him, then I'll do it.'

'I was more than capable of doing it myself, and would have done it, if you hadn't stopped me.'

Danny ignored Moray's reply. He passed across the filled glass, then glanced down at his watch. Christos was running late. 'There was something I was meant to tell you, actually, and I'd better do it, before they get here. I was with Freddie when he killed one of the Greeks a couple of months back.'

'What? And you've only decided you'd mention this now?' He stood back slightly, and ran his hand through his dark hair. 'Fuck me, Danny, you don't half pick your moments.'

'I'm only mentioning it now, because I'm going to tell them Freddie was responsible, and I don't want it to be the first time you hear about it.'

'Cheers for that.' Moray rolled his eyes. 'Anything else I should know about, while we're at it?'

'No, that's about it.' They would be here all day, if he started confessing to everything he'd done over the years.

* * *

'It was you… you killed Nico. You and Freddie Smith, together.' George was furious. He stabbed his finger forward, his dark eyes flashing dangerously. His instincts had been right all along. Hadn't he said it to anyone who would listen, that these were the two men who'd been responsible?

'I can swear to you, hand on my heart, I did not touch a hair on your nephew's head, but I know who did, and I can take you to both him, and the man who killed your brother.' Despite the hostile reception he and Moray had received from the two Greeks, Danny remained in control of the situation.

'You know where Lee Hart is?' George and Alexandros turned towards one another. To say they were stunned was an understatement. They had spent the best part of two months trying to hunt the slippery bastard down.

'We have both Freddie and Lee Hart holed up together. But before we hand them over, we want to come to an arrangement about the doors.' He took a sip of brandy, savouring the burn as he swallowed the liquid down. He wanted the two men to be able to digest what he'd just said, before continuing. 'We need your assurance that you and your family will steer clear of our doors. In other words, you'll stay away from our manor, and we'll stay away from yours.'

George leant back in his seat. He eyed the two men in front of him warily. He knew this was what his brother wanted, for them to sort out their affairs, yet he couldn't help but feel as though he was doing a deal with the devil himself. He tugged at his pinstriped tie, leaving it to sit askew against the white linen shirt, while he thought the proposition through.

'So, do we have a deal?'

George glanced towards Alexandros. He needed to process this. He was in half a mind to take the deal, and then double-cross them. When was business ever black and white anyway? The first rule he'd ever learned as a young man, was that you had to be ruthless and look out for number one. He could feel his brother's eyes boring into his skull.

The three men were waiting for his answer. As eager as he was to get his hands on Freddie Smith and Lee Hart, giving up the ambition and power he'd always strived for, was a different matter entirely. Finally, he nodded. As much as he disliked what he was agreeing to, Alexandros was right. They needed to put an end to the bloodshed.

'You have your deal.' Alexandros spoke for his brother as he leant across the table to shake both Danny's and Moray's hands. 'You have our word that the doors will come under no threat from us.'

Danny grinned as he shook the proffered hand and glanced across to Moray. This had been a lot easier than the both of them had expected. They had been expecting a backlash of sorts, maybe even a few punches to fly. At the very least, one or two idle threats.

'Now that the deal is done, when do we get them?'

'They're yours, whenever you're ready, but just a little warning for you, if you go back on this deal, then believe me, I will hunt you both down, and I can guarantee you won't like the outcome.' Danny's voice was suddenly menacing, leaving it clear to the two men that he meant every word.

Alexandros nodded. It was exactly what he'd expected to hear, and if the roles were reversed, he knew for a fact that they would have said the exact same thing. He glanced across to George, hoping his brother also took heed to the warning they had been given. 'You have our word.'

'Good.' Danny rubbed his hands together. The business was concluded. 'Whenever you're ready, both men are yours for the taking.'

* * *

Freddie's heart sank as he watched the Greeks walk through the lock up doors. He felt panic begin to rise within him, and moved his body this way and that as he tried to fight his way out of the thick plastic cable ties that restrained him.

Pushing his body against the now semi-conscious Lee, Freddie toppled over onto his side. His body and mind battled against one another, as a survival instinct inside of him took over. The numbness in his hands made it impossible for him to do anything other than lay squirming where he'd fallen.

The fury of the situation he found himself in began in his belly and pushed its way up through his chest. He roared in frustration. 'You no good fucking cunt,' he screamed in Danny's direction.

He could hear the men discussing him, as though he were nothing more than a piece of meat on the floor. In their eyes, he'd ceased being a human being. He was a nothing, a no one. Instinctively, he knew his days were numbered, and without a shadow of a doubt, he knew they wouldn't keep him alive for any longer than they needed to, yet the pride inside him vowed he would fight on, until the bitter end.

* * *

'Right, they're all yours.' Danny looked around him, then nodded his gratitude towards the Carter brothers. The business was concluded. Freddie's and Lee's fates were now in the hands of the Christos family.

George Christos nodded in acknowledgement. He'd dreamt of this moment for so many years. He could feel the hatred burning inside of him and knew each of his family members would be feeling the same emotion, as he himself was. He walked slowly around the two men, resisting the urge to kick out at them as he did so. 'Twenty-one years, I've waited for this moment,' he spat, crouching down beside Lee. 'Twenty-one years, I've waited to see you hanging from a hook, just like you left my brother, with his insides hanging out of him to rot.'

Straightening up, George walked back towards Alexandros. He stood beside him, watching as his nephews brought in through the lock up doors a heavy metal hook and a length of thick metal chain. 'Assemble it here,' he ordered them.

* * *

Watching as the Greeks assembled the makeshift execution structure, Danny took one last look towards Freddie and Lee. He felt no emotion towards them, whatsoever.

'Oh, by the way, your nephew was still alive when Freddie set him on fire.'

He watched as a flurry of different emotions crossed George Christos's face. The fact that he had just set in motion Freddie's own method of death, meant nothing to him, and why should it? He had warned the man not to do what he had done.

Nodding his head towards Moray, Danny indicated it was time for them to leave. They shook hands with George and Alexandros, ignoring the desperate pleas to spare his life, which came from Freddie.

Without even a backwards glance, Danny walked out of the lock up for the final time, leaving the man he had worked for, for over twenty years, behind him. As far as he was concerned, Freddie was already dead to him. In fact, the man's fate had been sealed, the day he had plotted his own death sentence with Big Tone, Terry Stevens and Lloydy.

20

Tracey Underwood had the shock of her life as the men burst through her front door. In terror, she had screamed and cowered behind the sofa.

It was Danny who dragged her out by the scruff of her neck. He pushed his face towards her. 'Do you know who I am?' His grip was tight, his voice menacing and loud, as he spoke.

Furiously, Tracey nodded. She was petrified. Of course she knew who he was. Everyone knew who Danny McKay was. In terror, she tried to wrack her brains as to what she could have done to annoy the man in front of her. As far as she was aware, she'd never had any personal dealings with him.

She felt a moment of shame as he took in the squalor around them. Dirty dishes were piled up in the sink and strewn across worktops. In fact, every plate, cup and bowl she owned, had been used, and were covered in thick dried remnants of the previous meal. She usually just gave the plates a quick rinse under the tap, as and when they were needed, and that was only if she remembered to feed her kids first.

Dirty soiled clothes littered the kitchen floor, and the dog she had bought for protection, had started using the corner of the kitchen as his own personal toilet, all because she couldn't be bothered to take him downstairs for a walk. She kept meaning to tidy up, really she did. There was just always something more important she needed to do first.

'This place is like a fucking pigsty, and you call yourself a mother? You dirty cunt.' Disgust was clearly evident across Danny's face, and he wrinkled up his nose at the foul scent of dog's piss, ground in dirt, and chip fat.

He beckoned for Matty to enter the flat. 'Find the boys, and pack a small bag of essentials for them.' He watched as the lad did as he was bade, then turned his attention back to Tracey. She'd been the first on their list today.

Throughout the course of the next few days, they would pay a visit to every single perpetrator on the sheet of paper Matty had given them.

'When the authorities ask you where the kids are, which they will, you are going to tell them that they've gone to live with a relative, because you're too much of a useless, selfish bitch to take care of them. I don't care where in the world you say they are, but if you breathe one mention of mine, or anyone else's name in this room, then I will come back here for you, and bounce you all over this poxy shithole that you call home. Am I making myself understood, in that drug-fuelled brain of yours, or do I need to punch it into your skull so that you understand?'

Tracey nodded. 'I understand,' she stuttered. She watched, helplessly, as her two boys were ushered out of the flat. Typically, her first thoughts went to the money she would be missing out on, now that the boys were gone. She began to cry as she realised she would not even receive her child benefit money, which she often used to go out and score. She relied on that money for a midweek pick-me-up to get her through, until her social security giro arrived on a Friday.

Throwing Tracey away from him, Danny watched as she fell in a heap at his feet. 'If you were a bloke, I would have knocked your jaw clean off your fucking face, so think of yourself as lucky.'

Through her tears, Tracey nodded. She didn't need telling twice. She already knew she'd had a lucky escape, if you could even call it that.

Walking from the flat, Danny breathed in lungfuls of fresh air. How people could live like Tracey did, he had no idea. He wiped his hand down his jeans, not wanting the grime of Tracey's skin to linger on his fingers. She repulsed him.

As they waited for the lift to reach the ground floor, he turned his attention to the two terrified little boys clinging onto Matty, and could feel the anger begin to bubble inside of him once again. His thoughts turned to Logan and his unborn child; he'd do anything to keep them safe, he'd even die for them without giving the matter a second thought. How could any parent use and abuse their child like Sam and Jack's so-called mother had? He had to physically stop himself from taking the lift back up to Tracey's flat and destroying the sorry excuse for a human being that she was. Instead, he ushered the terrified children towards a navy blue transit van.

'They've got five minutes, then they need to leave.'

Danny nodded. He watched as Moray went to speak to the driver, and opening up the back doors, he helped the two little boys climb inside. He then turned to Matty.

'These people are Moray's kin, his family. You're going to travel the country with them. Where they go, you go. Do you understand?' He waited for the lad to digest what he'd said, then continued. 'Now, I've already given them money to sort you out someplace to live, and I want you to take this money to tide you over for a couple of weeks. After that, you'll have to work along-side Moray's cousins. It's going to be your responsibility to provide for and look after these boys.'

Matty looked down at the large bundle of notes Danny was holding out in his hand. He could already see it was a small fortune, and more than enough to tide them over. 'I don't know what to say.'

Danny shook his head, dismissing Matty's words. 'You don't need to say anything. You just need to look after those two,' he said, nodding his head towards Sam and Jack.

'Danny, time's up. They need to get going.'

Glancing towards Moray, Danny smiled gently. 'Go on, get in the van and take care of yourself.'

Throwing himself into Danny's arms, Matty smiled. 'I will do. Thank you, and I promise I'll look after the boys.'

Danny nodded. He watched as Matty climbed inside the van and then closed the doors behind him. Already, his heart felt lighter, knowing he had done the right thing in helping all three of them escape. He thumped his fist on the back door, signalling for Moray's cousins to drive on.

As they watched the van pull away, Danny turned towards Moray. 'I owe you one, mate.'

Moray nodded. He began to walk towards his car. 'Yeah, you do,' he called over his shoulder. 'I had to pull a lot of strings for them to take the boys.'

'Well, I'm more than grateful.'

'I know you are.' Moray cleared his throat. They were both becoming soft with age, that was half the problem. 'Right, where to next?'

Danny took out the sheet of paper from his pocket. This was going to be a long day. 'Drive towards Upminster. We're going to go and see our old adversary, Detective Chief Inspector Williams.'

'Now this, I am looking forward to.' Moray grinned.

* * *

Martin and Geoff Scanlon took short puffs from the cigarette they were sharing. They kicked the leaves from underneath their feet as they strolled through Epping Forest. The forest was one of their favourite haunts, especially when they were bunking off school for the day. Well-hidden and out of sight, they could spend the day at their leisure. They had their packed lunches to munch on when they became hungry and would share the few cigarettes they had stolen out of their mum's handbag. As long as it wasn't too cold or raining, it had to be better than going to chemistry lessons with that pompous old git, Mr Philips.

'Oi, come on, Geoff, it's my turn.' Holding out his hand, Martin waited for his turn to take a drag on the cigarette. 'You're a greedy sod,' he chastised.

Blowing out smoke rings, Geoff grinned sheepishly before handing over the cigarette. He knew he should have given his brother more of the smoke, but seeing as he was older, he had first dibs. It was an unspoken rule.

He sat down on a log and took out his packed lunch. 'Tuna again,' he groaned. 'Mum knows I hate bloody tuna. What have you got?' Snatching up Martin's bag, he rifled through his brother's packed lunchbox. 'Cheese sandwiches. I'll swap you.'

'Oh, no you don't,' Martin stated as he watched his brother stand up with the cheese sandwich in his fist. 'Oi, give it back,' he yelled, trying to snatch it back from him.

'If you want it, you'll have to take it.' Geoff laughed and ran from his brother. He took a bite, his teeth sinking into the soft, buttered bread and thick slices of cheese. 'This is lovely,' he teased. He turned towards Martin, expecting a thorough backlash.

Instead, he was met with his brother's eyes, as wide as saucers, and his face, a deathly shade of white. 'What?' he asked.

Martin didn't speak. Instead, he pointed his finger to behind where Geoff was standing.

Geoff could feel his heart begin to beat wildly in his chest. Slowly, he turned around, before falling backwards, in his haste to get away from what they had stumbled across.

Scrambling away, Geoff's eyes were now as wide as Martin's. 'Is it real?'

Martin nodded. 'It's definitely real. Look, you can see a face and everything.'

The two boys stared down at the charred remains of Freddie Smith.

'What should we do?'

Geoff began collecting up their school bags. 'We can't tell anyone. Mum and Dad will go mental at us for skipping school.'

'Yeah, but we can't just forget about it and not tell anyone what we've found,' Martin protested as he pointed down at the body.

'Listen, we say nothing. Now come on, get your bag. We need to leave. You never know, whoever did this to that bloke, could still be here watching us, waiting to kill us next.'

With his brother's words spurring him into action, Martin hauled his rucksack up onto his back. 'Come on.' He shuddered. 'This place is giving me the creeps.'

Without a backward glance, the two boys ran from the crime scene, leaving Freddie Smith's charred remains, half hidden by branches and fallen leaves, to remain undiscovered.

* * *

Detective Inspector Ronnie Dellow wasn't a happy man. In fact, he felt defeated. He'd put all of his man power into locating Lee

Hart, and the man had apparently vanished off the face of the earth.

He stared up at the pin board in front of him, the mug shot of the wanted man mocking him. He had to be somewhere. It should have been just a simple case of locating Hart, arresting him, and case solved. Only, finding Lee's whereabouts was proving to actually not be as simple as he'd first thought it would be.

Pushing his hand through his wiry hair, Ronnie took a deep breath, before unpinning everything relating to the case from the board. This was the first case to have gotten the better of him, and after months of trying to solve it, it was now being scaled down.

Lee Hart's mugshot was the last item he took down. He looked down at the photograph in his hand. 'I will find you,' he muttered, before flinging it inside the brown cardboard box with the rest of the paraphernalia relating to the case.

With a heavy heart, he sealed the box, and waited for it to be moved to the storage room, to sit alongside the rest of the cold cases.

* * *

As usual, The Tavern was crammed full with punters. Moray, Danny and the rest of the lads, had gone there to drown their sorrows. They had just come out of court, after the sentencing of Aaron and Colm Garner. Fourteen years apiece, the two lads had received.

Moray had shaken his head sadly as his two boys were taken down. As easy as it was to put all of the blame onto Lee Hart, he had to blame his own sons, too. Their greed had caused this, and as a result, they had been caught, bang to rights. As much as he hated to admit it, the boys would have to pay the price for their actions, and ultimately, as a result, they would lose their freedom.

Raising his arm in the air, Moray gave a little wave. Leaning into Danny's ear, he spoke. 'Now she,' he said, grinning for the first time that day, 'is the future Mrs Garner.'

Danny was stunned. He followed Moray's gaze and watched as Sophie walked towards them. 'I thought you said you'd been there, done it, had the T-shirt, and that you'd never marry again?'

'I did.' Moray grinned. 'But now, I need to make an honest woman of her. She's pregnant.'

Danny's mouth fell open. 'Fucking hell, mate! Congratulations,' he said, shaking Moray's hand.

Grinning like a Cheshire cat, Moray hugged Sophie towards him. 'Let's hope it's a girl; a lot less trouble.' He winked.

'I'll drink to that.' Danny grinned back, knowing full well that if the baby was indeed a girl, then Moray would never know a day's peace again. Over-protective father wouldn't even come into it.

* * *

Big Tone laughed as he listened to one of Callum Riley's stories. The man was a natural-born storyteller, and was sure to have everyone in fits of laughter. He sipped at his pint of lager, mindful not to drink too much. He, Terry Stevens, Lloydy and Mick Johnson were off shortly to do a big job for Danny, and it felt good to be back in a trusted position, once again.

He knew this was an important job they had been chosen to do, and he'd felt a sense of pride, when Danny had stated that he'd picked them out specifically, because he knew the four men from old, therefore, knew he could trust them explicitly not to talk about the task in hand to anyone, not even Moray.

All they had to do was wait for the nod from Danny, and then they would set off towards the border of Essex and Suffolk. From there, they were to drive to a disused country pub to collect a stash of guns, which Danny planned to purchase.

Laughing once again, Big Tone tipped the remainder of his lager into his mouth, before wiping the back of his hand across his lips. He couldn't remember the last time he'd felt this happy.

* * *

Glancing at his watch, Danny made eye contact with Big Tone. He nodded, indicating it was time for the four men to leave. He watched as they drained their drinks, then followed them out of the pub.

'You know exactly where to go?' he asked.

'It's all up here.' Big Tone grinned, pointing to his temple.

Satisfied, Danny smiled. He shook their hands, and watched, as they climbed into Big Tone's Range Rover. As they pulled out of the car park, he leant against the door frame, and waited until he could no longer see the car's tail lights in the distance. Only then, did he allow the smile upon his face to turn into a snarl. If there was one thing he was, it was a man of his word.

The truth was, there were no guns. He'd vowed, a long time ago, that these four men would pay the price for the attempt on his life, and the murder of the Greek lad.

In fact, the only thing they were going to find at the Suffolk pub, were the Carter brothers, and the four men would definitely not be returning, he'd made sure of that.

The beauty of the situation was that none of it could come back on him. He had the perfect alibi. He would be staying in this packed boozer until closing time. More than enough witnesses would see him generously buying drinks for all and sundry.

He walked back inside the pub, in time to hear Callum telling one of his stories.

'And so my mate, massive West Ham United fan he is, and he's always wanted a season ticket. Anyway, Christmas comes along and the wife has only gone and bought him one for his present, but what the silly mare did was, she bought it at the start of the season, and kept it hidden until Christmas morning. Nearly half the fucking season he missed out on. That's women for you.'

Danny laughed along with the rest of the lads, before looking around him. With all of the top players of Freddie's firm dead, or very soon to be disposed of, he truly was the Top Dog now.

He downed his brandy before ordering them all another round of drinks. The devil himself couldn't have done a better job than what he'd achieved in such a short space of time.

In fact, he was certain that when people spoke about him, they would say the situation couldn't have turned out any better than if he'd planned it all out. Of course, he would laugh it off. How could he have known what Freddie was? The only wish he had was that he'd found out sooner. Nothing would have given him greater pleasure than to have brought Freddie down before he'd had the chance to even harm a hair on a child's head.

He patted the sheet of paper in his jacket pocket. He'd have his day; he would hunt every single nonce on the list down and dish out his own form of punishment. In fact, he was looking forward to it.

MORE FROM KERRY KAYA

We hope you enjoyed reading *Top Dog*. If you did, please leave a review.

If you'd like to gift a copy, this book is also available as an ebook, digital audio download and audiobook CD.

Sign up to Kerry Kaya's mailing list for news, competitions and updates on future books.

http://bit.ly/KerryKayaNewsletter

Another gripping gangland read from Kerry Kaya, *The Price*, is available now.

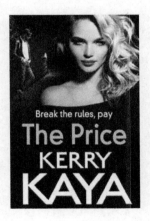

ABOUT THE AUTHOR

Kerry Kaya is the hugely popular author of Essex based gritty gangland thrillers with strong family dynamics. She grew up on one of the largest council estates in the UK, where she sets her novels. She also works full-time in a busy maternity department for the NHS.

Follow Kerry on social media:

 twitter.com/KerryKayaWriter
 instagram.com/kerry_kaya_writer
 facebook.com/kerry.bryant.58

ABOUT BOLDWOOD BOOKS

Boldwood Books is a fiction publishing company seeking out the best stories from around the world.

Find out more at www.boldwoodbooks.com

Sign up to the Book and Tonic newsletter for news, offers and competitions from Boldwood Books!

http://www.bit.ly/bookandtonic

We'd love to hear from you, follow us on social media:

facebook.com/BookandTonic

twitter.com/BoldwoodBooks

instagram.com/BookandTonic

Printed in Great Britain
by Amazon